harem

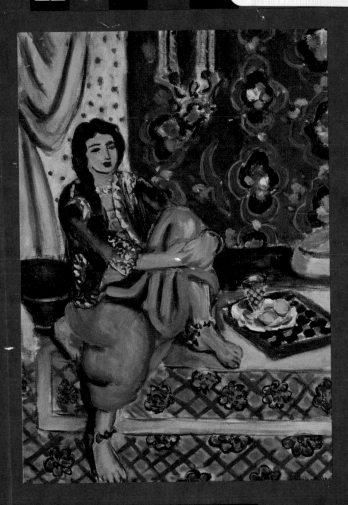

jan carr

"An erotic, poignant, and
slyly satirical debut."
—*Publishers Weekly*

"With lush language and a flair for real old-time-sit-by-the-fire storytelling, Jan Carr takes the complex threads of two epochs and two very different lives and weaves them together to create an intricately detailed novel." —*The Advocate*

"There is a wide-eyed kind of wonder to *Harem Wish*. . . . Carr is a talented writer and it will be interesting to see what she does when all her characters live in the same era."
—*Los Angeles Times Book Review*

"A deliciously fresh and evocative novel . . . Jan Carr playfully experiments with time, myth, and the wages of desire, and explores the preservation of a fragile, sensual love."
—Jenifer Levin, author of *The Sea of Light*

"A fresh voice, stylish writing . . . Carr moves from one world to the other with easy grace." —*Philadelphia Inquirer*

JAN CARR has written several children's books and young adult novels, and her work has been published in *Playbill, Stagebill, Variety,* and *Writer's Digest.* She lives in New York City.

jan carr

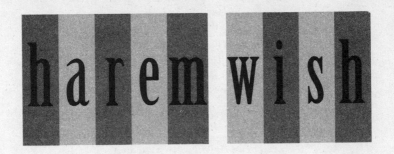

A PLUME BOOK

PLUME
Published by the Penguin Group
Penguin Books USA Inc., 375 Hudson Street, New York, New York 10014, U.S.A.
Penguin Books Ltd, 27 Wrights Lane, London W8 5TZ, England
Penguin Books Australia Ltd, Ringwood, Victoria, Australia
Penguin Books Canada Ltd, 10 Alcorn Avenue, Toronto, Ontario, Canada M4V 3B2
Penguin Books (N.Z.) Ltd, 182–190 Wairau Road, Auckland 10, New Zealand

Penguin Books Ltd, Registered Offices: Harmondsworth, Middlesex, England

Published by Plume, an imprint of Dutton Signet,
a division of Penguin Books USA Inc.
Previously published in a Dutton edition.

First Plume Printing, March, 1995
10 9 8 7 6 5 4 3 2 1

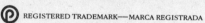

The Library of Congress has catalogued the Dutton edition as follows:
Carr, Jan.
Harem wish / Jan Carr.
p.   cm.
ISBN 0-525-93739-0 (hc.)
ISBN 0-452-27118-5 (pbk.)
1. Lesbians—New York (N.Y.)—Fiction.   2. Lesbians—Arab
countries—Fiction.   3. Harem—Fiction.   I. Title.
PS3553.A76286H37   1994
813'.54—dc20
93–30365
CIP

Printed in the United States of America
Designed by Steven N. Stathakis

PUBLISHER'S NOTE
This is a work of fiction. Names, characters, places, and incidents either are the
product of the author's imagination or are used fictitiously, and any resemblance
to actual persons, living or dead, events, or locales is entirely coincidental.

ACKNOWLEDGMENTS

With many, many thanks to all the good folks at The Writers Room, where a chunk of this book was written.

undertow (un der-to) *n.* The seaward pull of receding waves breaking on a shore.

Anwa was like no other. She was brown-skinned, nappy-headed, tall, sleek, and proud.

Once I threw a scent pot at her.

"You've pride enough to fill the sea," I shouted.

Anwa just smiled. That made her more proud still.

Those nights I could I slept with my cheek nuzzled in the soft fullness of Anwa's breasts. She would laugh at mine.

"Young figs," she called them.

But often I caught her gaze on them just before she'd fall on me with kisses.

Sweet nights, fleet nights, nights white with stars.

The night I threw the scent pot at Anwa was a night before a wedding feast, an event that moved us both to make vows it later turned out we neither could keep. I ran my fingers over her broad back on which was printed a map of the world. In strong light of day this map appeared more clearly as a welted web of scars. That night I asked her how she came by those scars, it was nothing I hadn't asked her before.

"You tell me first," she said, "by what miracle you were able to remain a virgin, you, just-ripe and nubile, traveling in caravan with lecherous traders?"

"By miracle of this," I said, and I lifted my robe to bare my young labia and new fur. "The trader in charge preferred this." Here I crooked a finger to indicate a different sort of sex.

Anwa threw back her head to laugh. In those days I still had power over her laughter and I took much pleasure in exercising it.

"And now your turn," I said, I had not forgotten. "Tell me who it was gave you those scars and what it was that happened."

"I can't recall," she said.

"Of course you can."

"There are different sorts of can't," said Anwa. "You, you are able to tell your life as if it's gossip that happened to someone else, but that is not my way."

Anwa's ways—they were all dear to me, though some were to cause great pain.

I can't account for Anwa's scars, but I can tell my own. I'll start with the story of how I was traded for a sack of spice. An event that transpired, as it happened, in Felix Arabia, a name that translates as Happy Arabia. Arabia rich, envied by its neighbors, the land blessed, in my lifetime, with what it was everyone wanted.

I lived there in the hareem of the Mukarrib's khan, the court from which the Mukarrib ruled over our tribe and all the loose assemblage of brother tribes, as his title bore testament. Mukarrib, Maker of the Covenant. All those in his reign were happy, all benefited from abundant trade. We all, in cult, worshipped the same god, the moon god, as our Mukarrib decreed. At least, we did so in his earshot. And the earshot of those who might represent him.

My own name was Sari, which means "fluid as riverflow, eloquent of limb." I was the Mukarrib's most prized dancer, born into a body that could pick up and express whatever music happened to pass in the air. I could easily express that which is conventionally acknowledged to be music—tambour, cymballine—but my body was also sensitive to more subtle strains, to the sensuous physical life that sounds all around. By this latter I mean that I could convey the skulk of panther, the ripple of wind. My body simply told those things that others heard, saw, and felt, those things all knew to be true. In the days I recounted at the start, I had seen thirteen summers.

I must've danced in the womb. I must've danced as an infant, even while bound in the cloth that rode my mother's hip. As a child I didn't reside in the khan. I lived in an outlying tribe with my family in a village, where I did simple work. It was my job, each night after dinner, to pluck insects and dried bits of manure out of sheep's wool, then to comb the wool's fibers into little ruffs, like weighted clouds. Each night I went to sleep with the greasy scent of the wool still upon my fingers. I liked to curl my fingers under my nostrils to take the scent with me into my dreams.

Mornings, my mother and I walked the herd of sheep to the river. Against the sun and sand, my mother would be heavy-robed and veiled. She carried the ruffs of wool I had prepared in a sack at her waist, and, as she walked, she spun the wool from a hand spindle, the fibers lengthening and drawing together to make one long strand, the spindle dropping dizzily. Each day, on our way to graze, we passed the village water buffalo, tethered to a water wheel. It was one of my young cousins who sat by the beast and encouraged his rounds with a switch.

As early as my village life I had reputation as a dancer. The night I first danced for audience, publicly, if you will, was at the celebration of a solstice. My clan had gathered before a great, sparking fire set for the occasion. The fire lit the faces of those around me and toasted my cheeks. I sat on my mother's lap, a position telling of my youth. Across from us, a circle of flat-handed men beat out rhythms on stretched skins. I wriggled free of my mother's arms, moved to converse with the drums. For days afterward, my clansmen remarked on my gift.

"Her hips play so fluid. Her arms might charm snakes."

Dance, you see, was my first language, my tongue without

3

words. I learned it not by instruction; its source was an inner spring, deep and clear.

My village life proceeded carefree and undisturbed until the day I was called upon to dance for my mother's life. One morning my mother did not rouse to the sun. She lay in bed sweaty, fevered, her eyes glazed. The other women in the village erected a tent and removed her to it. They built a fire inside on which they baked big round stones, then doused the stones with water so that steam filled the tent, which they meant as cure. As the daughter of the one ill I had license to run in and out of the tent, and this helped appease my strong fears. But I watched the steam with misgiving. It seemed only to match the fevered vapor already rising hot off my mother. It seemed to me more of the same.

"Steam won't cure," I said. I was right, it didn't. My aunts shushed me, then shooed me outside.

At the other end of the village, a group of men had gathered to chant and drum for my mother's health. I joined their circle to dance, the most powerful prayer I knew.

During the days my mother was sequestered in the tent, a caravan of traders arrived in our village, drawn, I suppose, by the scents of food and profit. My father fell on the traders with questions about the fever. He pressed them to tell if they'd heard of it, if they knew of cure. One trader ridiculed the steam as ignorant, misguided. He said fever required aromatics, that Mama was failing "for want of fragrant smoke." The trader produced a sack of spice he said was certain cure.

"Myrrh?" my father asked, hopeful. It wasn't. Nonetheless, my father grabbed at it, offering to trade anything from our stores of food, but the trader said the spice required something of more value. My father offered our cooking pots, he offered our sheep, he offered the leather camel saddle that was not even his, it was his brother's, but all these offers were refused.

The trader had been watching me dance.

"Is she a virgin?" he asked my father.

"She's my daughter."

"Is she a virgin?"

"She's ten years old."

"For the trade of this young girl, herbs enough to cure your wife," the trader proposed.

My father turned from me. After which, in the heat of the day, I was slung with a satchel and set on a camel.

"Where am I going?" I asked. My father would not look at me. "I have to go to the tent!" I tried to jump down, but the trader sat behind me and crooked his arm around my waist. "I must speak to my mother!"

"She's fevered," my father answered. "You mustn't go near her. You'll catch it."

My father knew that I had spent this morning, as the ones before, at my mother's side, helping to mop her sweat and wipe her spittle. It may well have been his guilt I heard speaking. Whatever its spur, it offered me last hope of escape.

"But I *have* been near her," I said loudly. "I was just in the tent."

"She's lying," my father addressed the trader. "She's been cared for by her aunt. She's not been near her mother for two weeks."

"Yes, I *have!*"

The trader pulled on the reins of the camel. No surprise. He chose to take a man's word over a child's, a girl child's, at that. He turned the camel around and led the caravan out of the village.

"Mami!" I screamed as we rode past the tent. My aunt opened the tent flap and watched as we rode past. "Mami!" I screamed again.

My aunt closed the tent flap. I never knew whether or not my mother heard my cries.

That night, when we camped, many men came sniffing around, but the trader who had made himself my keeper kept them at bay. He himself had with him a young boy and preferred the boy's flesh to mine. In that way, I myself was saved. I listened to his moaning and the wet slap of skin against skin. I worried about my mother and wondered whether she was yet well.

It was many days' travel till we reached the Mukarrib's court. Down the green strip that bordered the river, and then across the parched, bleached white sands. I had heard of the desert, but never before had I crossed it. At first, it frightened me, as it seemed to support no life. But at night I was kept awake by high-pitched croaking sounds, the mating calls of ruby-throated lizards. Days, as we traveled, I watched an old and wizened wind wave across the sands and shift the dunes. By the time we again met a river, the desert inhabited me. Grains of its sand matted my hair. At the river, the men bathed, but not me. I sat tensely on the bank, waiting for the ferry they said was to come. I did not want to yield any of the land I had traveled. I was already learning about loss.

The ferry came. Our caravan was large and required four crossings. I fixed on the long pole that cut the river and argued the current. After that, we trekked alongside fields—green, irrigated, cultivated—sure evidence of man. And it was not long after that we arrived at the wall of the city, a snakelike stretch of stone. The stone was etched with a legend, an inscription touting the deeds and accomplishments of the Mukarrib who ruled there. He repaired the dam, the inscription read, he erected a temple, extended the wall. The wedgelike characters told all this and more. To anyone wise to their key.

We passed through a great, yawning gate, one of seven animating the wall's perimeter. Inside the gate were streets teeming with people, more people than I had imagined were alive. The caravan stopped to water and feed, though I was not to rest. The trader pushed me ahead and pressed through the throng to the citadel nestled beyond that walled off the khan.

In the khan, I was traded once again, this time for more parcels than one. And not for sacks of any dubious spice, this time for baskets of the aromatic responsible for the famed happiness of my homeland. Frankincense, the most precious commodity of all. Having now glimpsed the city, I understood why the need for it was so sore. So many people crammed into such concentrated quarters. Something had to sweeten the stench. The fragrant smoke was a mask.

The trader put his hands on my shoulders and turned me to face two men, one a steward, the other a scribe.

"A virgin," the trader said.

Or at least that's what I surmised. They spoke a language I understood but barely. The two men questioned him and the trader answered back. Only some of their words bore relation to the ones I had learned in my village.

The trader pulled down the underlids of my eyes. He pulled back my lips to show my teeth. He bared my skin to prove it wasn't scabrous. Then that man rapped me on the rear and bade me, "Dance."

I swiveled my hips, it was not much. My ear had dulled to passing music. But it must've been enough, for I was delivered from the men to a coarse-handed woman who bathed me and oiled my hair. She walked me through the honeycombed quarters where lived the other women, dancers and members of the Mukarrib's hareem. That first night, in the long hall, I recall passing Anwa.

"Nubian," the woman said to me, a new word completely, but I discerned from the context what it must mean. Dark-skinned. Never before had I seen skin the color of Anwa's. Truth be told, on first sight, I didn't like the way it looked. Foreign, not the way I knew. I worried she could give the evil eye.

The woman deposited me in a small room, which was nearly bare save for a reed sleeping mat set against one wall, and left me there alone. The sun had set, and the day's light was fading. I sat on the sleeping mat and stared out the adjacent window at the courtyard, which was a whole story below. From my vantage, the people walking there looked like schools of waterfish, darting and swarming. In my chest, I had a tight feeling where, in the past days, all my yearnings for my village had lodged. I was thinking that, if I were back in my village, my hands would be busy with wool.

I put my head down on my new mat and comforted myself with thoughts of my mother. I wondered if she was still sick. Quickly, in my mind, I made her well, and imagined her herding our sheep down the quiet river path. It occurred to me that if I wasn't there, she might now take someone else to accompany her, but that thought caused a sharp pang, so I decided that she took no one, that I was irreplaceable, that my mother now went alone. I pictured her, a tall solitary figure astride the bleating herd. I watched as on her walk she passed the village water buffalo.

When I was very young, my mother had daily lifted me up to the buffalo's woolly snout and bid me kiss it one, two, three. I'd kiss that gentle animal who each day wore the same plodding, circumscribed path, knowing no other. His path secure and constant.

As I'd once thought life to be.

2

"Too many cats," I tell Anwa when she asks. "There were too many cats in the khan, and hungry, every one."

"And what else is it you recall from those earliest days?" Anwa likes me to tell her stories, entertain her with my life.

I am resting my head on the round mound of her belly. I run my tongue lightly over the thin line of coarse black hair that traces a path from her navel to her pubis. I press my cheek against the soft give of her flesh.

"Cats," I repeat. "Feral. Everywhere underfoot."

"Go ahead. And . . . ?"

"And the summer sun blinded the sky and withered the days."

I don't always like to tell about the cats. In any event, they didn't figure into the story so early on. Water did, a small pool of water I discovered in the garden of the khan. Lily pads floated on its surface, rooted, or perhaps not. I call it a reflecting pool, for it was on its silvered surface that I first caught the sad reflection of my face, pale and wan. Eyes lifeless, mouth tightly pinched.

I was a girl in tow, passing through the garden on my way to the metalsmith who was to fit me with the circlet I would be required to wear on my ankle. I did not know this, though. Not yet. I knew only that the coarse-handed woman had come to my room to get me. It was my first morning in the hareem, and the heat was barely sufferable. I had been startled awake only a short while before by the sound of my mother calling out my name.

"Sari!" I'd heard my mother's voice distinctly. "Sari!" she called.

I'd jumped, sweat-drenched, out of bed to answer her, but it was a strange room met my open eyes. It took some moments before I remembered where it was I had been brought.

The cry came again, though it was not my mother's voice as I had thought, the voice was a man's. And it was not my name he was crying out. He was hawking wares.

"Stra-a-a-wb'ries!" was what he cried. "Redripe stra-a-a-awb'ries!"

The cry was coming from my window, from a man in the courtyard below who had at his feet a large basket of the sweet summer fruit. When I looked out I saw that adjacent to my window was a line of other windows, and in them there were women, leaning out, laughing, calling back to the vendor. Some were lowering small baskets down by rope to fetch their share of his wares.

"Well?" Someone was asking me a question. Someone behind me. "Would you like some?"

I spun around and saw that it was the Nubian girl addressing me. She was standing in my doorway, and I was surprised to see that up close she looked young. Though she carried herself with stature and authority, she could not have been more than two or three years older than I. The girl put a strawberry to her lips and sucked the fruit off its leaf. Then she held one out to me.

"Strawberries," she said, when I did not move. "You've not tasted the fruit?"

I shook my head no, not in answer to a question I wasn't sure I understood, but to indicate I did not want any. Not from her.

She took a step forward.

"I am called Anwa," she said. She paused so I could introduce myself in turn. I did not. "And you?" She pointed to me.

I pursed my lips, as if my identity were a secret I held tightly inside. A strange taste rose from the knotting in my stomach. Much later, Anwa would tell me that I looked at that moment like a wild rabbit, cornered and frightened.

"But you loved me immediately?" I would ask.

And she would answer, "I sensed the softness of your fur."

"You must have been prescient," I would laugh. "I was yet tender. I had no fur."

"Then it was your scent." And she'd nuzzle me at that scent's very source.

"What are you doing here?" That first morning, the coarse-handed woman appeared in the doorway and addressed Anwa. "Have you come for purpose, or did you catch the scent of fresh meat?"

"Maadr," Anwa greeted her. "You ask me the very question I might well ask you."

"The girl is in my charge," said Maadr. She pushed past Anwa and dropped a knotted bundle on my sleeping mat. "Off with your clothing," she nodded. The woman didn't wait for me to comply. She yanked up the sides of my robe and wrangled it over my head. Then she unknotted the bundle she had brought. Out spilled a cascade of garments. All were brightly dyed and finely woven. Some had decorative stitching and beads. I grabbed up my homespun which she had tossed to the floor. It was cloth my mother had made. I hugged it to my chest.

"Grain sacking," Maadr said, dismissing it. She snatched the robe from my hands and pulled a new one from the pile. "I'll give that to the stableboy for grain sacking."

Anwa stepped between the older woman and me. "Give it or sell it?" she asked. "I doubt that you plan to give it to the stableboy. I don't think I've ever seen you give anything away."

"You have some interest in this robe?"

"I just don't think you need take it from the girl. Dress her

11

in new cloth, if you will. Cloth that more appropriately suits her for court. But why not let her keep the garment she arrived in?"

Anwa slipped a ring off her middle finger. In it was set a faceted red stone that caught the light. She held the ring out to Maadr.

"I suppose this would make a nicer trade still."

Maadr eyed Anwa a moment, then took the ring and tucked it into the fold of her sash. "Keep the robe," she said, tossing it back to me. "You have a benefactress. Keep it but don't let me catch you wearing it. It could cost me my station."

Anwa laughed aloud. She took a single strawberry out of her basket and set it on the small stool near my mat.

"In case you want later to venture a taste," she said to me before she left.

When the sound of Anwa's footsteps receded down the hallway, Maadr picked up the strawberry and popped it into her own mouth.

"Be careful of that one," she warned me. "She beds most nights with the Mukarrib. They say she has his ear. If she hears something, it is likely that he does, too."

When Maadr had me freshly suited in one of the new garments, she, too, started out the door. "Come," she said. I ran to catch up with her and on impulse reached to take the skirt of her robe in my hand. Maadr tugged the robe away.

"You're not in your village," she snapped at me. "I'm not your mother. Behavior is different here."

I reached down and clutched at the fabric of my own clothing. The silk felt as weightless in my hand as it did against my skin. I bunched up more of it and squeezed tighter.

As Maadr padded down the hall, I trailed behind her. The other women in the hareem leaned out of their doorways and eyed me curiously. They called to one another over my head across the hallway, their chatter sounding high and shrill, like the buzz of insects in high summer reeds.

"A village girl," said one.

"She's young."

"No younger than I when I arrived."

"Yes, but this one's a bud. You came in full-bloomed."

"And you? The edges of your petals were already browned."

A sandal sailed over my head, hurled by one woman at another, who caught it with both hands and shot it back. Maadr led me past them, through an arched doorway. We passed from the shade of the building to an assault of sun in the garden, which was where I saw my face reflected in the pool of water. After which I found myself in the metal shop where a man measured the circumference of my ankle with a rope in order to fit me with the circlet worn by all the women of the hareem, a circlet that marked us as property of the Mukarrib. I watched the man hold the band of metal with a long pair of tongs over a fire. The room was close with the sour smell of perspiration, both Maadr's and the metalsmith's. When the piece was pliable, the man took it from the fire and hammered it into shape. Though he set it to cool, it was still hot when he clamped it on me. I cried out from the shock of it.

"Careless fool!" Maadr shouted. She ordered the man to get her a small cloth. "And make sure it's clean!" She dipped the cloth into a basin of cool water, then slipped it between the hot metal and the skin it had singed. "There," she cooed, tender, suddenly maternal. "There, my daughter, there." She ran her hand over my hair to soothe me.

The skin of my ankle was hot, tight, and smarting. With the old woman leaning so close to me, the strong smell of her no longer just flirted with my nostrils, it seemed to flood my mouth and throat and gag me. In an instant, I lost control, doubled over and began to retch.

My skin blistered, the contents of my guts heaved on the floor. It was in that graceless, unhappy fashion that I began my career in the Mukarrib's hareem and was first marked as his property.

"Go on," says Anwa. "I know you remember more."

I put my lips to her breast. I take its full, dark nipple in my mouth and suck hard.

Anwa laughs. "You were taken from your mother too soon," she says.

But Anwa was not like my mother. She was altogether different. Something fresh-scent, wild.

Which is, as it happens, only half the story.

One night I sat bolt upright in bed. I turned to the lover who lay at my side, her brown skin tinged by the blue flicker of the TV. I told my lover the dream I'd had. That we'd lived together other lives.

"Oh yeah?" she said. My lover's name was Dee. She set down the remote control to the television set. "Where?"

"In a harem," I said, the detail of the dream seeping through to my consciousness. "We were lovers in that life, too."

"Codie," Dee said, tough-like, skeptical, which was the way she liked to talk, "you just *wish* we lived together in a harem."

"So what if I do?" I cocked my head. I had some weak idea it might inspire Dee to grab me up and kiss me. "Where's the harm in wishing, I ask you?"

Dee aimed the remote control back at the television and flipped through the channels, as if half a world away. I turned to the window and stared out at the maze of traffic that was our view. On the long expanse of wall opposite ours, some tale-telling youth had painted an ornate flourish of graffiti. In the half light of night, the writing looked to me to be indecipherable. The letters didn't look like the alphabet, but garbled. More like characters to some language long forgotten.

A car alarm sounded. A siren shrieked. Through it, I felt I heard the faint thrum of tambour.

What drifted in my window was ancient and sensuous, suggesting even more. Fatted smoke from the night fires. Women wailing in the name of song.

Moonspill, of course.

And flies. . . .

3

No doubt, by now, everybody in earshot's itching to find out who this is who's telling the tales, spinning the yarns, so to speak.

Someone sorry, that's who.

Men on the street they call to me as I pass. "Smile, sweetheart! It can't be that bad."

How do they know?

One day when I've had about enough, I spin around and shout back. "Oh yeah? Today alone, my mother died and she took my lover with her!" Though actually it's been quite some time since I've had a mother. And lovers seem to disappear like water on a griddle.

Dee up and left me. That's the real beginning of this story. And the end as well. After she was gone, I had six words for crying. Which is two more than the Eskimos have for snow.

Wren, good friend that she is, has done double duty counseling me not to worry. She's tried to tell me it's a juncture I'm at, is all. But me, I've not been so sure. What with crying just about as constant as breathing, and me barely knowing which way to turn, let alone where to start.

"Look in the mirror," says Wren.

Whatever that means.

"Start at the beginning."

The beginning . . .

From the start, I'd have to say that jokes have been what's hardest. I get to the end and forget the punch line. Even with coaching I could never remember what it was exactly that some Polack said to some black guy said to some Jew.

"She's not my daughter," my father would say, grinning, shrugging, to whatever group of relatives or friends was assembled. His own punch line.

Oddly enough, one thing always good for a laugh was my name. In a decade when other girls had names like Debby, Suzy, and Linda, my parents christened me Kodiak. I shortened it as best I could and answered to the nickname Codie. Though the name they gave me had an insistent way of surfacing.

"Kodiak James," the nun would read from the roll each year, the first day of school. Then, confused, she'd quickly reverse the last name with the first, assume that I was a boy, that the list had been typed wrong.

"Present," I would call out, as we had been taught. The nun would squint at me. Me, a thin girl with hair dark and broody, braided tightly off the face. A girl wearing a loose uniform jumper, ill-fitting.

No rhyme or reason.

None of this took place anywhere too exotic. A town called Middletown somewhere between the O's in Ohio. My family lived in a Gold Medallion All-Electric Home. I knew because there was a bronze plaque beside the front door that said so. Embedded in the brick, right above the milk box.

When we moved in, we had a yard, but no lawn and no trees. The house sat on a staked lot of raked dirt, and all the other lots on the block were as barren. Our lawn was delivered one day on the back of a flatbed truck. It came as pieces of sod which were rolled up, grass-side in. Workmen unloaded the truck and stacked the sod against the side of our house, like a woodpile. I climbed to the top, Queen of the Mountain. The rooted dirt was cool against my bare calves and I liked the earthy smell.

My father unrolled the pieces of sod and laid them end-to-end across the yard, fit them together like puzzle pieces. The sod looked green, lush, tuft-y. Who was to tell it was just sitting on top of the dirt, not rooted at all? Later, my father added saplings to the yard. It was years before they provided any shade.

No one seemed to wonder at the irony. Every morning I woke up to the low groaning of bulldozers. The contractors had completed our street, but behind us were acres of undeveloped woods. The bulldozers leveled the land and uprooted all the trees.

I have snapshots going back even further toward the beginning. There's one, for instance, of my parents on their Florida honeymoon. My mother lying on a lounge chair by the hotel pool, bundled feet to neck in a heavy wool blanket.

"It was cold," she explained. "It was January."

My father, in the same picture, stands beside her. He is tanned and bare-chested. His hair and swimming trunks are dripping. He smiles up at the sun.

My father smirked whenever I brought out that picture.

"Your mother thought I was a Russian spy," he'd say.

"Because you *told* me you were," she'd complain.

"I told your mother I was a Russian spy and she believed me."

The way my mother told the story, she didn't know much about my father before she married him. They'd gone out only a few months before they were wed. That first night in Florida my father had taken her to a candle-lit dinner in the hotel dining room, and my mother was feeling girlish and shy, it being her honeymoon and all. But while she was buttering her breadstick my father turned suddenly grave. He lowered his voice and said there was something he had to tell her. "You've got to promise to stick by me and never breathe a word," he said. And that's when he told her he wasn't an electrical engineer at all, he was really a Russian spy.

"And she *believed* me," my father would bellow.

I can tell you what I see in the picture. My mother blue-lipped and shivering in the winter sun.

"It wasn't funny," she said. "I was really scared."

So my parents named me for an island off Alaska. It's where my father was stationed during the war. Which illustrates so beautifully, doesn't it, how war expands horizons?

"Did you kill any Japs, Daddy?" I once asked, spurred by the boasting of a friend. But my father didn't have war stories like other fathers. Alaska had seen no active fighting. What my father did bring back was a box of photographs he had taken, eight-by-ten prints of volcanoes, aerial shots taken from Navy prop planes, the camera looking straight down into the mouths of smoking craters. My father had been a photographer during the war. The Navy had set him up with a camera and a dark-room and enlisted him in a mapping mission, had him charting territory in case the war in the Pacific escalated and Alaska be-came strategic.

Something about the photographs my father had taken fas-cinated me. I found them one day in a thin gray box stored in the basement. Often I stole downstairs by myself to look at them. In my favorite photo, my father had caught the wing of the plane in the frame. The wing was crude, boxy, a silver slash against the snow-crusted, open-mouthed peak. I imagined that the war had been about landscape, that men had been con-scripted and mobilized to capture such commanding forces of nature.

"And what about the shower?" my mother interrogated me. *"What happened in the shower?"* Her accusations whizzing by like ammo.

When I'd chanced into my mother's room, I'd found her staring vacantly into the mirror, sitting at the dressing table be-side the large garbage can that belonged outside. My mother looked somehow different, though at first I didn't realize why. Until I noticed that where once she had had eyebrows there were now only little red bumps. My mother had plucked out her eyebrows completely, and all of her eyelashes, too.

"Mommy?" I said.

I wasn't sure she heard me. At first she didn't answer.

I'm telling you, Mama. Nothing happened in the shower.

"Nothing?"

Not that I remember.

Dee. Sometimes Dee called me Tat. As in, "Tit for." One reason I loved her. One of plenty.

Dee wrote stories, New York stories, ones she collected each day driving her cab. I fell in love with the cocky way she wore a baseball cap, the ease she had behind the wheel. She drove—no, wove—the grid that is Manhattan. She knew the streets, the warp and weft of them. I fell in love with the child-like way she posed requests.

"Tat?" Dee asked one day, all innocence, ingenuous. She was at my house one morning before we actually moved in together, ironing a Yankees T-shirt and a pair of jeans. Ironing them, at least, as best she could given that all she had to work on was a dishtowel laid flat on a corner of the table. "Tat," she asked, "when we have an apartment together, can we get a real ironing board?"

"The biggest board they sell," I promised. "With a flame-retardant cover." I would've promised Dee the skies, the oceans, whole continents. Peninsulas and seas.

What can I say, Dee appeared in my life and made magic. We were two people in love, so happy to have found each other that that summer, when I did move in with her, we called a celebration. For party favors, Dee bought a bag of tricks. Paper flowers that bloomed out of breast pockets, and little wire puzzles, the pieces impossibly entwined. Friends came to our apartment, toasted us with champagne and showered us with gifts. Three knife sharpeners, we got. We got other gifts, too, but three friends independently came up with the idea of knife sharpener. I was polite about the first two but I laughed out loud when I opened the third.

"What's that they say about coincidence?" I asked.

Dee returned to the room with a fresh pitcher of punch.

"You should've seen Codie's face," she told our guests. She didn't care that she was changing the subject. She was all smiles, so proud I half expected her to hand out cigars.

"When I walked back into that bakery?" I said. "Are you talking about when I walked back into the bakery?"

"I should've got a picture," said Dee. "The look on your face."

What Dee was bursting to tell was the story of the wedding cake. The idea to get one in the first place had been mine. It went with the dress I'd found to wear. White. Tea length. Just a touch of lace.

To add grist to Dee's story I turned to our friends and feigned offense. "I couldn't believe what I was hearing. I left the bakery for a minute, no more, and when I walked back in, there was Dee, chatting away with the baker like he's her long lost brother or something, and then I hear Dee say, 'Actually, we don't want a bride and a groom, we want two brides.' 'Two brides,' she says."

Dee shrugged, all nonchalance. "The baker had a carton full of those plastic ornaments you stick on top of cakes, but they were all bride and groom combinations. So I just asked him if he could give us two brides."

"Two brides," I repeated for effect. "Dee T. Matthews, before we even called up this bakery to make an appointment, I made you promise that you wouldn't breathe a word about the cake being for us."

"And I never did," Dee said. She smiled at our friends. "I never explicitly said it was for us."

Tricks up her sleeve? Dee had plenty. At the bakery, she'd sent me out to check the parking meter, so she'd be alone in the room with the baker.

"Actually, I never told you the best part, Codie." Dee was grinning. "When you were out at the car, the baker asked me did I want a black bride and groom or a white set. 'One white and one black,' I said. And that's when you walked in and I explained to him two brides."

I groaned. I covered my face with my hands.

"So what happened?" asked a friend.

"The guy barely blinked," Dee went on. "He fiddled with the plastic bride and groom to see if they would come apart and when they wouldn't, he fished back into the carton and pulled out the ornament we got. 'I've got two bells,' he said. 'Will that do?' "

"Two belles," I said.

Dee put both arms around me and hugged me from behind. Then she reached into my pocket and pulled out a paper flower I hadn't even known had been planted there. "It's a beautiful cake, huh, baby?" she said. I wriggled around to face her so I could kiss her full on the mouth.

"The most beautiful cake in the world," I answered. In my experience, when your heart is full to overflowing, the corniest things spill out of your mouth.

Someone snapped a picture of Dee and me kissing like that and then another of the two of us cutting the cake. Dee's hand was grasping mine as we steadied the sterling silver cake knife Wren had brought over, borrowed from her mother for the occasion. Around us, friends held glasses high, a toast. Me, I was leaning into Dee, drawn into her orbit as if by magnetic design. Both of us were beaming.

Tide turning.

Anwa was bright sun to my pale moon. Reflected light.

After we moved in together we took two of the three knife sharpeners back to Macy's and exchanged them for an ironing board, a big one with fold-out legs.

"We'll store it in the broom closet," said Dee.

Though of course we never did. We left it open in the living room. Half the time it stood in the middle of the floor. Dee used it every morning, I hardly ever used it. To tell the truth, I seldom ironed my clothes.

"Seldom?" I can hear Dee now. "You mean never."

"It's a look," I would say to defend myself.

"What, the rumpled look?"

"I work in the Village. I'm *supposed* to be rumpled. They expect it."

"Codie, I've visited you at work. No one else dresses like you. Everyone else dresses like they're going to a *job*."

"So I'm an individual."

"Yeah, well, you're gonna get that individual ass of yours *fired*."

"I thought you liked this individual ass of mine. I always sort of got the impression you were partial to it, in fact." I'd stick my rear out just a little, so it looked kind of pert and inviting.

"Get your butt over here," she'd say.

"Make me."

Then Dee would grab me up and kiss me and say something like, "That's just what I was planning on doing."

Newlyweds. Always the same. Everything's endearing. The very things that later turn fodder for fights.

As if to confirm our status, one night, early on, Dee turned on the television and there he was, Bob Eubanks, host of *The Newlywed Game*. I took that for what it clearly was, a patriarch's firm blessing. I got out a pad and pen so we could play along.

"Which of us is going to be the husband?" Dee asked.

I rolled my eyes for effect. "I only see one macha in this room."

"Okay," Dee agreed, "I'm the husband." She straightened

up in her seat to give her attention to the screen. One thing about Dee, she never could get any of the questions that required the least observation of detail.

"The color of her toothbrush!" she shouted. "Who the fuck knows the color of their wife's toothbrush?" Bob Eubanks's smile never faded.

We played until the first commercials. Until Dee, fed up with the questions Bob Eubanks posed, made up her own questions, wild and silly. "Husbands," she asked, her voice deep and authoritative, "husbands, which of the following fruits would you say describe your wife's breasts: oranges, mangoes, or cantaloupes?" Dee didn't miss a beat, she shouted out her own answer, "Lemons!" though that had not even been one of the choices. "No! No! Not lemons!" she squealed, a better idea coming to her. "What are those little, pointy, squishy fruits the Korean stores sell in the summer? Figs! That's it! My wife's breasts are like figs, Bob."

Dee pulled up my shirt right there on the couch and fell to nibbling at me.

"Judges!" I shouted toward the TV. "One of the husbands is nibbling at the wives! Disqualify her!"

I shouted over the ironing board, which stood between the couch and the TV. Dee had set it up that day like a coffee table. On it stood three beer cans, two empty.

Dee scrunched her head under my shirt and pretended to slobber all over me.

"Hey, I just ironed this shirt," I protested weakly. Both of us knew that was a lie.

Just beyond me: three beer cans in stark relief. Beer cans all in a row.

That night in bed, I curled around Dee like a vine.

"Do you remember the first time I went down on you?" Dee asked. "Do you remember what you did?"

"Probably I got all squirmy with pleasure, huh?"

"No. You wrenched away and said, 'Whoa! Let's not get carried away!' "

"I did not."

"You did, too."

"Well," I said defensively, "it was my first time. I was never in bed with a woman before."

" 'Let's not get carried away,' " she scoffed.

"Listen," I said, "don't ever tell anybody I said that."

"Hey, don't look so worried."

"Really. Don't ever."

"I won't, baby. I'd never."

Those first nights I slept at Dee's apartment, I had a nightmare, a recurring one about breaking glass. The dream seemed to get triggered every time I was there. I didn't say anything about it to Dee, though. I'd wake up before her, with traces of the illusion still lingering. I'd lie in bed and worry about why I had the dream. What it could mean or foretell.

One night, though, I woke up in the middle of the night and the sound was right in the room. Glass. Shattering. It was real, coming from somewhere outside, just beyond the window.

"Dee." I shook Dee's shoulder to rouse her. "Dee, what's that noise?"

"Hmm?"

"That noise. The breaking glass." I sat up in bed and shook Dee's shoulder harder. "What is it?"

Dee hugged me around the waist and laid her head in my lap. "The bar downstairs," she said sleepily.

"What do you mean?"

"They do it every night. At closing. To fit the empties into the can."

"Really?" I asked, not reassured.

"Don't worry," said Dee. She shifted her head, nestling into me as if I were a pillow. "I'll protect you."

Dee fell right back to sleep. I stayed awake a while. The room was lit by the spill of the street lamp outside. And loud with the sound of breaking glass.

The night I first followed Dee to her room, she'd draped a sheer length of silk across my face, then kissed me through the veil. Harum-scarum.

25

So where's the harm in wishing? I'd later wonder, looking back.

"What are you thinking?" Dee interrupted.

The radiator hissed. The night was still, snow-sodden, heavy with winter.

"I was thinking of the seasons," was all I could tell her. "How they pass so quickly."

Jake poked his head inside my cubicle, stack of mail in hand.

"Hey, Codie," he said. "What's the talking bunny count this morning?" Talking bunnies was our running joke. Jake knew I was going through the morning's unsoliciteds.

"One," I said. It was true. I held up the manuscript for my boss to see. "Proof."

"*Fluff N. Stuff,*" Jake read off the cover page. "By Bern Acinder of Blaze, Colorado." He winced at the obviousness of the name, then returned to our pet point. "How do they all do it? Thousands of story-telling hopefuls across this great, free land and they all come up with the exact same idea."

"Not all. Here's something original." I held up another manuscript. "A talking *toothbrush.*"

"Variation on a theme," said Jake. And he was gone.

This was what I did for a living. I worked in the editorial offices of a children's publishing house, and part of my job was to screen the manuscripts submitted. I leafed through the talking bunny story that had come in that particular day. My eye fell on a paragraph at random.

"Fluffy wiggled her cute little pink nose and hopped quick as a bunny into Farmer Parsnip's garden."

"Quick as a bunny?" I said aloud. "She *is* a bunny. And it's *wriggled*, not wiggled."

I put the story in the envelope the author had included for its return and tossed it into the out box. In the long window that faced my cubicle I could see into the windows of the building across the street. The one directly opposite mine opened into a dance studio. The dancers were wearing rehearsal clothes and were bunched in the center of the room, watching a teacher who was demonstrating a step. I watched as they spread out and waited for some cue, then themselves began to dance. For me, of course, the dance was mute. Movement to music I couldn't hear.

That night, late, Dee was working on one of her stories. She was propped up in bed, a legal pad on her knees. At the foot of the bed sat the television set, which was blaring, as was the radio. Dee's doing, not mine. She always liked a lot of noise. I stared dutifully at Movie of the Week, trying hard not to pay it attention.

"Hey, Code," Dee said. She didn't look up from the sentence she was writing. "Can you swipe me some more of these legal pads from work? I'm going through 'em like water."

"Sure," I said. Actually, I had a story idea of my own brewing. And it was not in the talking bunny genre. "Will you tear a couple of sheets off for me there, too?" I asked.

Dee ripped a few pieces of paper from the back of the pad and handed them over. On Movie of the Week a cop was pursuing a couple of drug smugglers who were making a helicopter drop-off on a rooftop. The helicopter took off with the cop hanging from the runner. The cop had his gun drawn as if that would help.

"Can I turn off the TV?" I asked.

"I like it," said Dee.

"You're not even watching."

"Yeah, but the music is perfect. I'm writing a car chase. I got the idea this afternoon when I had two Mafia fares."

"Mafia? How do you know?"

28

"Had to be. One guy was packing a pistol and kept talking about 'the job,' and 'the family.' And I distinctly heard the other guy say 'whack.' "

"Whack? What's whack?"

"Rub out, Codie. Get with the program."

"Come on. He said 'whack'?"

"Honest to God."

Sometimes the details of Dee's day were alarming. "One guy had a pistol? You have fares with guns? You're driving the Mafia to rubouts?"

"They said 'dese, dem, dose,' " said Dee, as if to clinch her story. Her attention trailed back to her paper. She hummed distractedly along to the movie music, rocking back and forth with the beat.

I wasn't sure whether I believed Dee or not. My not-so-private opinion was that she watched too much television. I decided, myself, to escape its influence. I picked up my paper and pen and went to run a bath. I liked writing in the bathtub. Reading, too. So much so that I had developed something of a reputation around baths and Dee wouldn't let me take any of her books into the tub with me. "If we break up," she'd once said to me, "we won't have any trouble dividing up the books. All of yours have crinkled pages."

That night, the idea that proposed itself to me was a children's story. I positioned my paper on the lip of the tub and began jotting down what came to mind—character traits, possible scenes, turns of phrase. I did so, that is, until distraction showed her face. Distraction by the name of Dee.

Dee barged into the bathroom and unbuttoned her shirt. She shed her clothes onto the tile of the floor. "Move over, Rover," she crowed, holding her arms wide and shaking her tits. " 'Cause Dee's comin' over." The doctored lyric, apparently, of some song.

Dee wasted no time in climbing into the bathtub with me, nor any time complaining. "Ouch!" she said. "It's too hot! If I wanted to poach, I'd turn on the stove!" She reached behind her to the faucet to add some cold, and then she fidgeted around trying to get comfortable in the cramped space we were now supposed to be sharing. She tried to stretch her legs out on either side of me, but they were too long for the tub and her knees stuck up out of the water. "How're you supposed to get comfortable in one of these things?" she asked. "I never understand what it is you see in these baths."

Taking a bath with Dee was like sailing in a squall. The water got all choppy. You couldn't just lie back, let yourself be lulled. That's what I was thinking, so I told Dee so, then and there.

"That's why you love me," she said.

"Yeah, but couldn't you every once in a while just get into a bath and be calm? Maybe like once every six months or so? I know it's a stretch."

Dee made a face and shifted again. "The faucet's sticking me in the back," she said. "How are these baths supposed to work?" Dee took hold of the paper I had been writing on and tugged it out of my hand. "So what's this?" she asked. "What're you working on anyway?"

"I got this idea for a children's book," I said.

"Great!" said Dee. She threw her arms around me in broad, tipsy show of affection. "What have I been telling you? 'Write a children's book, Codie,' I said. You've got to do better than all these other people you tell me about."

Dee studied the paper. My handwriting coiled out in an illegible scrawl, arrows pointing every which way. Some of the ink was smeared. Dee knit her brow. "So what's the idea?" she asked.

"It's about a young girl who's a temple dancer in some ancient time and some exotic place."

"Your harem idea," Dee said flatly, as if that explained everything.

"Well, not harem exactly. She's more like a temple dancer."

Dee leaned back in the bathtub and squinted at me. "Codie, you can't write a children's book about a harem."

"I just said it wasn't a harem. She's some sort of ritual dancer or something."

"Well, where is it?"

"I don't know, someplace kind of Middle East-y."

"And when exactly?"

"It's not going to be any time exactly. It'll be the ancient . . . I don't know . . . the ancient Arabia of my imagination."

"You mean like generic ancient?"

"It'll be imaginative, fabulous."

"You can't do that, Codie. You have to set it."

"It's a story. I don't have to do anything. I can write whatever I want."

"Now listen, Codie," said Dee. She'd switched to her lecture voice, a tack which did not make me want to listen a whit. "Kids are going to read this and they're going to wonder, 'Where exactly is this? And when?' This will go to young, impressionable minds. You have a responsibility to be historically accurate."

"I disagree," I said flatly.

"Anyway, what's this harem fascination?" Dee pressed. "You're really getting a thing about this harem."

I slouched down in what little bathtub space was left me so that the water covered my neck and lapped at my chin. Dee stuck her toes into my ribs, a sort of underwater tickle. Across the tub her face looked too big to me, assuming, like a full moon looming in a starless sky.

"The water's getting cold," I said. "Turn on some hot."

I didn't play with the story anymore that night because there was Dee in the bathtub. The next day, it occurred to me to pick up the notes I'd made and play with them, but, when I had the chance, I didn't do it. Some voice in my head had begun whispering doubt. Crisis of faith, as the nuns would've said. Crises of faith running rampant.

The next morning, on my way to work, I stopped at the newsstand on the corner and bought myself a *New York Times*. I didn't usually read the paper in the morning, and I didn't exactly intend to read the paper that morning either. What had hit me was a sudden, inexplicable craving for articles about volcanoes, and I thought I'd scan the paper on the off chance.

As the odds makers might have predicted, I didn't find any volcano articles that morning, but I did find one that caught my attention. A small article, buried in section C. It concerned a pod of stranded whales.

"And how are you this morning, Ms. James?" Jake asked as I passed him in the hall.

"Ten whales have beached themselves!" was my furious answer. "On the Oregon shore!" I waved the paper in front of him for context. "Rescue workers tried to tow them back out to the deep, but when the whales got free, they swam right back to the sand!"

What frightened me most, I think, was it seemed the whales wanted to die.

After my assault on Jake, I holed myself up in my cubicle. I uncapped my take-out coffee and nursed it a long time before I started work. I sipped slowly from the cup and stared into the windows of the dance studio across the way. There, dancers were warming up. Their movement was slow. Hypnotic as surf.

Eventually the mail cart came around and I got a stack of unsoliciteds. The first one I opened was a story about a talking clam. It was submitted by a Barbara S. Deed of Shanghai, Virginia. In her cover letter, Ms. Deed wrote, "I think the story could be quite revealing. Especially for readers who live inland of the sea."

I snatched up the manuscript and strode down the hall to Jake's office, the most purposeful thing I'd done since last we spoke. The conversation he and I would have was already raging in my head. "Talking clam!" I would shriek. "She thinks it could be quite revealing! Especially for readers living inland of the sea!" But when I got to Jake's office and knocked, he didn't answer. I twisted the knob and cracked open the door.

No one was there.

6

Anwa doesn't mind me telling stories, she's just wary of me inscribing them for the ages. She wants me to tell about the blood that colored that time. There was blood, I won't deny it. But there were also events of a different cast. More sanguine, if you will. As when Iman pushed me forward as a dancer. The khan was set to celebrate. And it would be my good fortune to be spotlit, suddenly graced with attention.

It was Iman who first brought us news of the feast. We women of the hareem had assembled together to dine, as was our custom. The weather was hot, the breeze aromatically spiced. We lounged outdoors in the garden at long, low tables overhung with trellises and vines. Banter darted among us as quickly as the bowls of food.

"Look at Somhe pile pigeon on her plate."

"She thinks eating pigeon will round out her breasts. It won't, Somhe. It'll go right to your hips."

"And the Mukarrib likes ample-breasted women, not ample-hipped."

"Well, then, pass the pigeon over here. Perhaps if I add enough girth that man will keep his hands off me."

"Yasamen has girth. Nine months of girth."

"Close your ears, Sari. The one virgin among us."

Flies lit on our food. Cats rubbed against our legs, not for affection, but for the meal on our plates. We tossed scraps to our favorites. The others we knocked back.

Our directress had not yet arrived in the garden. When the bowls were cleared and a tray of sticky sweets set down to replace them, she came to join us.

"Iman," someone greeted her, "where have you been?"

"With the Mukarrib."

"Don't tell me. Called for coupling? At your age?"

"No." She shook her head. "As priestess. May the gods help us. He's had another dream."

The Mukarrib had had a dream, certain enough. A dream about a serpent. Upon waking from which he'd decided that we should hold a feast to honor the animal, and should do so with haste. The snake was the symbol of the moon god, we knew, who must be propitiated now that summer was high, the dog-star upon us. For summer was the season in which the workers tapped the trees, cut into the bark of the sweet wood frankincense, coaxing it to ooze its precious resin. And whose trees were they if not the god of the moon's?

Beyond us, in the dry beds of the garden, gusts of wind kicked up the arid soil. Sand swirled. Dust devils. We covered our eyes.

Iman, though, sat distracted among us. As well she knew, this whim of the Mukarrib's would fall to her employ. When the food was cleared, she excused herself and went alone to the Hall of a Hundred Columns. There she waited for night to fall. What Iman traded in was visions, ones that came to her moonlit, in solitude. Though mysterious, these visions translated, for us, into practical work. This night, the vision that came to her was of a snake wriggling about, shedding its skin. When she called us to our first rehearsal, Iman told us her plan—that we should all move together in unison, so our movement would read as one serpent.

"Was this instruction given you by the gods," someone asked, "or did you come to it out of expedience?"

"The gods," answered Iman.

"How fortuitous that they would suggest an ensemble piece at just the time when Yasamen"—Yasamen was her principal dancer—"is near to nine months with child and barred from the bounds of the temple."

"Indeed."

"You have witnesses to these supposed gods?"

"You know as well as I that the gods descend when I'm alone. You all are asleep. I'm the one who stays awake all night in the Hall."

"How many of these gods were there, then?"

"Four, I think."

"And how did they appear to you?"

"They alighted from a cloud and whispered in my ear."

"And what did they say?"

"They said, 'Iman, your principal dancer is unable and impure. Best do an ensemble piece to serve expedience.' "

"Oh, I see. These were practical gods."

"And what other kind?"

"Dancers!" At the first rehearsal, this flew out of Iman's mouth like an epithet. Already we were frustrating her desire to have us move as one snake. It is an odd fact, curious to the profession, that dancers can sooner balance on one finger than move synchronously. Iman leaned her forehead against one of the columns for which the Hall was named. "Whatever possessed me to dream up movement so simple?" she asked.

"I thought it was divinely inspired," someone called out.

"It was." Iman turned to us. "But the gods forgot to take into account the distinct and individual styles of my dancers. I am on my knees to beg you." (Which anyone could see she wasn't.) "Many dancers, one serpent."

It took the full afternoon of rehearsing, but by the time the light was rosy with the suggestion of sunset, the group had achieved the effect, or at least more nearly. There was only one dancer who, try as she might, could not move in unison with the others. And that was me. Iman stopped the flautist who accompanied our rehearsal and pulled me out of line.

"Sari," she asked frankly, "what are you doing?"

"I thought I was doing as directed."

"Then why does my eye go to you whenever the line starts up? I tried squinting so as not to see individuals or faces, but still my eye goes straight to you."

"Are you going to instruct the Mukarrib to squint?" I asked.

"No need," she said. "He'll already have had his wine. Come. Do the step. What is it you do that's so different?"

I did the step as she asked, and Iman could find no fault. She pulled the musician back over to again accompany me. "Stop," she said. The fault was the flute's. "When the music plays, you complicate the step with extraneous movement. It looks as if you've got a snake living inside you, wriggling to get free."

"Well, at least my error is thematic."

"Can't you contain the serpent?"

"Apparently, the music calls her out."

"And you have no say?"

"It appears not."

"Well, if you can't do as directed, what do you propose I do with you?"

"I know what you want me to say, that you'll need to remove me from line. But if that's your decision, I am afraid you'll have to say so yourself, for I like to dance."

At this retort I was banished to a carpet at the far end of the room. Iman returned her attentions to the work. She dragged a bin to the center of the room, out of which she pulled long lengths of fabric. "Cloaks," she explained, shaking them out. "In the second phase of the choreography, the snake sheds its skin." She distributed the cloaks one each to the dancers, and demonstrated how they should drop them one by one in swift succession. She then instructed Somhe, the dancer at the head of the line and therefore the one posing as the head of the snake, to flick her tongue—quickly, in and out. Somhe's tongue was nimble, the glint in her eyes suggestive. "Well done," approved Iman. "That will be the punctuation of the piece. And now?" She raised her hands. "Enough. Out of here, all of you. Give a tired woman some peace."

As my friends trickled out the Hall, I stood up to follow
them. "Not you, Sari," said Iman. "Let's see you dance to the
flute again. What happens if we free this snake you seem to
have inside you?"

I did as asked. Iman waited a long time before she spoke.
I was still unsure enough to worry about my employment at the
hareem. It crossed my mind that Iman could dismiss me then
and there. But what she said was, "You'll be soloist. I hadn't
planned for such a role, but there seems to be no quieting you."

"Soloist?" I said. "Me?"

"You heard me. Now go. I'll work with you tomorrow. And
Sari!" She called this to me as I was almost out the door. "Someday I'll teach you how to do the step correctly if you'll teach
me to do whatever it is you do with those shoulders of yours."
Iman wriggled her shoulders to mimic mine.

"That's poor imitation," I laughed.

"Go!"

Anwa's at my ear again, impatient. "Tell," she prods. "Tell what
it is really happened."

What she wants me to tell, still, is the part about the blood.
In those days blood was everywhere. Everywhere leaking between lips. One moon-drunk night, I looked on as a tangle of
cats first fought over, then ate a fresh and glistening placenta.
This was no veiled symbol in some despot's dream. It was Yasamen's last offering to those yet alive.

Nights in the hareem were seldom quiet or still. But the
night Anwa wants me to tell about was distinguished from the
others. By birth and death and the vigil that attends them. Over
time I'd become accustomed to the din of women crying out.
Night sounds, a dissonant lullaby. But this night, the sounds
weren't the moaning or impassioned pleading I'd grown accustomed to. They were screams.

When the screams awakened me, I clothed myself and followed them to their source, as if they were the call of some
siren goddess. Though clearly they were mortal. As would
prove the woman from whom they ushered.

It was Yasamen screaming. Near to nine months and no more room to hold the baby daily growing, daily pushing out the too-tight skin of her belly. When I got to the room, many of the women were gathered there already, come together to witness something. A birthing, is what we suspected.

Beside Yasamen was Somhe. She held Yasamen's hand and smoothed the sweat-stuck hair off her forehead. For Yasamen was Somhe's lover, the woman with whom she'd nightly practiced the flicking of her tongue.

Two women scrambled about making preparations with water and cloths for washing the baby when it would emerge. Another crouched between Yasamen's legs, ready to facilitate the birth. The rest of us, helpless of task, stood around in the light, diaphanous clothes we wore around the hareem, looking for all the world, in that midnight light, like attendant spirits.

While we women clung to one another, the cats were braver, those cats who were everywhere. They roamed the room freely, in and out our legs, undisturbed by Yasamen's screams, or perhaps deeply disturbed, but by nature driven to a different sort of behavior. Yasamen's bare legs trembled, her weight light and inconsequential, as against a fierce, aboriginal cold.

As happens from this sort of effort, a baby was born. Its head crowned between Yasamen's legs. A naked, wrinkled body followed, and when that baby had irretrievably been expelled from its dark, liquid womb, the woman who'd been midwife took it in her arms.

"A girl," someone murmured.

It was just after that that the cats leapt up wildly. I think it must have been the smell of all that blood, and the sight of a new thing looking defenseless enough to be dinner. The midwife held the baby out of the cats' reach, but when the afterbirth came flushing out from the open wound that was Yasamen's sex, the cats pounced on it. The midwife grabbed the baby's cord, and another woman took a knife to it more quickly than she otherwise might've. It was then that Anwa arrived, straight from the work that kept her away at times the rest of us were bedded down. She pushed through the crowd, grabbed a basin of water and tossed it on the cats, sending them scattering.

The baby born of Yasamen began to cry, a fitting response, I suppose, to its new circumstance. And though Yasamen had expelled the baby, still she bled. Blood continued to flow out of her wildly, like a river seduced by demons off its rightful path. This frightened the midwife, and Somhe even more. They raced to stop the blood with fresh cloths and the robes the rest of us tore directly from our bodies. But all the fabric in the world could not stop the blood that was flowing out of Yasamen, along with her life.

That night, as I hinted early on, Yasamen died. With Somhe at her side, clutching her, begging her not to.

And this on the eve of The Feast of the Snake. A feast that would seem, to any hearted soul, a bit frivolous of a sudden.

If not outright sacrilege.

Dee never told me her middle name, but anyway I knew it. It was "Trouble."

After Dee left, Wren was at a loss for what to do for me. Or say. One day, to cheer me up, she told me, "Actually, Codie, I think maybe you look better after you've been crying all day." Another day she got reckless. "What the hell," she said. "Sounds to me like women are bad news. What about—dare I ask it—men?"

But Wren knew my stories. She'd been my friend when I'd gone out with men—my share of them. "Guys with names like John, Joe, Bob, Bill . . ."

"Tom, Dick, and Harry?" Wren cut me off.

The real trouble was that my affections stayed trained oh-so-tenaciously on Dee. Didn't seem to matter I found strands of blond hair in a bed supposed to be mine. So sue me, I missed her. More than once I called her up to tell her. The last time I called, the blond answered the phone, which got me all un-hinged. When she passed the phone to Dee, I lost any sem-blance of the composure I might've deceived myself into thinking I had when I'd made the call, and I started shouting. Dee did the predictable thing. She hung up on me. So I called back and shouted some more.

"Jeez, Codie, what are you getting so upset about?" Dee asked, all calmness and reason.

"Unconscious," was Wren's assessment when I reported back this particular detail. "There's something about Dee that's unconscious."

Well, a six-pack a night'll do it.

During that phone call I got the chance to loose a lot of things that'd been amassing in my chest. I could actually feel them there, a tight lump under my breastbone. I asked Dee if she'd added my photos to her trophy page. "You wouldn't recognize love if it danced right up in your face!" I shouted.

"Like some Halloween harem girl?" she shot back.

And that was when I really lost it. Dee knew full well Halloween was a sore point.

All the while I was carrying on, my cat crouched under a table, keeping well out of my way. When finally I hung up, it hit me that I was now alone. Suddenly, the hum of the refrigerator was the loudest sound in the room, a quiet that scared me even more.

"The pain won't stop," I cried to Wren. "I can't seem to stop missing her. *Why?*"

"I think," Wren suggested, "that this is not about just Dee. You may feel that she wronged you, that it's her and her alone you're missing, but it's more."

(Beat) So who asked her?

The night of the feast, we dancers reported to the stone temple that flanked the khan, the sacred precinct in which the offering would actually be made. The altar in the temple was bronze, fashioned with a hollowed depression to serve the needs of blood sacrifice, though by my day sacrifice had grown less visibly barbaric. Statues were now the fashion. Statues in the likeness of the offerer. The temple was crowded with them.

We'd left Somhe in the hareem, grieving over Yasamen, in no condition, certainly, to dance. Or so we thought. As we gathered in the small vestibule off the side of the temple to purify ourselves before entering, Somhe surprised us all by appearing in the room as we took our turns at the ritual.

"Somhe," I protested. I stepped back from the brazier of incense. "You needn't dance tonight. One of us will take your task."

But Somhe stepped up to the brazier herself and cupped her robe over it, letting the fragrant, purifying smoke billow up to cloud her head and hair. "It will do me good," she insisted, "to play the head of the serpent."

The lot of us shrugged, getting on with more frivolous tasks, fussing with our kohl and the henna patterns that stained our hands and feet. We felt, collectively, content and whole in that way of a body that has all its working parts. Foolish girls. We took the word of one distraught and grieving.

Somhe took her place. We followed her in line through the imposing propylaeum that fronted the temple, and, without thinking, let Somhe step out onto the vast, vacant floor in front of the officials gathered there by the Mukarrib. To lead the line, to punctuate, as Iman had termed it. How surprised could we really have been when, at the end of our dance, the time at which Somhe had been directed to flick her tongue, something sharper came out her mouth?

Somhe wheeled toward the Mukarrib, spewing out the truth as she knew it.

"The Mukarrib killed Yasamen!" she cried loudly. "Let him pay!"

As Iman had earlier directed me, the last gesture of Somhe's was to be my cue to dance. But at her outburst, I stood stone still, as did everyone else. Somhe turned and stared at me, defying me to proceed. I looked quickly to the Mukarrib. He waved me on, but I could not move. The Mukarrib then turned to his guests and laughed. The guests joined in, out of nervousness or relief it must have been, there was not much amusement in that temple. "Dance on!" the Mukarrib commanded me. The corps of dancers fled the floor like some scattered herd, enveloping Somhe, spiriting her away. "Dance, I say!"

And so I took my place as soloist. As one culled from many. Momentous change, for me, has often been linked to feasts and their celebration. The important turning points in my life have had a curious way of attaching themselves to special events.

The better to remember them by, I suppose.

Death and fear will quiet a place, even a hareem. For weeks after The Feast of the Serpent, we were subdued. Perhaps we felt no need to speak, knowing that there was not a lot any of us could add to the truth that Somhe had already spilled. Or perhaps it was a cowering quiet we kept. Cowering because Somhe still walked among us, not punished in any way. It seemed a miracle, one no one wanted to call attention to for fear that castigating gods had simply overlooked their opportunity, left Somhe her life by oversight, nothing kinder. Only the cats were wild, brave. Emboldened yet by blood, I suppose. One mute night, with the air close and we dancers dining outside under the trellises, the cats jumped brazenly into our midst. We knocked them back, a gesture that seemed, suddenly, to free us, to push back whatever obstacle had dammed the flow of our speech.

"Get back, you scroungy beast," one started. "Keep your flea-infested carcass away from my plate!"

"Cousin to the lion? *Distant* cousin!"

"Teeth and claws to scare mice, not humans!"

Laughing, talking. Knocking back the cats. Life returned to normal.

Mocking the Mukarrib.

One of the female cats was in heat, and had been yowling throughout the serving of the meal. When we shooed her from our food, she climbed the vine-covered trellis that overhung our low-legged table. A pack of male cats scaled the trellis to pursue her, as was their sport.

A light breeze rustled the vines. I ate from the plate of spiced rice and pickled eggplant. The cat above yowled louder. We looked up to rank the males who chased her, casting bets on which would win.

"I think the orange tom has the biggest member."

"I hear it's bigger than the Mukarrib's."

"Yes, but the orange cat won't win. The tiger is much bigger and more of a fighter. Look, he's already pushing the others out of the way."

A fight ensued between the two males. As one of us had predicted, it was the large tiger who had his way and mounted her.

I was distracted from watching the event when another tray of food was set before us. On the tray was some sort of meat. It was odd that the slave from the kitchen served another tray. Usually we did not get more after the first platters had been set down. I noted also that the meat was a sort I did not recognize. It had a bumpy pink coating and the inside looked soft, unusually tender. I judged it must be a delicacy, reached for a slice, and took a bite. But when I looked up, I noticed that no one else was eating the meat. The faces of the others had paled and some of the women were edging away. Above us, the tiger was copulating with the female while the orange tom tried to claw his way back to her graces. The orange tom succeeded, interrupting the other mid-thrust, just as he was about to ejaculate. The jism which should have tunneled up the female spurted, instead, down from the trellis. All over my meat, it went, whatever that meat was.

I had not more than a moment to react before two men from the Mukarrib's guard came out, each taking a place on either side of Somhe and grabbing her up by her forearms. Somhe struggled to break free, but they put a knife to her throat and led her away. As we all witnessed. Helplessly.

"Tongue," someone next to me whispered. "The meat is tongue."

I did not know what any of this could mean. No other took a bite of the meat, but neither did they get up and leave. Everyone seemed to be waiting. For what, I could not guess.

Until the guards returned. They again had Somhe by the arms. Her body shook and shivered in convulsion. I thought perhaps she had the jinn, but then I saw her mouth, open now, stained red with blood. Somhe's eyes rolled back in her head.

"No!" cried Iman. She jumped up to catch Somhe, who

could not keep her balance and was lurching back. Somhe opened her mouth wider to try to speak, but what came out was not recognizable as a word, it was the cleft part of a word, a vowel. And that was when I saw, through the blood that still streamed from her mouth, that Somhe had been severed of her tongue.

Which is why I now burn aromatics in homage and chant upon my knees. To extend my sincere thanks to the Mukarrib. For supplying such a clear lesson to all of us, and to me at such a tender age, that severe punishment will befall a person who somewhere finds in her the voice to speak the truth about another. The lesson as crystaline as water from a well.

"Blood," insists Anwa.

Blood. Yes, it's true. But, despite it all, I danced in the khan. And how can I reconcile that?

In what seems like it might've been another life, time was innocent, or at least it felt so. Saturdays, I used to sit out on my fire escape scrubbing the strong scent of males off my window. When Dee first started coming around, she quickly got used to me balling up strips of newspaper and crawling out the window in my sweatpants. The first time I did it, she sat back and watched me curiously, as an anthropologist might observe the quirky behavior of some isolated island tribe. But the second time, she reached down under the kitchen table to pet Clue. Already Dee was part of the family.

"Codie's out there washing away all traces of your beaux," she said to Clue. Her eyes were glinting, devilish; she was trying to stir up mischief.

"Don't worry, Clue," I called in through the window. "I'm making it so you'll have *fresh* spray to sniff at. This stuff's stale, caked-on. Your boys'll be back in no time."

Two grown women vying for a cat's attention. Clue paid no attention to either one of us. She cleaned her paws, then lifted her hind leg to lick her genitals.

"Because she can," said Dee, the head of the joke unspoken. I climbed back inside. "How come you named her Clue?" Dee asked.

I glanced at Clue, who was moving to a patch of sunlight and arching her back. Clue's coat was black, but in the sun it took on a reddish henna cast.

"I named her Clue," I said, "because when I adopted her I didn't have a one."

"That was before me," Dee said proudly.

"B.D.," I agreed, my new way of marking time.

The truth was, I took in Clue because she had been waiting for me when I came home from my mother's funeral. She was a stray who'd visited my window before, though I'd never done a thing to encourage her. Actually, I'd been afraid to feed her. I was afraid that if I fed her, I'd have to keep feeding her, that I'd never get rid of her, find myself responsible for something, and I didn't think I wanted that. But the night I flew back from my mother's death—it was late, sometime between midnight and morning—Clue was at the window. Though I'd been gone for over a week, she was waiting. As if she expected me. Or maybe she'd been waiting all along. Whichever it was, it seemed like devotion. So I let her in, fed her a can of tuna fish, then picked her up and cried into her fur. The next morning when I woke up, I noticed flea bites dotting my breasts. I went out and bought a flea collar. After that Clue was mine.

"Black cat for Halloween," added Dee, this just occurring to her. I'd noted that from the start. "Let Clue out," Dee urged. Clue was looking happy enough stretched out in her spot of kitchen sun, but Dee had a different idea. Early on, I'd figured out something about Dee. That she liked me to give Clue whatever it was she herself wanted. It soothed something in her, so, often as not, I obliged her. I opened the window and Clue jumped out. Clue was domesticated, but she still liked to be a wild thing at least a couple of times a day.

"Look," I said, to call Dee to the window. I pointed to Clue, who had scaled a chain link fence and was running along its thin top edge. As we watched, she stopped short. She pricked her ears at a sound we couldn't hear before she ran off again, out of sight.

"A wild life," said Dee. "She does like her wild life."

"Yeah," I said. "I'm just never sure what to say to her when she comes back with bird on her breath."

"What do you mean?" Dee asked, alarmed. "You smell her breath? You can't smell bird."

"I see feathers in her claws. Same thing."

That's when Dee asked for another story. So I told her the tale about how, the week after I adopted Clue, all the other strays in the neighborhood came parading by the window, strays I'd never seen before and hadn't caught a glimpse of since.

"These days there're only two or three toms who spray the window," I said. "I know which ones they are. But the week I adopted Clue, there must've been fifty or sixty cats that came by. They just came up to my window and peered in, wanting to see for themselves what had happened, I guess. I think, that week, Clue's adoption was the hottest news on the cat circuit."

"Yeah, but how did they know?" asked Dee. This was what we asked each other every time I told this story. "How did they know you adopted her? How do they communicate these things?"

"Maybe it's through smell," I said. We both stood there, staring out the window. We watched as, in the building next to mine, another cat, a male, climbed out of the basement well and ran in the direction in which Clue had gone.

"You'd better get her fixed," said Dee.

"I already did," I said. "First thing."

I took the coffee off the fire and poured us each a second cup. We were sitting at the kitchen table that had once been my mother's. It was the table I'd grown up at.

"What's this?" asked Dee. She was pointing to a place next to her cup on the surface of the table. I leaned over to see. It was the word "Kyrie" in a child's loopy scrawl, etched into the soft pine like a relic, or a fossil.

"I used to do my homework at this table," I said. "I must've written that on a piece of paper and pressed through."

"Kyrie?" asked Dee.

"Kyrie eleison. I'd thought the words were 'Keyring-a, a lady's son,' so I had to write it twenty-five times."

When I was a child, I used to like to play orphan. I used to strip down all my dolls and put them in the bathtub to soak. Poor little orphan dolls. Dirty, grimy.

The day after my mother walked in on the naked orphan dolls—and me and my father naked as well—she drove me to confession. I'd tried to tell my father, "I take baths, not showers." I knew I had sinned, but it had happened somehow despite me.

Right around that time my mother began to forget to feed me sometimes and herself as well. When we did eat, she'd open one can of something for the two of us. Canned spaghetti, maybe. Chef Boyardee. One night, late, I walked in on her in the kitchen. The overhead light was off, but my mother was lit by the bulb in the open refrigerator. She was in her nightgown, stuffing fistfuls of cold rice into her mouth. The two of us, foraging for food, furtive, spectral, surprising each other in the night.

"Life is a test," she'd said to me. Or, to be more accurate, she'd screamed it at me. In the parking lot outside of class.

You want to know what happened in the shower, Mama? Nothing happened in the shower. How many times is a girl required to explain?

In case my mother hadn't noticed, it wouldn't have been in my interest to stray down a sinful path. Not as I saw it. I had lofty ambitions. Raised in the Faith as I was, I aspired to be a saint. Saints wore lighted crowns and had hearts pierced seductively with swords. I took nourishment from processions, events I could be sure of, events guaranteed by a Catholic education. Schoolchildren snaked their way through church aisles, singing hymns to the Virgin, laying bouquets of spring flowers at her feet, or at least at her statue. I was a child who craved procession. I recognized magic as soon as I glimpsed it, was hungry for every shred of ritual. I loved the church most when it was shrouded in purple and thick with incense.

The only snag to sainthood was that I'd have to come up with a miracle in order to win the attention of the Vatican, a necessary requirement for canonization. Most of the best miracles had already been taken. Like forgiving someone who had defiled you. Maria Goretti had aced me out there, and in this century. Or speaking in tongues. Twelve men had captured that one.

For no particular reason, I loved the story of Pentecost. A tale of twelve men, fearful, cowering together in a room. After the death of their beloved Jesus, they found themselves bereft, lost, overwhelmed by the task that lay ahead of them, and thinking it would be impossible ever to be able to express intelligibly to the world who it was they had known, what it was they had experienced. But into this room, from the heavens, tongues of fire descended. *Spiritus ex machina.* The tongues enkindled something in the apostles, and the men found themselves suddenly, mysteriously, able to speak in the language of whatever land they traveled.

Abracadabra.

"So there's these two chinks," my father says.

"Chinks?" I feel, for some reason, like being a stickler, though where will it get me. "Asian is the correct term," I say.

"No." My father grins. He's got me now, it's a setup. "I'm talking about chinks in a wall. I'm telling a story about *pla-a-a-s*tering."

"Oh yeah?" He's got the root right. "So go ahead and tell it."

Once again I had taken to the bathtub, my insistent reiteration. Dee was snyde. "With you, Codie," she said, "the only thing that changes with the seasons is the water temperature."

I'd taken refuge in the bathtub because Dee was in the bedroom with two televisions. Ours was on the blink, so Dee had borrowed another from a friend. When I got home from work she had stacked the new one directly on top of the old.

"Totem TVs," I said.

Comments like this were getting barbed.

In the bathtub, I nicked my legs with my razor. Twice. "Two chinks," I thought, out of nowhere. The nicks were deep and blood flowed out of them and into the warm bath in thin, lazy streams. When I lifted my leg out of the water, bright blood ran down my wet shin, and I was worried because of something I feared almost as if it were something remembered, though how could that be—that blood draws sharks.

That night I fought off fear by going ahead with the original plan I had had for my bath, which was to again try my hand at a story. I had a fresh idea. This one was about a young girl who is studying to become a ballerina and how she is wrenched away from what she loves by circumstance beyond her control, perhaps the Russian Revolution.

I was busy writing and didn't notice that Dee had appeared in the doorway.

"What are you working on?" she asked.

I tore the page off the top of the legal pad and tucked it in the back. That night I just didn't feel much like having Dee tell me my story was a bad idea.

"Nothing," I said. "Just a letter."

"Who to?"

"My mother," I said.

As both Dee and I knew, my mother was dead. I was never a very good liar.

My mother died on Halloween, though I was senseless to the day. The night before, I'd sat up all night in the armchair next to the hospital bed that had been set up in her room. The dress I was wearing was white cotton with pale stripes. It was unseasonal, too thin against the nip in the air, and it smelled because I hadn't changed it all the week since I'd arrived. I'm not sure why I'd suddenly grown so attached to it. I guess there'd be deeper reasons, but the only one I can think of was that the pattern of the fabric reminded me of the uniforms that candy stripers wear, candy stripers being those fresh-faced girls who volunteer in hospitals, ministering with magazines and the mail. All night long I'd listened to the rattle that passed as breathing in my mother's cancer-wasted chest. Once she'd reached up her stick-thin arms toward the ceiling as if it were the heavens and I'd heard her cracked whisper ask aloud, "Why, God? Why?"

Early in the morning my father came back up from the living room couch, where he'd been sleeping, and spelled me. I suppose I could've taken a shower then and changed my clothes, but I didn't, and the only other thing I ended up wearing the whole time I was there was the black dress I'd brought for the funeral.

I went down to the kitchen, where my father had set up the television, and turned on the set. All I could find were cartoons, though I was well past old enough to know better. The cartoons were not as instructive as the ones I remembered from my childhood. Quite irrelevantly I found myself thinking about the parlance of cartoons, the reassurance that certain things were sure to represent certain others. When a cartoon character hits his head, he sees stars. Daybreak is always signaled by a music cue, a chipper little excerpt from "The William Tell Overture." If a character gets an idea, a light bulb appears over her head. I thought a while about the lexicon of animation and then stared dazedly at a commercial for a sugary cereal that advertised decoder rings as a prize, which got me thinking. At that point, I'd been at the house a full week, come to stay when my father called, because everyone could tell it would be soon. That week I'd watched my father attend my mother with no trace of enmity between them, as if it had been erased, but it didn't seem so simple with me.

Sometime into my reverie, my father called me up to the bedroom because my mother was dying, and it wasn't pretty like on TV. She was gasping. Her head and chest heaved suddenly up off the pillow. Her eyes rolled back and blood trickled out the corner of her mouth. The whole week I'd been there I'd waited, waited for my mother to call me over to her bed, take my hand, and tell me that I'd been an ace daughter, that I'd made her proud, so proud, and that she'd love me beyond time. But suddenly she was dead and nothing of that kind had been said. I don't know what possessed me to expect it. I suppose it had been a lot to hope for.

After the doctor came to issue a certificate of death, we called the undertaker. I'd met the undertaker a few days earlier when my father and I had stopped by his office to finalize the funeral arrangements. I'd had to pick out the holy cards that would be available at the funeral mass. The undertaker said he'd print them up with my mother's dates of birth and death and a prayer. Did she have a favorite, he wanted to know? He fanned a stack of holy cards and held them out to me. They were gilt-edged, each with a picture of a different saint. I waved them away, it felt like a card trick. I said, "An assortment will be fine." Then he told me that I'd need to pick out a dress in which to lay out my mother, something pretty, something becoming, he suggested.

Becoming? I felt at sea. "Like she might wear to a wedding?" I asked.

"Perhaps something a little more sober," was his answer.

When we got back from the funeral parlor, I spied my mother awake and watching us from her window as we walked up the front drive. We'd told her—my father's idea—that we were stepping out to get groceries. Now we'd been gone over two hours and had no bags getting out of the car, also my father's idea. "Aren't we going to stop for some groceries to at least carry in with us?" I'd asked on the way home, and he'd said simply, "We don't need any." Then he'd drummed his thumbs on the steering wheel and stared straight ahead at the crisp, bright leaves that littered the road.

When I walked back into my mother's room, she eyed me, suspicious. "So what'd you get?" she asked.

"The store was closed," I said.

"Closed?"

"Bomb threat." The alibi just slid from my mouth. I never know how I come up with these things.

I averted my eyes from my mother's and wondered how I was going to manage to hunt through her closet for something pretty and becoming with her dying right there in the same room. And it was not so long after that that the undertaker came to our house with another man and wheeled a stretcher up to my mother's bed.

The undertaker put his hand on my shoulder in an avuncular way to suggest to me that I "might want to leave the room." I guess he wanted to spare me the sight of my mother's lifeless body being lifted up and strapped down. But when they had done what they had come to do, I returned to her bedroom and stood at the window, the same window from which my mother had watched me, but this time I watched her. I watched her being wheeled down the walk to the hearse that was parked right in our driveway, should any neighbors want the news. The men slid her into the back and drove down the street and then my mother was gone, and I stood there thinking I don't know what, though I do remember thinking, "So that's all?"

In the kitchen the TV was still on from when my father had called me away, though cartoons were long over, they seemed like a dream. Because it was Allhallows Eve, our bell would soon be rung by a tireless parade of skeletons and ghosts. "Too late," is what I'd say when I'd answer the door. "The Grim Reaper's come and gone." Of course, that wasn't actually what I'd say to impressionable children begging candy. It was simply the sorry response I entertained in a too-quiet house.

I turned off the TV. The telephone rang. I knew I had to pick it up and answer. It would be relatives wanting to know.

After the death, I stayed with my father alone in the house and busied myself organizing the food that appeared unexplained in our kitchen as if left by angels, though I suppose it must have been neighbors. What they left was comfort food: creamed casseroles with egg noodles, iced butter cookies, piping hot bread. I gobbled up the food hungrily, starved for what it was it offered. My father sat in the living room nursing his scotch.

The flight I got back to New York was for a Sunday, two days after the funeral. I had wanted to go back earlier, but my father prevailed upon me to stay for the weekend, and since I didn't have to work until Monday, I didn't have much of an excuse not to. After all, I figured, the man's wife just died. During that time I didn't talk much with my father, I mostly just wandered around the house, looking through things, touching them. I rifled through the silverware drawer and hefted the knives. I held the etched, tinted wine glasses my mother had received as a wedding present up to the light, I wasn't sure why.

After that I found myself in the basement, looking to see if a certain box was still there. Behind the furnace is where it would've been, is where I'd hid it years ago when I was younger, a slight, willowy figure slipping downstairs in the dead of dusk to hide a box which would otherwise have been pitched into the garbage along with everything else. And who would blame me for wanting to save something flashing sequins and boasting pink netting?

All those years later, though, the box was no longer where I'd hidden it. Found by whom? I wondered. And when thrown away? When no answer suggested itself I went back upstairs and buried my attentions in a mound of photo albums, wiled away a whole afternoon. There were the photos of me, of course. Toes pointed, legs turned out. A whole book of those. And then there were the photos of people I didn't know. When I was a child I used to question my mother about the people in those pictures. "Who's this?" I might ask, getting my smudgy fingerprint on the face of some strange man, third from the left. My mother would set the pot she was washing back into the suds and come over to look. "Oh, that was a friend of your father's," she might say, wiping her hands on her apron. "They worked together when we were first married."

There were still a lot of people in the photos I didn't recognize or remember—a woman standing next to my grandmother, a man with his arm around my aunt. I guess that's just how it goes. When someone dies, though it's no longer possible, it often comes up that there are still a slew of things you need to ask them. Ask, and tell as well.

The things I want to tell dead people. . . .

Later that afternoon I got in the car and drove in the direction of town. I didn't know I was going to stop, but when I passed the Natural History Museum I pulled off the road and into the parking lot. The first room I wandered into had a sign posted, HABITATS. In front of me was a glass case in which were displayed a variety of bird nests. What struck me was not the odd shapes of the nests or their varying sizes, but the materials the birds had used. Woven into each nest was something man-made. One incorporated a thin strip of insulating material. The side of another was threaded with a jagged piece of plastic wrap. There were also bits of tinfoil and odd Styrofoam pieces. A plaque next to the display explained that, in building their homes, birds use whatever materials they find. I sat down on the cushioned bench in the center of the room. I didn't want to look farther, but neither did I want to drive home. There was something rising in my chest like panic. Death was all around.

The night before I was to leave I stayed up late reading in bed, the bed I had grown up in. The bed had a daisy bedspread and a daisy dust ruffle, bought to match the daisy wallpaper. My mother had decorated the room one year without consulting me, and she'd done it with a vengeance. She'd primed the walls and slapped down wallpaper paste. She'd cut out daisies from the half roll of wallpaper left over and glued them onto my lampshade and the windowshade, too. The truth is, I never really liked daisies. I was thirteen and worried whether there would be any room left for my posters of rock stars. I had always felt uneasy about sleeping in that room. As much then as now.

After the funeral my father moved back into the bedroom he'd shared with my mother. The hospital bed was gone, picked up by the company that rented it out. Which made me wonder how many other people had died in that bed. Ghosts were on my mind.

I'd been reading by the dim light of the small lamp on my night table, one small pool of light warding off the dark of the room, of the house, of the wide night outside. I closed my book, ready for sleep, but climbed out of bed first to visit the bath-room at the far end of the hall. The house was quiet. I flushed the toilet. The night absorbed the sound as if the darkness were padded.

When I got back to my room, I was surprised to find that

the room was completely dark. The lamp had been turned off. I stood in the doorway. In the darkness I could make out a form. A man. It was my father. He was standing by my bed.

"Daddy," I said. I froze in the doorway.

My father didn't say anything. He just stood there, looking at me. When my eyes adjusted to the dark, I could see that he was wearing a bathrobe and that his legs were bare. My heart was racing, adrenaline was pumping through my veins, an instinct for flight. I wanted to scream, "What are you doing in my bedroom? Why is there no light?" but I didn't. Instead I asked, "What's up?" affecting nonchalance.

"Your lamp burned out," said my father. "I came in to change the bulb."

I didn't believe him. "It was working a few minutes ago." I didn't believe my own father.

"I was passing by your room . . ."

On the way to where?

". . . and the lamp blinked off. I got another light bulb out of the closet, but when I went to screw it in, it dropped and rolled under the bed. Maybe you can reach it for me. If I get down on these old knees I'll never get up."

"A minute ago it was working," I repeated. I was sweating, my armpits were swamps.

"It rolled under here," said my father. He pointed to a spot next to him at the edge of the bed.

I did not want to walk into that room. It felt foolhardy, like taking a shortcut through a graveyard on a full-moon night. But I couldn't say that to my father. I couldn't articulate any reason why I shouldn't do what he asked. A refusal would've implied that I was afraid. "Afraid of what?" my father would ask. I couldn't say; it was a trap. So I walked into the room, to the spot my father indicated, and I got down on my knees. My father didn't move out of my way. He stood right behind me, towering above me, too close. Though I didn't really believe there was any light bulb, I groped under the bed, feeling around for it. My hand touched something round and smooth. I curled my fingers around it in relief and stood up.

"Here it is." I handed it to my father. He took it and screwed it into the socket. The light went on. The room was lit.

The light bulb had been there, under the bed, just as he said. But if there had been another one that had burned out, where was it?

"Where's the old light bulb?" I heard myself ask.

"I threw it away," said my father. His lips cracked into an uneven smile. "Good night," he said. He left the room.

I closed the door behind him and checked the wastebasket by my desk. There was no burned-out light bulb. I latched the lock on my door and got back into bed, but did not turn off the lamp. I lay there wondering, "Why was I so afraid of my own father?"

That night it was a long time before I could get to sleep. Some wild and early instinct had shot adrenaline into my bloodstream.

And adrenaline takes some time to fade.

One night dark and stormy Clue bridged a great gap between species to communicate something of importance to me. Afterward, when I described to Wren what had transpired, I'm not sure she quite believed me. Or that she saw in it the same significance as I.

"So?" she said, her expression as uncomprehending as a wooden decoy. "The meowing could have meant anything. It could have just meant Clue wanted out."

So, indeed. What we have here is a situation in which a cat told me something which I then tried to communicate to a member of my own species, but had not the words, apparently. Tell that one to Sister Dymphna.

"Sister Dymphna?" asked Wren.

"Sure. She's the one drilled me about animal nature. She's the one told me not to listen to my instincts. Said I have a higher, God-like nature. With reason and intellect."

Wren squinted at me, impatient. "What's this sidetrack?" she asked. "Weren't you about to tell a story?"

Story? Truth has it all over fiction. The incident I present as evidence involved Clue, and it's one that to this day I find inexplicable, peculiar, and remarkable. It happened one night in that sorry time after Dee had left. I had taken to my bed, propped only by my pillows, alone in the world, for crying out loud. To say that I was crying, though, barely expresses what it was I was up to. As was more frequent than not at that time, I was wailing. Of its own accord some untamed sound surged out of me. From some core, primal place.

While I lay there wailing, Clue perched on the windowsill opposite, watching. She watched as I doubled over my bedcovers. She pricked her ears the loud, long while I heaved up the sound. I continued wailing until there was no more of whatever it was inside I had to expel. But Clue never took her eyes off, not a moment.

"How could she, with you dealing out all that drama?" asked Wren.

But Clue wasn't watching me exactly, her eyes were fixed on the place on the bed over which I'd been leaning. And when whatever it was seemed to have passed through me, when I finally fell back, spent and glassy-eyed, Clue sprang up and raced over. She circled the spot on the bed she'd been watching and meowed insistently.

"What is it?" I asked, but she wouldn't stop. She kept circling and complaining, stopping only to catch my eye, a communication I read as her demanding that I do something. All of this gave me the feeling that Clue saw something there that I didn't. And the something she saw disturbed her deeply. "What's the matter?" I asked. "What do you want me to do?"

Clue couldn't provide me with any sort of explanation that might put my rational, human mind at ease, but neither did she rest. Finally, because I couldn't think of what else to do, I went to the bathroom and brought back a roll of toilet paper. I unrolled a wad and used it to blot up whatever it was that was there. I blotted it gingerly, as if what I was mopping up was vile, like vomit. It was hard to tell how long I should keep this up since I couldn't actually see anything, but when Clue seemed quieted, I balled up the mess and flushed it down the toilet. After which Clue sat back on her haunches and licked her paw. Then she went back to her perch on the windowsill and fell asleep. Worries put to rest.

I went back to the bed uneasily and ran my hand over the

sheets. To see if there was any difference there that I could detect. In the vibration, perhaps. In the temperature . . . I wasn't sure what I was looking for. Something bile-colored, maybe? Something fetid? All I knew was that where I'd felt pain, Clue'd seemed to sense something actually physically there.

"Hmmm . . . ," mused Wren.

So there you have it, Sister. The true story. It's why I just can't seem to get behind this Heaven of yours in which no cats are allowed.

11

And me arching up to her fingers like a bridge to sky.

"*Cielo,*" I called Dee for unvoiced reason. My vision went all star-studded. Azure sighs.

"*Cielo?*" Dee asked afterward, suspicion in her voice. "Where'd you pick that up?"

I ran my lips all over Dee's, which is what I loved to do after, my lips kept alive next to hers. But Dee demanded answers.

"What're you doing, going out with some Latina on the sly?"

"Latino," I said. "And it's not on the sly, it was before."

"Oh."

Something Dee and I did, on occasion, in bed, was tell stories about going out with men. Dee would consider whether or not she wanted me to go on. Then she'd ask, "So what was he like?"

"Nothing to speak of," I told her this time, which was true. I was relieved Dee didn't ask his name because I'd have been hard-pressed to remember. "No. Wait a minute," I said. I'd suddenly recalled something that might bear telling. I put one of my hands palm down on Dee's forehead and pressed hard, trying to push down her head, as men used to do to me when they wanted me to suck them.

Dee laughed. She knew exactly what it was I was signifying because, no coincidence, men used to do it to her, too. A little something we discovered one night when comparing notes about our sexual pasts. Now we had a joke without words. The best kind.

"So tell another story," said Dee. I fed Dee's need for bed-time tales, a need she never outgrew. Over the months I'd told her many stories—all about men, and none of them the warm milk, tucking-in kind. I told Dee the story, for instance, of the man I once dated who wrote an ethics column for a prominent magazine. This guy came on to me in line at the supermarket, asked for my phone number, then called me up and asked me out. We went out a few times and I found myself starting to like the guy. Although I did find it curious that he'd only give me his work number. (At this detail, Dee drew in her breath expectantly.) Then one night I came home to a message on my machine from this fellow. In the message he said not to call him anymore, that he wouldn't be able to go out with me that weekend or any time after because—

"He was married!" Dee shouted out. She liked to try to guess the punch lines.

"Well, almost," I said. "It turned out that that Saturday he was *getting* married. He called to say he couldn't go out with me that weekend as he'd led me to expect because he had to go to his wedding."

"His wedding? So, I don't get it. You were what, his last fling?"

"Must've been," I said. I don't know why I started up these stories. Always at the head I forgot about the pangs that accompanied the tail.

"Well," Dee considered. She was going to try to appease me. Pacificatory tack. "Look at it this way, Codie. The man had his standards. He wasn't going to go out with you once he was married."

"Ethics column," I said. "Right."

Even as my words lingered still moist in the air between us, Dee was off that story and ready for another. More. She wanted more. I was beginning to feel queasy, as if I'd eaten too many sweets at the fair with no real meal in sight, but Dee was pulling me along, so I thought fast and went for another. "Did you hear the one about the guy at the party?" I asked. I set up the joke. "He and I were talking, and in the course of conversation he asked me how old I was. I thought we were flirting, so I didn't really feel required to answer him straight. When I hedged, the guy took my chin in his hand. I thought maybe he was going to flatter me, say how pretty I was, something like that. But what he did instead was lift my chin for closer inspection and what he said was, 'You can always tell how old a woman is by her neck.' "

"Jesus!" Dee exclaimed.

Just a sampling. I've got a million of 'em.

By this time Dee was past restraint. I could see it in her eyes. She was crazed, wanted more. It was bloodthirst.

"You're not my *cielo,*" I said to her. "You're my vampire."

Dee bared her teeth and bit me on the neck.

"Okay! Okay!" I cried. "Anything you want! I'll tell one more!"

Dee puffed up her pillow and leaned back into it. The way she looked, all nestled and cozy, I felt as if I should start the story, "Once upon a time." But that's not the lead I had in mind. A quick glance at Dee to make sure she was listening, and then I went for it.

"His name was Guy," I said, "which makes it all rather generic."

After a string of stories on this order, Dee was never ready for bed. She got all high and wild-eyed. She usually "wanted some," as she herself would put it. And chances were she wanted it in story mode.

"Let's pretend we're meeting for the first time," she said. I knew this game. It was Dee's favorite, but not mine. Something about it worried me, did not sit well.

"You just like to pretend we never met in the first place,"
I complained. "You like to pretend we haven't gotten to know
each other."

Besides, the way Dee and I met was at a bar. Smokey, stale,
a failure of the imagination.

"Sit back, babe," I ordered. "I have better ideas."

"Who you talkin' to?"

"You."

Anwa tried to tell me it was words wooed me, words that pref-
aced kissing, Anwa's quickest tongue. (And me wriggling
against it, as I'll tell.)

This installment of our story begins before we'd kissed,
when still I barely knew you. Barely knew and barely noticed.
In the time since I'd arrived at the khan, I'd emerged as its
principal dancer. And developed every bit of self-absorption
requisite to my position.

One morning—a day when the air was soft and the breeze
flirtatious—I stood at my basin, splashing water over myself
chirpily, like a bird at bath. The next day was to be a feast.
Never any lack of celebration in the Mukkarib's court. This time,
we'd be feasting off the excess of the tithe, a little show of
ostentation that took place yearly, barring deterrents, like pes-
tilence or war, though these were rare in Felix Arabia. Our city
was blessed. With all the excess that engendered. And all the
dropping of guard.

As opening ceremony to the feast, we dancers would be
engaged to parade long trays of spices among the assembled
guests. Some of the spices were aromatics grown locally for
export. Others had arrived from India, come begging passage

through our lands on their way to others, the taxes and tariffs on which richly fed us all.

I rummaged through my trunks, searching for my bracelets, an element of costume. I clasped the bracelets up my arm and threaded lapis earrings through my lobes before I padded barefoot down the cool tile flooring that led to the Hall of a Hundred Columns. My arena.

I was late for rehearsal and well aware of it. I pushed open the doors to the Hall. Inside, all stopped and turned to see if it was me. I paused a moment in the door frame, a posture to mean, "It is."

In my quick glance around the room, I spotted you, and your presence surprised me, for you didn't work in our troupe. You were standing alone against one wall, your skin a rich brown against the sand color of the stone. I veered out of my way to walk past you. I asked, "You intend to perform?" I knew you did not, and waited for no answer. I strode past you, thinking I was Queen.

At the far end of the Hall the drummers were bunched in a tight knot, passing a small torch from one to another, heating the skins of their drums. In the center of the room were the dancers, scattered about, gracile-limbed, testing balance and other tricks. Among us all moved Iman, pacing about the columns.

"Sari!" As I entered, she called me to her. "We'll rehearse the death dance," she said. "The last shall be first."

I raised my eyes in mock annoyance. "Death, always death."

"You die well," Iman said to humor me.

"And you, best of all, must know that all I do is milk its drama."

The dance Iman referred to was one that involved the entire troupe. It was to be the culmination of the performance, and the climax to the story. Iman called the dancers and drummers to her. You alone remained at the far end of the Hall, leaning against the corner column. There was something about you that appeared impregnable. Deceptively so.

The dance rehearsed well. Those who were to perform

acrobatic stunts succeeded. Those whose task it was to juggle fire set neither themselves nor the Hall aflame. I waited for my cue, watching the others from behind a folding screen. For my entrance I was carried out in a curtained litter and set into the center of the circus. Just the sort of theater I was born to. Iman had choreographed a rather simple step for me to alight from the litter, so I substituted a leap—more dramatic—and tossed my hair from one shoulder to the other with the precise craft for which I was now reknowned. As culmination to the dance, I lifted my hand as if I held a knife and plunged this imaginary weapon into my heart, contracting sharply to mime the pain.

The dance done, the lot of us dropped to the ground, like so many camels resting in the sand.

"Well done," Iman nodded. "But, Sari, in the last gesture your shoulders were hunched. Take care to keep them down."

I jumped up, hand on my hip. "You mean," I said, "that even as the knife punctures my ribs and perforates my heart, I need be worried about the position of my shoulders?"

"In this Hall, even death is correctly placed."

I raised my hand to mime the gesture again, this time with care to keep my shoulders in line. I collapsed to the floor and raised one hand in mock supplication to the heavens.

"Life," I said. "So bitter, so sweet."

Some of the performers began to ululate to applaud my performance. Their ecstatic, shrill call filled the Hall. I glanced in your direction, curious for your reaction as well. Your expression was difficult to read. Characteristically so, I was to learn.

The other dancers began to drift out the archway to the adjacent garden. They walked in pairs and threes, small snippets of their conversations trailing lightly after them in the air.

"I didn't know if I would catch that last rod of fire."

"Are we supposed to tumble at the last cue of the drum or the beat earlier?"

"Sari," Iman called me to her. "Have you tired?"

"On the contrary. I am warmed. Work me till the sun sets and rises once again."

"Youth!" Iman laughed. She dragged a small carpet from

the edge of the room and set it where the Mukarrib would sit during the feast. "I would like to work the dance you do alone, the one played to the Mukarrib, and then I will have finished with you today."

"That carpet is to stand for the Mukarrib?"

"Direct your dance to it," she instructed. "He sits there, his hand is raised. He's commanded you to dance."

"I cannot dance to a bare carpet," I said. "I require someone to sit there."

Iman looked to the garden to summon one of the dancers.

"No," I said quickly. "Let it be Anwa." I surprised my own ear at this request, and myself believed the jest in which I couched it. "Anwa has audacity to come today to the Hall without intent of working? Let us put her to task. She will play the better Mukarrib. She has, after all, known him most intimately."

I said this loud enough for you to hear, though you took no visible notice. Iman shrugged. She walked to you to pose my request.

"This is not my hour of work," I heard you say.

"So you refuse?" I called across the Hall.

"I have my labor," you replied.

"If you call taking pleasure labor."

You crossed the Hall, understanding from the first that our exchange bypassed Iman. "I don't take pleasure," you said to me. "I give it. You're the one with luck enough to take pleasure in work. If you wish me to pose in the Mukarrib's place, that's what I'll do, but you'll find that it is not the Mukarrib who sits there. Have no illusions."

You took your place on the rug, sitting straight and proudly, as you always sat.

"Sit slumping," I instructed. "The Mukarrib's tendency is to slump."

You sat taller still. "I know how it is the Mukarrib sits."

"I'm sure you do," was my retort. "Or at least how it is he lies."

"Sari," Iman interrupted. "Keep in mind that the point of this dance is flirtation, seduction."

70

I pulled the thin strap of my sheath off my shoulder and winked suggestively at Iman. She ignored my clowning.

"I know you're not unaware that the swivel of your hips has an effect. In this dance, simply use that to its full."

I thrust my hips lewdly forward as I had seen the other women of the hareem do when mimicking the sexual habits of the Mukarrib.

"Your eyes stay on the Mukarrib," Iman instructed. "As you dance, you draw in the chord of desire that stretches between you."

I laughed loudly. "You sorely test my skills as actress."

Iman tried to silence my impudence with her glance, lest it be overheard and reported. I tossed my hair, caring not. Iman signaled the drummers to begin.

At the sound of the drums, the dancers who had been outside in the garden began to drift back in to watch. I closed my eyes. The music began to move in me. Slowly, my head rolled from side to side. A wave rippled across my back, quaking my torso, shuddering my arms. By the time I again opened my eyes, I was fluid and dancing. Note that I say, "fluid," for what I had become was water, and water has specific properties, obeys certain physical laws.

When I looked to the Mukarrib's carpet, as Iman had directed, I was surprised to see that it was you sitting there; it was as if I had forgotten what I had wrought. Your eyes caught mine and the directness of your gaze unnerved me. A current shot through me, and with it, sudden shame. I'll tell you in what sense I hold water responsible. There was lightning in that room. It was crackling. I had simply and unwittingly primed myself to attract it.

Your eyes wandered down my body. It felt as if you were handling me.

"Sari! Your cue!" It was Iman, calling out to me. "Move to the column! Drape yourself!"

I was sure that everyone watching must be aware of what was passing between us. I pivoted to the column and danced the steps I'd rehearsed, but my legs faltered, my feet were suddenly stupid.

"Look to the Mukarrib!" shouted Iman.

I did. Though it was not to the Mukarrib, it was to you, and it was as if I first recognized you. You, who'd been in my sight since the very first day.

I recognized something in me, as well. It was want.

For the climax of the dance, Iman had choreographed a passage shamelessly suggestive, the type of dance on which she'd built her reputation. She had me sidle up to the Mukarrib and, before sitting upon his lap, brush the tips of my breasts lightly across his lips. This I did to you who sat in his stead.

As I rested against you, you laid your hand on the back of my neck, as if you were taking possession. An audible moan escaped me. My body was no longer mine, it was shaking, and you held its sway.

"You express yourself well," you said, so I alone could hear.

"What I wish," I said, looking you in the eye, "is to express myself all over you."

I did not realize that the drumming had ceased. Nor that Iman had come over and was standing beside us. She put her hand on my shoulder to gain my attention, and at her touch, I fairly sprang off your lap. Iman noticed the quaver in my legs and the shortness of my breath.

"So," she said. "Youth tires at last."

I bit my lip. I'd no idea how to behave.

"Go. Take some refreshment," said Iman. "You danced well. But we have more work to do. The seduction was not quite convincing."

Not convincing? There was nothing not askew, neither my feelings, nor my perceptions. I turned to you and curtsied quickly, a silly gesture born of the blush burning on my cheeks. Then I walked out of the Hall, past the others and through the garden. My feet, not consciousness, led me. They took me out of the courtyard and through the small, undefended portal that foolishly, temptingly, led out of the citadel, to the river that watered the khan. Blindly, I followed the path to the river, the guard of palms on either side a blur. I cringed at the memory of my words.

"What I wish is to express myself all over you"? Had I actually said that? A jinn had gained control of my tongue, there could be no other explanation.

At the river's edge, I shed my costume in the rushes and dove into the waters. As my body drifted weightlessly back to the surface, my hair floated up around my head like frond.

My body felt ajangle, astir. . . .

I paused a moment to think where I might take the tale from here.

"Go on," urged Dee. She liked a slow hand and her stories ornate and florid.

Where in the world indeed.

13

Very quickly it happened that I began to feel foolish. What was I doing treading water in a brackish river? When the drama of the moment faded, I had nothing other than gooseflesh and soaked skin. A mosquito buzzed at my ear, needling my dignity. I swam to shore and put on my robe, then headed up the path that led back to the walled womb of the hareem.

Outside my room, in the hot, white sky, the sun began to fade. Sounds drifted in my window—the braying of donkeys, the clanging of pots. I thought I heard children, the high, reedy voices of the infants spirited away from the hareem to be tended by aging women, not their young mothers, as if they'd been no more than desert mirage. But it was not children, it was voices, the voices of my friends gathering for dinner in the garden.

I was hungry enough and plenty to join them, but decided against it. If Anwa was drawn to me as powerfully as she'd have it seem, I reasoned she'd come to find me. And when she did, it would be better if she found me alone. I sprinkled some incense on the coals I'd set burning in my brazier and fanned my hair above the smoke to scent it. I dimmed my lamp for sultry effect.

Time passed. There came no soul to my door. The women

of the hareem began drifting from dinner back to the living quarters. I heard their footsteps and chatter. Finally, a figure rustled the carpet that curtained my door.

"Who is it?" I called out, sure that I knew.

"It is Iman," said a voice.

"Iman? What do you wish?"

"Can I speak with you?"

When I pulled back the carpet, Iman looked at me queerly, noting my dim, smoky room.

"When you didn't come to dinner I became concerned," she said.

"Concerned?"

"For your health."

"Only because you need me to perform tomorrow."

"Well of course for that. But for you as well. Are you all right?"

"I'm feeling tired, is all."

Iman put the back of her hand to my forehead to satisfy herself I was not fevered. "Perhaps you're nervous about your performance?"

"Why would I be nervous? One feast is like another."

Footsteps sounded in the hallway. I peered out anxiously to see if they were yours. They weren't. It was another, going to her room.

Iman questioned me a while longer, then left me alone, realizing, I suppose, that she'd have little success wrangling answers from one so obviously obstinate. And though I continued to wait for you that night, you didn't arrive.

The next morning, starved out of my warren, I went to breakfast, hoping to see you there, though it wasn't common for you to breakfast with us. Usually, you stayed with the Mukarrib for that meal. Still, I lingered a long time at the large bowl of clear water set at the edge of our meal, rinsing my hands of the mango I'd eaten. Once, twice, three times I ordered the slave to perfume my hands, stalling my ablutions in hopes that you would show. You did not.

It was not until the feast itself that I saw you again. Seated next to the Mukarrib, pouring him spiced wine. The Great Hall was lit by flaming torches anchored high on its walls. I stood beneath one and stared at you a long time before finally you turned in the flaring light and glanced my way. Your expression was impassive, a quality of yours that, over time, would madden me greatly, though I suppose it suited perfectly the demand of your job.

When the performance began, I stepped forward with Iman's instructions nagging at me to direct my dance to the Mukarrib. The Mukarrib was already drunk. I knew his perception would be blurred and that he'd ill be able to distinguish the exact focus of my gaze. So, though I faced him, it was your eye I caught. If you'd made your feelings clear at any point, I might not have had to go to the lengths I did. Might not have brushed my breasts against you before brushing them against the Mukarrib. Might not have drawn up my legs and extended them across your lap when I sat upon the lap of the Mukarrib. Sat in the Mukarrib's lap and leaned back in his arms. All the while looking at you.

Later, you tried to impress upon me that I'd been playing with fire. And not our fire, rather one that would threaten to char me. The Mukarrib kissed me drunkenly on the neck. When the drummers played the roll which was my cue to exit, I stood up and took my bow, but did not go.

"Leave!" you hissed. You fairly spat it at me.

As I quit my performance, I glanced back. The Mukarrib was gaping after me, reaching out his arms like a lost child. As I took my place in the circle I'd been assigned and received my plate of roasted lamb I looked again. You were twining your fingers in the Mukarrib's hair. I watched you tease his attentions back to you. And what I thought was, "She lied to me. Her heart is the Mukarrib's." There was something in me, it started that night, that loved you and hated you both.

The nights that followed were fat with frustration. I lay in bed, unable to sleep, and so took to walking the halls like some somnambulist. A somnambulist, though, who has taken obvious care to dress for the situation. Any interested soul could've seen my naked form silhouetted beneath the scant clothing I wore, and I was hoping you were the soul interested and more. I passed your room many times and peered in, but your mat was always empty. "With the Mukarrib," I thought in despair. "She's every minute with the Mukarrib."

After a string of nights spent wandering about this way, the sleep I deprived myself of began to tell on me. One irritable morning, I slogged down to breakfast without freshly plaiting my hair or even washing my face. At breakfast, my friends were engaged in their usual morning gossip. I sat at my place too grog-headed to participate. Until I heard them mention your name.

"Anwa? What of her?" I asked, as casually as I could. "Where has she been? Has she taken up permanent residence with the Mukarrib?"

"If she has, she's there alone. The Mukarrib is away."

"Away?" I asked.

"Off to oversee the second incision."

"Of the trees?"

"They now tap for frankincense two times a year, not one. The Mukarrib's gotten greedy."

"Then the Mukarrib left directly after the feast?"

"And you ought be glad, Sari. If he'd stayed, you'd no doubt have been dragged to his bedchamber. It's small miracle you escaped as it was."

"But where is Anwa?"

"With him, where else?"

"Think of it as Anwa's saved you," another suggested. "Your maidenhood in her hands."

At this reference to what was in your hands, the subject veered to stories of a sexual nature, stories in which you were prime player. Every woman at the table had some sexual exploit of yours to relate, many reporting ecstasies they'd received from you in the Mukarrib's chambers. I know you'd like me to prolong this portion of the story, have me repeat every virtuoso feat attributed you. But I won't. You know them all already.

They were based on your reputation, and that you know as well as I. It was you who created it.

I felt a bit of a buffoon having paraded myself nightly, with you not even on the premises. I left the table, still unwashed, still in the mussed state in which I'd roused myself from bed, and returned to my room. The room I encountered was as unkempt as I. My clothes were scattered all over the floor as I'd left them when I'd rooted through, looking for just the right costume for seduction.

Spurred by a sudden impulse to cleanse away the stagnancy I found myself mired in, I gathered up the clothes and decided then and there to wash them. I dropped the bundle into a sturdy reed basket, balanced it atop my head, and headed down to the river.

At the riverbank, I upturned the basket and plucked out a garment. Then I hiked up the robe I was wearing, knotted it above my knees, and waded into the water. There, I bent over a rock and beat my clothing, my robe knotted up, my hair still snagged. Such was my state when I looked up and saw you on the riverbank. You stood staring at me, watching.

"Anwa," I said.

You stood astride my clothes, which lay in tumbled clumps about your feet. "Ready for another?" you asked. You tossed me a robe. Catch.

The gods only know what came over me, perhaps accumulated days and nights of frustrated desire, but I tossed the robe back at your feet. I unknotted the one I was wearing and pulled it over my head so I stood there bare-fleshed, knee-deep in the water. I tossed that robe to you, too. You caught it flush against your chest.

"No thank you," I said in answer to your offer. "*I'm* the one next. I want to wash *me*."

When I calculated that you'd had a good look at me, I turned and dove into the deeper part of the river and came up dripping, my long hair free and wet and sticking to my breasts and ribs, which were heaving from the shock of the chill water. I climbed back up onto the bank and faced you.

"Now I am clean," I said.

I pushed out my breasts provocatively, and cocked my head at a challenging angle. I wanted you to do something, grab me up right there and kiss me, throw me to the ground. I actually had only the vaguest idea what it was we might do, but I knew it must be something and you, after all, were the experienced one, the one spent every night, so it seemed, in the Mukarrib's chambers. But, you, shrewd strategist, did nothing of the sort. Instead, you pressed a scarab into my hand. A promise, one made of stone. "I like you wet," you said.

Then you simply turned on your heel and walked back toward the khan. Left me standing there dripping and cold and feeling foolish, my whole body pulsing with desire. I sat down naked in the shallow bank of the river. The mud oozed around my buttocks, and the cool water lapped my breasts.

A small fish slithered past me, glancing my thigh.

"You know what just occurred to me?" I said to Dee.

Dee tugged the covers around her, irritated that I'd interrupted the flow, broken the spell. "What?" she asked.

"About my mother . . . I wonder why she took to wearing that stained white nightgown day in and day out."

"What stained white nightgown?"

"I've *told* you."

Dee frowned. "Am I wrong, or weren't we just involved in something a little more animal here? Something a little more exciting than The Codie James Case History Hour? Can we just get on with it?"

"It must've just been too much for my mother," I said, "thinking he was a spy."

"Code," Dee said flatly. "You know what the trouble with you is?"

"What?"

"You have to understand everything. Everything has to have an explanation."

"So?"

"So whenever you don't have one, you just make one up."

Damn right.

14

The night after you materialized on the bank of the river as enigmatically as if you'd been an apparition, I was in my room, again unable to sleep. For lack of better occupation, I picked up my mirror. It was polished bronze, graced, at top, by the figure of an ibex. My mirror, prettier than I.

But I was comely, I thought as I studied my reflection, wasn't I? Well, if I was, I was apparently not comely enough, or you'd be responding to me in the full measure that I hoped. I took out my jars of paints and set about lining my eyes thickly with kohl, staining my lips with cinnabar. I resolved that, thus made up, I would stalk into your room, lie down directly beside you, and say plainly, "Take me." This, of course, would be predicated on your being there when I arrived. And what precedent had I to expect that?

Nonetheless, it was with determination I strode to your chamber. Vacant. I wondered how much more of this I could bear. I knew I couldn't return to my room. That small chamber had not the space to contain all the energy making its restless home in me. I walked toward the opposite reach of the quarters, and pushed open the door to the Hall of a Hundred Columns.

The Hall was empty and eerily quiet. It was forbidden for

me to go there except for feasts and their rehearsals. Nonetheless, I entered and began to dance, in increments giving vent to more and more of my frustration. Soon I was flinging my arms about, whipping my head, spinning around the columns, shouting, wailing. When finally I stopped, I felt as if I had exorcised something. At last I could return to my room. I'd exhausted myself enough to hope for sleep.

Through the slender arch of my door, I was startled to see a dark figure seated on my mat. The shock of it stopped me. It was you.

"Where have you been?" you asked. Your words slid toward me like fish through dark water. I hesitated, unsure how safe it was to tell the truth, my brazenness gone.

"Looking for you," I said.

"I am here."

You stood up and walked toward me. When you were flush up against me, you tangled your fingers in my hair and combed the moonlight through. Then you wet a cloth in my basin and held my head steady to wash off my makeup, which the sweat of my dancing had caked and soiled.

"Let it shine through," you said.

"What?"

"Your desire."

At that, you wrapped me in your arms and I climbed up you as if you were some palm I'd shimmied up in childhood. We kissed, and it is that way that you carried me to the mat, where you unlaced my robe and began to work it over my head. Here I would love to draw a curtain on the scene and let my listener suppose that it built without obstacle to ecstatic conclusion. But that is not what happened. When you bent to remove my robe, I started.

"What are you doing?" I asked, nervously, quickly.

"Making love with you."

"No," I said, stiffening.

"Why not? Don't you like me? Aren't you enjoying my attentions?"

"Yes. I mean no. I mean to say, I don't know you."

You eyed me curiously. "Is this the same girl who threw off all her clothes at the riverside just this afternoon, whose actions fairly challenged me to take her right there on the bank?"

"That was different," I said, tugging my robe back down.

"Why?"

"Because now you are here in my bed, and somehow that seems to make all the difference."

"You are suddenly shy?"

"Shy?" I said, trying to feign indignation. "Not at all."

"Well, this is a shift. I forgot to consider how young you are."

"Not so young," I said. "I'm nearing thirteen. It's just that some of us do not spend every night in the Mukarrib's chamber."

"Have you never been touched before?" you asked.

I avoided your question by throwing out one of my own. "If you knew I was challenging you to take me this afternoon on the riverbank, why didn't you?"

"You're a virgin," you said, as if this notion just occurred to you.

"Why didn't you?" I insisted. "Why didn't you take me?"

You took my hand in your mouth and sucked on the fleshy mound underneath my thumb. "I had just returned with the Mukarrib," you told me. "He required my service. But I begged a few moments' leave and in those I went to catch glimpse of you."

"Oh." Sensation pulsed through my body.

"Sweet Sari," you said. You kissed the tips of my ears and sucked at my neck. Then you again lifted my robe and this time I allowed you. You touched your lips to my breasts and down my belly. "I want you to annoint me," you said. And then you worked your head in between my legs and licked your tongue full across my sex. At this, I jolted away.

"What are you doing?" I said, my body taut and coiled like a serpent. "Why are you putting your mouth on me?"

"I'm sorry," you said. "Was that too sudden?"

"Too *something*," was my skittish answer.

You placed one hand on my belly and rubbed it softly to soothe me, all the while keeping your lips between my legs, but now you kissed me softly, just light kisses on my sex and on the soft skin inside my upper thighs.

"Your fur is sweet," you said. "As sweet as I imagined and sweeter still."

"You've imagined it?" I asked.

"Many times. Did you not know that I have waited through seasons to be with you as we are now?"

"Through seasons?" I asked. "You have? How many?"

"Enough," you said, laughing. "Long nights I've imagined the taste of you on my tongue. To taste you now is simply confirmation."

As you spoke, I felt my body soften. You slipped your fingers into me and wriggled them around.

"Look how wet you are," you said. Your voice hushed to a husky whisper. "Like a succulent in the desert." You drew your fingers from me and wiped the wetness across the inside of my thighs, then across my belly. "I'm cooling you with your juices," you said, "and now I'm going to get them on me." You put your mouth back on me full, and this time I no longer wriggled away from it, but toward and against it.

After, you would laugh and tell me that it was the sweet talk you employed that had brought me willingly to you. "Fortunate for me I learned early on the key to your body. Honeyed words are all it takes."

"You didn't mean those words then?"

"Of course I meant them. Your fur is sweet. Sweetness itself."

"It is?"

"Come here, little one. I'm going to lick you again. I want to eat confection."

I did as told. When you lifted your head from between my legs, your eyes were laughing. "You see?" you said. "You see how easy it is for me to get you in this position?"

However it was you coaxed me, I no longer cared. That

night you made a willing lover of one reluctant. Is it that you tamed me or is it that you made me wild? We spent the full span of the night kissing and rubbing. If the length of it had been a lifetime, we would have used it all.

Late the next morning when you slipped out of my room, I closed in my palm the scarab you'd given me. It had indeed been a promise. As was the air we breathed, the rise and set of the moon and sun.

The tint of morning sky.

15

The morning after our exotic interlude, if that's what I may pre-
sume to call it, I woke up singing. Cole Porter, I think. Dee's
pajamas were strewn all over the bathroom floor as she'd left
them when she'd gone to work, but I didn't get angry, not a
whit. Matter of fact, the very sight of them made me smile.

The time I woke up singing was actually the second time
that morning I'd awoken. This time around, Dee was gone.
Which could go a long way toward explaining why I was able
to get a kick out of her pajamas. I sat on the toilet emptying a
night's full bladder, thinking that it was often easier for me to
deal with traces of Dee than it was to deal with Dee herself. In
her absence, there was quiet, and a space for sentiment to seep
in, the fondness I felt for Dee, the affection. I stared at Dee's
pajama tops, the very pajama tops I'd unbuttoned the night before so I could brush my lips against her stomach, across her
breasts, and across the vaccination mark that stippled her upper
arm. "Look," I'd said, waxing cosmic. I'd bared my own arm
and compared it to hers. "You and I are marked. Anyone who
would see our bare bodies would know exactly when to place
us on a time line. Before we were born, people got smallpox,
and after us, they'll probably develop a less crude method of

immunization. But in the second half of the twentieth century, countless infants were branded with a pox and sent forth in their newly armed bodies to live their lives." I'd paused a moment to marvel at the significance of my observation. "I guess we sort of belong to our time, huh?" I'd said, looking to Dee.

"You belong to me," she'd said. She'd rolled out from under me and positioned herself on top. She'd pinned my arms back with the strength of hers. "Who do you belong to?" she'd asked. She'd rubbed her sex across me, trailing her juices across my stomach, marking me invisibly, indelibly.

"You," I'd answered, no hesitation. Happily. Hopelessly happy. Dee and I tumbling through time.

As I sat there on the toilet, musing on the events of the night before, I picked up the roll of toilet paper from the back lid, where we kept it, and began, idly, to unwind some. At that point, to my utter shock, a waterbug fell onto my crotch. The bug must have made its home inside the toilet paper tube and when I'd disturbed it, it landed, scrambling, on my exposed vulva. I was so startled that I jumped up off the toilet mid-pee and screamed bloody murder. I didn't have the coordination or presence of mind, though, to stop peeing in the bargain, so I ended up urinating all over the bathroom floor.

Though I was alone in the apartment, I looked around sheepishly to see if anyone had seen what I'd done. The waterbug was paddling in the water of the toilet. I flushed it down. I stood there a minute before I mopped up my puddle, and then I started laughing. I was relieved that no one else had witnessed what had happened, but there was also something in me couldn't wait to tell Dee. Intimacy does have its quirky compensations.

"And right before it fell on me," I said when I told her, to cap the story, "I was thinking how pleasant it is in the apartment when you're gone and how it's somehow so much easier for me to love you from afar." I thought I delivered this clever little remark affectionately, in an elfish spirit, but Dee took it badly, she bristled.

"You liked it all right when I was in the house last night," she said. "You like it fine when I take you to bed."

True. I liked nothing more. "But mornings . . ."

Mornings, Dee was scheduled to get up long before me, though inevitably she slept through her alarm and woke up late. Which meant no more sleep for me. Dee liked to make a lot of noise, liked me to be well aware that she was behind schedule, and there always seemed to be something she couldn't find— a certain shirt, the sugar for her coffee, her keys. She'd bang things around in hopes that I would get out of bed and become involved in the search, and, if I didn't of my own accord, she'd draw me in directly. "Codie!" she'd shout from the bathroom or the kitchen or sometimes right next to my ear. "Where's my . . . ?" Clean socks, deodorant, comb, wallet, whatever. Somehow, it was my lot to always know the whereabouts of what it was she'd lost.

"What'll you give me if I tell?" I'd ask, still crusty-eyed and muss-haired from sleeping, still sassy from the night before.

"A spanking on that alabaster ass of yours," she'd say. That was fine with me.

If I were lucky, when Dee left, I'd be able to get back to sleep for maybe another half hour or so. But even if I didn't, it was cozy lying there in bed with traces of Dee's presence lingering all over our apartment, like fragrance.

I was in love. Pure coincidence, it happened it was spring.

The morning of the waterbug, when I left the house for work, I noticed that the trees lining one of the side streets were full with pink blossoms. I veered off the avenue and took that street. Some of the blossoms had blown off the branches and were skittering with the breeze along the sidewalk. Up close, the flowers looked perfectly formed. The edges were pinked, as if with shears, and the color was a brilliant too-pink. All of which made the blossoms seem unreal, dyed, manufactured. Like fabric flowers torn off the bodices of pastel prom dresses. Kitsch tumbleweed.

All this frolic in the air, all this gamboling, got me hungry, so I stopped in the Greek coffee shop outside the building where I worked and ordered a fried egg sandwich on rye toast to go.

"Double fried on whiskey!" the man behind the counter shouted back to the kitchen.

"Whiskey *down*," I corrected him, short-order savvy, lingo-wise.

"Whiskey *down!*" he called back.

When I got to my cubicle I opened the big sliding window that faced me. The breeze flirted with the papers on my desk and I liked the spring smell of it, but fresh air was against the rules. The week before a memo had circulated advising all employees that it threw off the office thermostat to have one part of the building "receiving outside air intake," as the memo had worded it. Ever since, the building manager had been roaming the halls, policing the offices on the lookout for open windows, a man with a mission. I figured he'd be around soon enough to close mine, and I was right, he was.

"Who opened this window?" he growled. I shrugged, deaf, dumb, and blind. I don't know nothin', sir. The man shut the window, irritably, since he had no one to blame. And when I was sure that he had long passed to enforce his strictures farther down the hall, I got up, looked both ways as if I were crossing the street, and opened the window up again to let in more fresh air.

A mother bird flew by, winging breakfast to her hatchlings. "I will not live enslaved," is what I thought out of nowhere. The strength of the sentiment surprised me.

16

"Look at all them womens," said Dee's mother. She clucked her tongue in disapproval. Or, as Dee would correct me, she kissed her teeth. "All them womens wearing corsages. A waste of money, that's what that is."

We were in Dee's taxi, driving through Harlem, a neighborhood in which there was no mistaking the day. All the women on the street were wearing flouncy, brightly colored Saturday night dresses, though it was mid-morning Sunday, and many had on wide-brimmed hats to match. Most of the women also had corsages pinned to their bosoms, as Mrs. Matthews was tireless in pointing out.

"Look at that one!" She craned her neck out the window to point to a woman wearing a large corsage with ribbons, pertly curled, dangling down.

Mother's Day in Harlem. I was as wide-eyed as Dee's mother, taking in the whole spectacle of it. Downtown, where we lived, the only evidence of the day was a creased Hallmark poster taped in the window of the corner card store.

"Is that two orchids she gots?" Dee's mother spied the most ostentatious corsage yet. "Is that two?" It was indeed. "I can't see spending all this money on corsages," she sniffed. "Orchids, no less. What these people made of? Money? *Last* thing I want is a corsage." She paused a moment before repeating it. "*Last* thing I want."

I was sitting in the back seat of the taxi. Dee and her mother were seated up front. When Dee stopped at a red light, I leaned up and whispered in her ear, "I think your mother wants a corsage." This was one of the few times I had met Mrs. Matthews, but even so I had divined that, with her, rules were different. Yes meant no. Saying that she didn't want a corsage meant that she wanted one badly. I congratulated myself for so quickly cracking the code. Dee caught my eye in the rearview mirror. "Really," I said, secretive, hushed-voiced. "I think we'd better stop and get a corsage."

Dee's mother eyed us suspiciously. "What you two whisperin' about?" she said. "This ain't no library."

I knew from living with Dee that this kind of talk was mostly for effect, not to be aggravated with an answer. As we drove down the avenue, I kept an eye out for florists. When I spotted one, I tapped Dee on the shoulder. "There," I said. Dee double-parked the car and ran in. I watched her pull her wallet out of her pocket before she even got in the store.

"Where she goin'?" asked Mrs. Matthews.

"She just had to stop a minute," I answered.

Mrs. Matthews squinted, trying to watch her daughter through the florist window. "I hope that girl's not getting me a corsage," she said. "*Last* thing I want is some raggedy corsage."

When Dee came back, she handed her mother a small white box with gilt edging. "What you get me?" asked Mrs. Matthews. "A corsage? I told you I don't want no corsage." Mrs. Matthews opened the box. Inside was a single carnation. She lifted it out, puckering her features in distaste. "A carnation!" she snorted indignantly. "That all? All the other womens got *orchids*!"

No winning. I was beginning to see where Dee came by the trait. We drove another couple of blocks to the church where we were taking Mrs. Matthews for Mother's Day service, and I thought, in passing, of my own mother. I thought of a particular night when, because my father had promised to take her to dinner, she herself got dressed up. I remember watching, transfixed, from the edge of her bed as my mother fastened stockings to garters, clasped pearls around her neck, dabbed perfume in the crux of her elbows. I remember watching, insensibly, as my mother lunged at me in her stained white nightgown and called me Whore of Babylon.

No. That must have been another night.

And time hurtling on like the slow erosion of stone. . . .

Mrs. Matthews continued watching out the window of the car, commenting on the women and their corsages. She was smiling now, though, having moved into the ranks of the acknowledged.

I, too, was giddy and excited. Soon I would be in the church, where Mrs. Matthews would show off her corsage to anyone who'd give her a moment's notice, everyone around me would sing hallelujah, and I would wonder self-consciously if I could join in, the sole white face in a spirited and celebratory crowd.

"Look at all them corsages," said Mrs. Matthews, radiating a pride I recognized from elsewhere. "All the womens sure is dressed up today."

I liked this kind of talk and expected that all day I was going to get to listen to this language that sounded like colorful cousin to mine. From the moment we picked up Dee's mother, she'd been talking about "womens," and in my white way I was half a step removed, busy calculating formulas for how to make language as she did. Take one irregular noun, a noun already plural by a change in its stem, and add an "s" anyway. Make the exception the rule. Just for the play of it. For the sheer joy of bounty. As if one plural alone is stingy, tight, too hopelessly impoverished to even bother with.

Did I mention we lived in The Orienta? That was the name of our building. Before I met Dee, I lived in another building that had a name as well. The Vulcan, it was called, carved in the stone over the doorway.

After Dee left, I admit I may have gone a little overboard calling her on the phone. Once I yelled at her, "What are you doing? Don't you know I'm in love with you, you jerk?"

Dee yelled back. "What's the matter with you, Codie? Don't you understand English?"

English? What English? She wasn't saying anything, not in English or otherwise. She never even said a proper goodbye.

I wanted Dee waking me too early, I wanted her chopping up my bathwater. I even missed her yelling at me, telling me I wore the wrong clothes. Sometimes, and don't think I am unaware how choice this admission is, what I did was chastise myself in my mind, in the ways that Dee used to. To make the loss less raw:

"Codie, you better get yourself dressed if you're going to get out of here."

"I am dressed."

"Dressed? You call that dressed?" I didn't answer, which Dee took for assent. "That's what I was afraid of," she barreled on. "And where you think you're goin' like that?"

"You know where I'm going. I'm going to work."

"Where you work, in a circus?"

Dee was home, sick supposedly. She'd decided that that day she was not going to taxi anybody anywhere. Instead, she was sitting up in bed, monitoring each step of my morning routine. I'd brewed her a cup of tea. To make her happy, I thought. But when I'd brought it to her she'd handed it right back and told me it was cold.

"If you're so sick," I said, "how come you have so much energy to give me a hard time? Why don't you just lay there and sniffle or something? Better yet, go back to sleep."

"Sleep? Who can sleep with you making all that noise you make and bringing me cold tea?"

I went into the bathroom because being in the same room as Dee was exhausting me. "I'm brushing my teeth now!" I called out to her. "Just thought you might want to know!"

But when I had my coat on and was ready to kiss her goodbye, Dee got out of bed and put her arms around me, not like goodbye, like hello. Me with my coat buttoned, her with no clothes.

"What are you doing?" I asked. Dee had slipped her hand between my legs and was rubbing there and grinning at me, too.

"Stay home with me," she said. "Play hooky."

"I can't." I had scheduled a meeting, a writer was coming. "Why didn't you ask me yesterday or the day before, we could've planned ahead."

Dee slid her hand from my crotch, pulled it out as if she were extracting a knife. "You know what, Codie?" she said. "You know what's the matter with you? You're a rigid personality. You are the whitest, most straightlaced soul to inhabit this planet. If you ever let loose, I swear, I'd keel over from sheer shock."

Calling me white. A little bit below the belt, that's what I thought about that. I tried to ignore what Dee was saying and kiss her goodbye, but when I did, she pulled away and made for the medicine cabinet. I left her in the bathroom. Tippling Nyquil.

At work, the writer I had scheduled to see showed up promptly for her appointment, and it turned out that the book she'd brought to peddle wasn't a real book, but a "product," a book based on a character she was trying to license. In addition to the book sale, she was trying to negotiate a television show or a movie for the character, in order to create an even larger market so the character could appear on tote bags, beach towels, lunch boxes, the lot. I sat stiff-smiled at my desk while the woman explained to me how she'd first got the idea for the character. I don't know what had possessed me to ask.

"It came to me first as a color," she said. "I was dozing off in front of the TV when I awoke with a start and saw an expanse of green. 'Green,' I said to myself. I knew then and there. 'The character's definitely green.' "

The next step, she explained, had been to christen the character. She'd hit upon "Greenback," the significance not lost on me. She'd stayed up all that night writing a manuscript for a picture book which, she said proudly, she'd completed by dawn. She pulled the manuscript out of her briefcase and slapped it down on my desk. I picked it up and paged through. The text she'd written aped the tone of a legend, though none too successfully. "Once there were green creatures who grew on trees," it began. It ended with a moral. Something about filthy lucre, money being the root of all evil. Worse still, the story was written completely in rhyme. I was trying to think how I might break the news gently.

"Hmm," I said. "You know, it's awfully hard to both tell a story and rhyme, too." The woman had rhymed Greenback with sweepstake. Unabashedly. On the first page. "There's always the temptation to sacrifice the rhyme for the story," I said. "Or the other way around."

"Oh, well, that's not a problem for me," she said. She pulled out another sheet of paper, on which she'd projected the licensing revenue, then looked me directly in the eye. "Not a problem for me in the least," she said. "I'm a poet."

After she left, I stared numbly at the title page: "The Story of Jack-Jack Greenback." I might have stayed frozen in that position all afternoon had Jake not stopped by to ask me would I like to go to lunch with him and a friend of his, Cliff somebody, an editor at some other house. We ended up at a restaurant a few blocks away, and Cliff and Jake talked acquisitions while I ate nachos and sipped my soda.

"We're closing in on the gorilla book," Jake told his friend.

"The gorilla book?"

"I told you. The talking gorilla? The woman who taught the gorilla sign language?"

"Oh yeah."

"We're aiming it, say, third grade. Hardcover. Glossy paper. We'll stick a photo glossary in the back, the gorilla demonstrating signs. The book's got human interest, one gorilla's story. But of course, you've also got your animal information and a bit about language. . . ."

"Soft science," said Cliff.

Jake smiled. "Eiderdown," he said. He checked his watch, ordered another espresso. "Wait till you meet this woman, Codie. Sturdy Northeastern stock. Lives alone with her gorilla in Vermont up near the Canadian border. Log cabin, probably, I don't know. The point is, she's totally tied up with this gorilla." Jake was looking for someone to write the book. Ghostwrite, he meant. The woman with the gorilla would be the one to get her name on the cover.

The waiter brought our lunch. I spooned up my spaghetti and listened to the soft clink of silverware and counterpoint conversation in the small Village restaurant.

"So," Jake said to me suddenly. I could tell he thought I was being too quiet. "Tell Cliff what you did in high school." I wasn't sure what he was talking about. "The study hall thing," Jake prodded.

"Why?" I asked.

"Because it's funny," said Jake.

"You tell." I knew Jake would just as soon.

"Get this," he said, his tone all confidential—he was about to tell the one about the Catholic girl. "Codie here went to Catholic school all her life," he said. "Except every so often her parents would ship her off to her grandmother's in a neighboring town, and then she'd go to public school."

"Why?" asked Cliff, trying to make sense of Jake's introduction. He looked to me for an answer.

"God knows," I said. Jake hadn't asked for that story.

"So, of course," Jake went on, "the public school was much looser. But Codie had had years of nuns." He stopped short, his expression puzzled, he'd forgotten the details. "What did you wear?" he asked me. Details crucial.

"Saddle shoes," I said. "Circle pins. My hair was in a pageboy."

Jake smiled, the picture clear. "She thought you were supposed to," he explained. "But these public school kids were wearing torn jeans, smoking dope, and none of the girls were virgins. Right, Code? They might as well have stuck you on the moon."

"Mars."

"Exactly. Anyway, she gets sent to her grandmother's at the end of her senior year, so, as it happens, she's at the public school for the very last day of class. Senior year. Last day, last period. And Codie has study hall. So she goes. Just like she thinks she's supposed to. Of course, nobody else has bothered to show up for study hall. No kids, no teacher even. But Codie sits down and opens a book to read. *Jane Eyre?*"

"Probably."

"So, Code," Jake asked, stopping short to get something straight, "in your whole school career you never cut class?" He sounded incredulous. "Not even once?"

"Nope."

Jake shook his head, considering this, then charged on. "Meanwhile, see, the teacher happens to walk past the room and spots Codie sitting there. 'What the hell are you doing here?' he says. 'Go home!' " Jake grinned. "Classic, huh? You can take the girl out of Catholic school . . ."

96

Cliff looked expectantly from Jake to me, figuring there must be more to the story, but Jake was shaking his head in a kind of afterglow, satisfied. "Yup," Jake said, by way of summary. "Codie's the ideal employee. My policy is always hire girls who went to Catholic school. Especially ones from Ohio."

Jake gave me an affectionate nudge. Cliff looked at me blankly. I had a sharp pang in my chest that felt like missing Dee. So when we got back to the office, I excused myself from Jake as quickly as I could and rushed back to my cubicle to call her. I had the idea that maybe I would feign sickness, go home from work early, be with Dee after all. As I should have been, I thought, all that morning.

"Hi, baby," I said, when she answered the phone, my voice creamy as pleasure. "I miss you."

"Hey," Dee said. Her own voice was businesslike, perfunctory. "I'm in the middle of something here." I could hear what she was in the middle of. I could hear it in the background. Dee was watching television. "Jesus!" Dee cried into the phone. It was the sort of thing she usually yelled when a televised batter hit a home run.

"What?" I asked.

"You won't believe this show!"

I stayed on the phone while Dee watched the show and described it to me blow by blow so I could get some sense, however blind. It was one of those programs with a controversial subject and a provocative host, the kind they run in the afternoons after the soaps.

"I can't believe it!" cried Dee.

"What?" I asked. "What's going on?"

"I just can't believe it!"

Dee explained that the host had been interviewing a woman who was describing the sexual abuse she'd experienced in childhood at the hands of her father. The woman described the abuse in detail, Dee relayed the information to me, and when we were thoroughly outraged, the program cut to a commercial.

"Oh my God!" said Dee, when the show came back on.

"What?"

97

Dee told me there was now a figure sitting behind the woman on stage, a figure masked by a scrim. The host introduced him. It was the woman's father.

"Can you believe it?" cried Dee. "He's right there with her on stage! He's listening to every word!"

"What's happening now?"

Dee said the host was asking the father, "And how do you feel about all this, sir? How do you feel about what your daughter just told us?"

"He called him 'sir'!" Dee said, incredulous. "He called the scumbag 'sir'!"

"But what's the scumbag saying?"

The father, as Dee relayed it, defended himself. He said that he loved his daughter and felt it better that she first experience sex with someone who cared for her than with some pimply-faced, horny schoolboy in the back seat of some car. The host turned to the young woman. "And how have your early experiences with your father affected your subsequent sexual relationships with men?" he asked.

"I don't have sexual relationships with men," she said.

"You don't?"

"I'm a lesbian."

"All right!" Dee exclaimed. Her voice trailed off. It sounded as if she'd thrown the receiver into the air, a sort of triumphant baton. "The audience is going wild!" she yelled.

My vision glazed. I felt shamed by this one-step recipe for lesbianism broadcast on nationwide TV. A person's past reduced, as if it were a sentence. There was something I wanted to talk to Dee about, something nagging at me, but Dee was distracted, cheering the show along, a fan at a Yankees game, so I interrupted just long enough to say goodbye, that I had to get back to work, nothing more. When I hung up, I found myself no longer in the world I'd tried to inhabit with Dee but in the one that was really my own. My world, walled by beige partitions. In the window opposite mine, ballerinas leapt across the floor, legs split, arms wide.

"Jake," I said. I'd barged into his office. Jake was leaning back in his chair, feet crossed on his desk, blinking at page proofs. "Jake, do you think that I'm rigid?"

"What are you talking about?"

"I mean, do you think I'm too straightlaced, that I never take any risks?"

"What makes you ask that?"

"Oh, I don't know. A lot of things." Jake telling the study hall story at lunch, for starters, Dee accusing me that very morning. Once I started up the litany, it was difficult to stop. I stood there in my workplace, inappropriately pouring out my heart to my boss, and he heard me out. Jake was a pretty good friend that way. To reassure me, he told me some kind and comforting lies, that he'd always thought me plenty adventurous. "A regular Sinbad," he said, with a resolute rap on his desk. And then Jake sat forward. "Codie," he said, "you want risk? I've got risk for you. Right here. I was going to save the news for later, but I might as well cheer you up now. The gorilla book. I'm going to throw it to you."

"The gorilla book?"

"Enough of *Greenback* and its ilk. Enough of talking bunnies."

"Yeah," I said, not so sure. "From talking bunnies to a talking gorilla."

"A gorilla who *really* talks. A *real* book, not product. You'll be editor and writer both. Codie," Jake said, "this could be a major feather in your editorial cap."

18

Jake promised me a videotape of the gorilla and the gorilla woman in order to get me started on the project, and I couldn't refuse. But I wrestled with my qualms as if they were a lover. Or perhaps some sort of knotty past.

On the home front, things were eroding. Or at least sloughing off. What I'm referring to here is a tendency that Dee had. The tendency to lose things. Just a little habit she had. Dee lost small things like combs, small but important things like keys and slips of paper on which she'd written information she would need, and other, bigger, more valuable things. When that happened, she'd yell at me before I even had a chance to yell at her, who even said I was going to?

"Where's the cassette player?" I'd ask. An innocent question; I'd be thinking we might take it with us wherever we were going.

Dee would whirl around and fix me with her stare. "I don't want to hear anything about it, get it?"

And that was the way I'd know it was gone. Once Dee even lost a typewriter.

"It's not like I just left it somewhere," she said, defending herself. But she had. Where she'd left it was the trunk of her cab when she'd brought the typewriter back from repair. She'd left it there for more than a week because every night when she got home she was either too tired to carry it up or she couldn't manage that and the six-pack, too. The week she left it there was the week somebody decided to break into her trunk. I remembered then something Dee'd once told me, it couldn't have been more than a month before. "Never leave anything in the trunk," she'd said. "Just the same as kissing it goodbye." The typewriter was gone and the spare tire, too.

Dee's hold was as fluid as a riverbed in rainy season. Certain things flowed out of her life and other things flowed in, the latter being, mostly, things found at the end of the day in the back of her cab. Dee brought home a steady stream of hats, books, scarves. She accumulated enough umbrellas to set up a corner concession in a rainy rush hour. When Dee brought home single gloves and mittens, I asked, "What for?" but she was happy to wear mismatches since, likely as not, she'd lost her own the day before. I knew better than to give Dee gloves for Christmas if I was thinking along the lines of keepsake.

It made Dee's day to come home with something bigger, better. She'd fling open the front door. "Spoils!" she'd crow. Dee considered found objects one of the perks of her job. Hers was not, after all, a job with health insurance and it took some of the sting out of me not being able to add her to mine. So when it came to pass that conversation between us started to strain, it eased things when Dee came home one day with two sets of towels in a Bloomingdale's bag.

"They're beautiful," I said, fingering the merchandise. The towels were thick, fluffy. Puce wasn't exactly the color I'd choose, but I didn't dare voice that to Dee. As it turned out, finding the towels was just a warm-up. A few days later, Dee came home with the camera. It was 35 millimeter. Name brand. We looked it up in the newspaper ads. It would've cost us a pretty penny.

"Yes, ma'am!" cried Dee. "I'm on a tear!" She cranked up the radio full volume and danced around in her underwear. There was one shot left on the roll already in the camera, so I took a picture of her—wild-eyed, dancing. When we got that roll back from the developer, we threw away the first thirty-five shots. Somebody's bar mitzvah. A lot of people we didn't care about or even know.

"Codie," said Dee, "I just realized. We haven't had a camera the whole time we've been together, so you'd have no way of knowing. I'm a fabulous photographer."

"Oh yeah?"

Dee flexed her biceps. "Ace."

Finding the camera set off something in Dee. She started buying film at the corner store often, as if it were Lifesavers or packs of gum, and she took my picture every chance she got. I had to start taking care to look good all the time, because I'd never know when or where. Dee caught me going to sleep, she caught me waking up, she caught me soaking in my bath. Sometimes Dee snapped me lightning quick and other times she took forever to focus.

"Move a little to the left. Now tilt your head up just a hair. Can you part your lips? No, lick them first."

I knew how to pose all right, no problem there. My father'd provided the practice.

Taking photos became what we did together, like drinking coffee, shopping for groceries. I actually began to look forward to Dee being home, her attention focused on me, though sometimes I did worry about the flatness of it all. Somewhere in me I knew full well that things kept on the surface can skim away. One day after work, to stave off nagging worry, I bought a red lipstick and put some on, enough so that when Dee got home she'd want to kiss me, and not so much so that she wouldn't. It did the trick. I got kisses out of it and photos, too. Dee even set up one with a timer so she and I could be in the photo together, Dee with her arm around me, me with rouged lips. I always could catch Dee with a little flash.

After I'd got Dee naked and smelling like me, she climbed out of bed and pulled down a carton she had stored at the top of the closet. In it was a photo album that I'd never seen before or even known she had. Dee brought it into bed with us and opened it up to the first page as if to read me a story. On that page were pictures of Dee as a young child, school photos mostly, her hair parted neatly and braided. I laughed out loud to see Dee looking so reined in and tamed, the contour of her face round and smooth, just a hint of mischief in her eyes. There was one picture I wanted to take and keep in my wallet, but Dee had only that one page for all her childhood, so I knew there wasn't really enough to spare.

"I should take more pictures of you," I said, thinking maybe she'd just given me a glimpse of something she needed. "You hardly let me take pictures of you." It was true, I realized, not since we'd first gotten the camera.

Dee winced as if she'd just been offered a bite of something foul and shook her head to dispel the taste. "I'm the photographer in this family," she said. Then she turned the page.

On the spread that followed were a series of pictures of women, old girlfriends I found out, ones I'd heard about but never seen likenesses of. Dee pointed to and named them in turn. "Here's Joy," she said. "And Serena. Here's Bliss." One thing I knew about them was that Dee had left them all.

They were pretty, every one of them. "Why'd you leave this one?" I asked, pointing to the one with the jet curls and seductive smile.

"Serena?" said Dee. "She got crazy on me." That was as much as she'd say.

I was curious about these women, but uncomfortable, too. I chastised myself, told myself what's there to be jealous of, these women were in the past. Dee wasn't in touch with any of them, she'd left them all behind. So where was the threat?

Dee turned the page again, and again there was a spread of photos of the girlfriends, the same array of women, only this time they were all in a different setting, at the beach.

"What'd you do?" I asked, bald reality leering up at me. "You arranged the photo album so that all your old girlfriends are always on the same pages together?"

"These were at home," Dee said, nodding back to the previous page, "and these are at the beach. . . ." She flipped the pages forward for preview. "And these are at Christmas, and these are on vacation. . . ."

"You mean you stuck all the Christmas photos together, you mean you organized it not by girlfriend but by event?"

"Yeah," said Dee. "That way I can see them all together." She flipped to the Christmas page. "See? Look, I can compare all the trees." In each of the Christmas pictures a girlfriend was sitting in front of a Christmas tree. The trees and girlfriends changed, but the ornaments on the branches were the same. I recognized the ornaments. They were Dee's. We'd used them the Christmas before.

"It's a line-up?" I said. "You just lined up all your old girlfriends like they're trophies or something?"

"What're you, jealous?"

"If we break up," I said, "don't you *ever* stick me on a page with a bunch of other ex-girlfriends." The shrillness in my voice sounded not unlike a mother yelling at a child who's run out into traffic after a ball. And which one of us was that child?

"All right, all right," said Dee. "Calm down. Hold your horses."

"If we break up," I continued, "you put the pictures of me someplace separate. I mean it. Don't you ever add me to some page of ex-es."

Dee riveted her focus to the book. "I already said I agreed. What's the problem?" She pulled the album closer to her so that it no longer straddled the two of us, and continued to turn the pages of old girlfriends as if the photos absorbed her. I stared across her at the pictures. The penultimate spread was of girlfriends all naked. And the last page showed pictures of the couples, Dee with her arm around each girlfriend in turn, cozy portraits taken together, as if with a timer.

After the outburst I had that day, Dee no longer got out the camera as often. Once she tried to take my picture when I was washing dishes and I said, with no little edge, "For the domestic page?" Another time, out of the blue, unprovoked, I put on my bathing suit and said, "You don't have any of me at the beach." I skipped up and down the edge of the carpet. "Come on. Take one of me frolicking in the surf."

"You always have to spoil everything, don't you, Codie?" said Dee. "You can never just have a good time."

Shortly after that Dee brought the camera along with us one day when we took a drive to the country. Dee had taken to snapping more at nature, I think because sunsets and trees didn't sass her back. We hiked along a ravine, and Dee dropped her lens cap into the stream that flowed below. I could see where it fell, under rushing water, beside a rock.

"Aren't you going to go get it?" I asked. Dee just shrugged and walked ahead, resigned. Losing things. It was something she accepted, didn't even seem to care.

Not long after that we were going away for the weekend and I was looking for the camera, figuring to pack it. But it wasn't in the closet where Dee usually kept it.

"Hey! Where's the camera?" I called to Dee, who was in the bathroom brushing her teeth. That's when she came out all foamy-mouthed and yelled at me, something like, "I don't want to hear anything about it, Codie, all right? The last thing I need is you giving me a hard time for something that wasn't my fault in the least!"

It's gone, I thought, all our picture taking over. She never did get a picture of me at the beach.

19

When I was an undeveloped, less exposed young thing, my father one day brought home a present for me. It was a doll dressed in a sequined leotard and a pink net tutu.

"A looking doll," my mother proclaimed at my side.

"What's a looking doll?" I asked.

"She's meant to be set on a shelf, like a figurine or a statue. She's to look at, not for play." As if to stake my mother's point, included in the box, packed in with the doll, was a wire stand for just that purpose.

At my mother's direction, I set the doll on a shelf in my room, high up and out of reach. And for a long time I looked at her, and didn't touch. But when the adults in my life narrowed their sights and not on me, I climbed up, lifted the doll down, and played with her. With abandon. Regularly. Behind closed doors.

In my defense, a picture-perfect doll in fantasy dress has powerful appeal in a house cave-dark from every shade drawn and a mother's gaze gone vacant. I had a mother who now cowered at the sound of the doorbell and jumped at the ring of the phone, her face haunted, her hair a fright, and mine unkempt as well with neither one of us, it suddenly seemed, old enough to comb it. This mother found it hard to stomach much, sustained herself with cups of coffee and chocolate bars, foregoing meals, a girl laid low and took to bed. Mounds of things banked up around her—dirty dishes, newspapers, last week's underwear. A fortressed bed. It was nothing to be frightened of. It was just that my mother sometimes had these spells, see, was what my grandmother called them.

To take advantage of my newfound license and fortune, I painted the doll's cheeks with red fingernail polish, Crimson Alarm. I ratted her hair. I set her tutu afire.

Of course I'm lying. I loved my doll. It's only unfortunate family mythology that I don't take care of my things.

"You played with her, didn't you?" she noticed (at long last). "And when I explicitly told you not to!"

These days, with my mother dead and out of the picture, I telephone my father. "Hi, Dad," I say in the bright voice I muster from nowhere.

There is hesitation on his end of the line before he says, confused, defensive, "Who is this?" though I am my father's only child. The only person on this earth who would call him up and use those words to address him.

"It's me, Dad," I say. I feel my voice cracking. "It's Codie."

When Jake stopped by my desk to deliver the videotape he'd promised me, he spun my chair around and snapped an imaginary candid. "Codie James, Editor," he said, ennobling the shot with a title. Then he made some joke, the punch line of which was "Gorilla of my dreams."

"You'll love the tape," he assured me as he set the case significantly in my hands. "The sound is spotty. The camera jumps. Backwoods Research. A classic."

I laughed. Somewhere along the line, Jake had managed to win me over to this project of his. Seconds after he dropped off the tape, I dialed Facilities and reserved myself a conference room and a VCR. I strode down the hall to view the thing, every bit the picture of a motivated, industrious employee. I set up the machine, turned off the conference room lights, then put my feet up on the table and peeled back the wrapper of the candy bar I'd brought in with me. As if I were at the movies. I don't know what I thought I was in there to watch. Daffy Duck?

The tape opened with a shot of the gorilla woman sitting in her study, answering questions put to her by an off-screen interviewer, questions about the language work she'd been doing with the gorilla. The gorilla woman's name was Eva. The gorilla's name was Simeon.

"Simeon has been with me for three years," Eva was saying, smiling at the camera. Her voice was high-pitched and whiney. "And I am pleased to say that his vocabulary is still expanding."

"With a voice like that," I cracked, "good thing she can sign." I bit off a piece of my candy bar. On my pad I wrote, "Three years. Vocabulary still expanding."

Eva spoke a while about the significance of the sort of language research she was doing, then walked through the house to the room where Simeon lived, the camera following closely behind. She opened the door on Simeon, who was in a cage, slumped against the back bars. Eva signed hello. Simeon lifted his head and signed hello back. Then Eva let herself into the cage and, for the benefit of the camera, prompted Simeon to demonstrate some of the other words he could sign. Names of things, mostly, and action verbs. When Simeon got a word right, Eva gave him a reward, some kind of food, gorilla candy, I don't know. By the time the tape was over, something great and dark had descended on me. It weighed on my head, oppressed my limbs. I could hardly get out of my chair.

I didn't speak to Jake right away because I wasn't sure what I would say. I tried, first, to figure out what it was exactly that upset me.

"It's partly the cage," I was finally able to articulate, as I took a seat across from Jake in his office. "But I think it's also the language part. Teaching an animal to communicate as a human. It's . . . it's against nature."

"How can it be against nature?" Jake argued. "Eva is teaching him. It's right there on the tape. Gorillas *can learn* language. That's the point."

"She's caging an animal and forcing it to communicate as a human!" I knew as I said this that Jake was dismissing me. I knew he thought I sounded like the type of person who'd set up a table on a street corner and hand out pamphlets with pictures of beaten, bloody seals.

"It's a plum project," Jake said. "The book'll be the biggest thing on our list. You're the editor, Codie. It's something to show."

The office suddenly seemed tight, cramped. I looked down at my notes. They were few. "Simeon signs 'food.' Simeon signs 'kiss.' Simeon signs 'run.' "

A few days later I went back to talk to Jake. He'd hustled me out the first time with a pat on the head, some platitudes, and a peppy, "So let's get this gorilla book on its legs!" And honestly I tried, it's not as if I didn't. But the objections within me were boisterous and clamoring.

"Simeon doesn't want to learn to talk," I said, flat out.

"How do you know?" asked Jake.

"He wants to talk the way gorillas talk, not the way we do. Who do we think we are, forcing other species to bow to our ways? He's caged, for chrissakes! You can't tell me any creature wants to be caged."

"He's cared for."

"Cared for? Enslaved!"

"Codie, I think you're going a little bit overboard."

"I am not. I do not want to be responsible for any book that glorifies the self-involved egocentrism of the human race."

"This is a better book than the commercial projects you're usually thrown. Would you rather work on another *Greenback*?"

"The fact that it has a classy look makes it all the more insidious. Kids'll open it up and there'll be Simeon, sitting in a cage, talking like a human—aren't gorillas civilized? Why don't we do a book about listening to what *gorillas* have to say and the particular ways they say things? Maybe they'd actually have something to communicate to us, something a little more profound than 'Simeon kiss Eva.' "

Jake looked at me hard and long. He softened his voice, the gentle approach. "Codie, do you know how ridiculous this is? Do you know what you're doing here? You're identifying with a gorilla."

I knew it was true, but fat chance I was going to admit it to Jake. He made it sound as if there were something wrong with that. When all I was doing was saying what I knew, that any caged animal wants out, that everyone needs to express herself according to her nature. In the ways that well up within.

"Picture it," said Jake, "color spreads of Simeon, bleeding off the page."

It's like I always say, give a human being a lick o' language and he'll dig his own grave.

20

I'd told Dee the whole story about the boxed tutu and the ballerina fabric. That's why, for my birthday, she got me two tickets to the ballet. I didn't know where we were going, she just told me to look nice and that she'd be by to pick me up in the cab when she knocked off work.

"Look nice like what?" I asked, trying to weasel clues out of her. I was excited, a kid at Christmas. "Look nice like going out to dinner at a nice restaurant? Look nice like going to a jazz club? What?"

"A jazz club?" Dee snorted. "At seven-thirty?" I was hopeless. "Wear your black dress," she said, "the one that hugs your ass."

"Oh, I get it. Look nice like you're gonna put your hands all over me."

"You got any objections?"

"None at all." But I did want clues.

Dee told me she'd pick me up at seven, which meant seven-thirty—I'd lived with her long enough to know that. I was ready by six, and pulling back the curtains to check out the window by six-thirty. No surprise there, either. I'd lived with myself even longer. To pass the time I put on some scratchy

Rodgers and Hammerstein records. Maybe what Dee planned to take me to was something high-kicking and fun, a musical on Broadway.

When Dee picked me up, though, she drove up past the theater district to Lincoln Center. She drove around front where other cabs were stopped, discharging passengers. Just to get the taste in my mouth. The sight of all those women in high-heeled shoes stepping out of cabs got me giddy. Dee swung around back to find a parking space. She spotted a space on the opposite side of the street and careened the car in a U-turn.

"What are we going to see?" I asked.

Dee grinned. "What you need to know for?" She pocketed the car keys, leaned over, and kissed me. On the crotch. That girl was nothing if not maddening. "Come on," she said. "Curtain's at eight." It was two minutes of.

Dee had bought balcony tickets. "It's better from up high," she said. "The patterns." Dee relayed this information to me hastily as we stood at the entrance while she searched her pockets for the tickets. "Hmm," she stalled. The ticket taker eyed us impatiently. "I thought I put them in my jacket." She checked the lining. She checked her wallet. And finally found the tickets in her pants pocket. By this time, bells were ringing insistently to urge us inside.

When we took our seats, the house lights dimmed. My thoughts flashed on a certain pink tutu, the netting sticking straight out as if it had taken a fright. Dee reached over and surreptitiously took my hand. Dee and I, we loved to hold hands in the theater. House to black was our cue.

"Ballet is like a language," Miss Rose had said. She'd cupped her fingers to her mouth and drawn them effortlessly away, as if she were extracting a pearlized string of words. "At first you might feel a little lost, like babies just learning to talk. But as the weeks wear on, you'll find it will actually become easy to express yourself. A pleasure, in fact. Second nature."

The first time I'd laid eyes on Miss Rose, what she was

wearing was pink tights, a pink leotard, pink ballet slippers, and a sheer, pink chiffon wraparound skirt. Right away, I'd aspired to be as pink.

My father was the one who'd granted permission. "You want to take ballet?" he'd said. "Of course you can!" I'd mustered up the courage to ask one night when my parents were lingering at the dinner table, nursing coffees. My mother had answered, "We'll see," which I suspected would ultimately mean no. But my father overrode her with a broad sweep of his arms. "Never let it be said of the James family that we denied our daughter culture." My father lifted his coffee cup to my lips, "Here, Codie, take a sip," then laughed when I screwed up my face at the strong taste of the brandy it disguised.

The night Dee and I drove home from the ballet, I held a pair of toe shoes on my lap, wrapped in a bright bag. They'd been signed by the ballerina who'd worn them, the ballerina that, as I'd remarked to Dee, I thought to be the most graceful, most musical of the dancers. Dee had bought the shoes for me at the gift stand during intermission while I was on line at the ladies' room. When I'd come out, I'd looked all over for her. I figured she'd probably disappeared to get herself a glass of wine. But she'd snuck up behind me and slipped the bag into my hands. "Happy birthday, baby," she said. The pink satin ribbons almost made me cry.

In the car I took the toe shoes out of their bag. I was thinking I might try them on when we got home. Dee was talking about the one black ballerina in the company, a young one in the corps. The girl had first fed on stage in a line of other corps members *bourréeing* into position. Their backsides were to the audience, and it was hard not to notice that the tutu of the black ballerina was set jiggling by the step in a way that the white ballerinas' tutus, sitting on stingier derrières, weren't. Dee had nudged me and smiled. "Look!" she'd said out loud when the corps turned to face us. "She even has tits!" The woman seated next to Dee had looked askance. Dee never could keep things to any kind of whisper.

As we drove home that night, Dee hummed the coda to the ballet. "So," she asked, "did you like it?"

"I loved it!" I said. I slid closer to her so I could bite her earlobe to let her know how much. "Of course, we did almost miss it," I teased. "Three minutes after eight and there you were, searching your pockets for the tickets."

"Codie, how long you gonna be in New York before you figure out that curtain is never any eight on the nose. What you want to get there early and sit around in those seats for? Not enough room for your *legs* in those seats."

"For *your* legs maybe."

"That's right."

Lost (somehow): One partner for affectionate banter. Untold sentimental value. Rich reward.

After the ballet, I was struck with remorse for not having trusted Dee enough to have given her the story I was working on. It seemed stingy on my part, the story being about ballet and her having just given me the gift of it. So while my beneficent goddess was kicking through a pile of clothes at the foot of our bed, searching for the sweatpants that served as her pajamas, I pulled the story out of the folder in which I'd filed it and gave her a copy.

Dee didn't read the manuscript anytime soon, though. Or maybe she did and didn't say. For weeks I walked around expectantly, waiting for her to comment. Funny. That I never felt I could just come out and ask.

"What're you watching?" I asked instead.

"A movie," said Dee.

"Oh yeah? What?"

The title? *Philandering Women.*

If only I'd thought not to ask.

21

One afternoon, with the cast of light amber on the wash of wall, I walked in on Anwa chanting in a tongue I'd never heard from her lips, or from those of any other. I might've thought it was pain she was expressing, but for the soft slur of the sound. Later I learned it to be Anwa's childhood tongue. She had one same as me. And the sonance of hers was silken, tender. Like caressing, like mother's milk, like a lambkin's baby bleats.

"What was that?" I asked.

"What?"

"What you were singing."

"I wasn't singing anything."

"Yes you were. I heard you just now when I—"

"Praises," Anwa said suddenly, a change of tune. "Praises to the goddess rules the sea."

"It's a goddess who rules the sea?" I asked.

"And the rivulets and the streams." She nodded out the window. "A goddess rules your river there." This was news to me.

"What cult is this?" I asked. Apparently it was more than just language Anwa had imported.

Anwa started up telling me about all the various spirits, lore she'd learned as a child. The spirits she spoke of had names, and each had personality, history, and quirks. One was easy to anger. Another, considered a flirt. Human, they almost were, but heightenedly so. "There are more cults than you know," she said. "A person prays to different gods for different things. We need bow down to all who rule and guide."

In that, I did not disagree. The one who ruled me was Anwa, no question. Then and there I fell at her feet.

"Get up!" Anwa cried. "Why do you mock the gods so?"

"I devote myself to the goddess who stands here before me. It is her I worship."

"Hold your tongue!" she cut me off. "You'll bring the wrath of the gods upon us!"

Sure enough calamaties would befall us. In the days that would come, Anwa would think herself a prophetess of some power and would spare no breath reminding me what she'd predicted. Which was really nothing so specific as to foretell anything at all. Nonetheless, Anwa would assign me blame, trace everything back to my young choice to fall at her feet.

When, actually, I'd had no choice but to do so, never did.

her scent like earth-been-turned, like the cool, wet roots of plants

"What are you doing?" Anwa asked me.

"Practicing my characters," I answered.

As if it weren't as plain as the stylus in my hand.

There are many ways to worship, of course. As many ways to worship as there are stories to inscribe in clay. One sure way is to record the truth for the ages, which I did. I wrote everything down. The tale of how I did so is one that bears telling, as it was uncommon for its day. It was not usual for a girl of my station to apprentice as a scribe. Nor was it even within law. It came about by chance. The stillness on certain afternoons a call to something more.

Afternoons in the hareem, those afternoons not taken up by Iman and her rehearsals, were listless, indolent. My friends lay about, chewing on cardamon, swatting at flies which swarmed like a plague. Often, the only sound for hours on end was the quiet clack of polished stone against gameboard. Games were a popular pastime in the hareem. My friends seemed to enjoy them—the codified rules, the opportunity for strategy. I, however, played only on occasion, those occasions on which Anwa was otherwise engaged. Even then, I was never much one for chasing a stone around a board.

"Play again, Sari," urged my companion, offering me the ivory throwsticks. "Go ahead."

I bowed out as gracefully as I could and took leave of the game and my gamemate. I wandered out into the hallway, intending to take a walk, something I had begun doing often as alternative to what was offered. The hallways in the hareem were a maze, and I a moving gamepiece. Each of the hallways led to another, and eventually, beyond our quarters. The far wing of the khan housed the Mukarrib's stores as well as his accounting. Or so it was reputed. My walks there had always been stayed. The junctures between the hareem and those quarters were closely guarded. Each had a guard stationed at its door. Eunuchs, it was rumored. Men without much more to lose. Opponents on my gameboard.

That day, as the gods granted, I found one of the forbidden halls unguarded, its eunuch apparently taken ill. The saucer-eyed guard I was accustomed to seeing there was nowhere in sight, and neither had anyone thought to substitute another. I looked around. No eyes were watching. I sailed down the illicit corridor as easily as if I'd been beckoned.

The corridor did not yield the particular plenty I expected. At the end, a tall tamarisk screen shielded something beyond. I peered through its tightly carved lattice, expecting, I suppose, to see jars with stoppers, graduated weights and scales, the sort of gauges of wealth and property I knew from market and ba-zaar. What the screen blocked, though, was a small room which was shuttered tightly against the blaze of the midday sun. In the hot light that angled in, I could at first make out only dust, the sand that, during the dry months, thickened the air of the khan always. Soon, though, my eyes made out a man. He was white-haired, sitting on a mat. He was knuckling an implement, etching things in clay. When he looked up and saw me, he appeared taken aback.

"How did you get here?" he asked.

I took a little step to indicate I'd walked. Both of us grinned. At the improbability of it all.

As the gods designed, the man I'd found was a scribe in the Mukarrib's employ. It was his job daily to log the vast stores of the Mukarrib's wealth—to note the weight of frankincense, the variants and grades, to tally all the tariffs paid in trade. The scribe invited me in, gesturing toward his tablets. Then he set the implement in my hand, offering to let me try.

"What would you most like to say?" he asked.

I thought. Of all the things there were to express . . .

"Kisses sweet as suckling," I decided.

My first poem of many.

By some odd oversight, for some weeks that followed, the hallway that led to the scribe remained as it had been, free of guard. In those weeks I took up the eager task of learning what the scribe had to teach me. First he taught me to distinguish between the various marks, marks that at first seemed to me to be as impenetrable as stars. Then he set about teaching me to etch the marks myself.

"From this side to that, then back again," he instructed. "Like oxen plowing the fields."

I couldn't think of what to write.

"Why not something about frankincense?" he urged.

I thought a moment, then I did.

"The tears of trees," I wrote.

One hot, breezeless afternoon in the hareem, I unwrapped the clay tablets on which I'd practiced from the cloth in which I'd cloaked them, and bared my labors to Anwa.

"What's that mark there?" she asked, not happy and showing it.

"The mark for sea," as it happened. "Your beloved sea."

Anwa put her fist into the clay tablet, smashing it to shards.

She thought it smart to pound down any new knowledge I acquired. How did she think our story would then get told? A footnote in history, if that.

"And you?" I challenged her. "Do you do only what's permitted?"

We both knew the answer to that.

After that, I did the politic thing. I hid my tablets from Anwa as well as from the others. I continued to scribe, don't doubt that. And put it to use some would call sacrilege. I wrote verses to honor the woman who'd later leave my life.

One sweltry day that followed, I sat under the sweet shade of the acacia tree at the edge of the river that bordered the khan. Taper-necked birds swooped at the river's shores. Dulcet waters lapped her banks. I noted that, in thinking of the river, I'd made her female, and began to wonder if Anwa might not indeed be right. About it being a female spirit that inhabited her. When I ran back to tell Anwa the good news that she might have in me a convert after all, I found her once again chanting. This time I interrupted.

"Why is it you chant today?" I asked.

"To counteract your heresy, why else?"

I knew without asking to whom Anwa was directing her song. It was a song I'd heard her sing before and plenty. To the sea, Anwa sang. Always the sea. Because I knew it would please her, I asked her to describe it for me once again. And so she went on about the creatures who live there, some swimming freely, some ensconced in shells.

"As if anyone would believe such report," I said. Though, me, I clung to every word.

I looking to Anwa, she staring past me. "And the thrill of standing on a large ship," she rhapsodized. Stared through to someplace vague and misty.

"What sort large ship? Where?"

"Wave-worthy," was her abstracted answer. "Could spirit me away."

22

One morning I awoke from sleep and said, "Gold is the metal of the sun. And silver the metal of the moon." I don't know how I knew this, but I did. As best I could, I shook the morning haze from my head and roused myself to do the weekday thing—dress for success, knot my tie. Metaphorically, at least. I turned on the radio, and, as it happened, I caught drift of an interview cast upon the airwaves by my local public station. The interview was with a woman who was a psychologist, and the subject she was discussing was fairy tales. "The fairy tales we're read as children," I heard her explain, "serve as road maps. For the psychological journeys we embark on in life, journeys that are often quite difficult."

"I hear you, sister," I said out loud. Dee's influence.

"These tasks," the woman went on, "may, at the time we face them, appear impossible."

"I I.D. with that."

"Just as we ourselves do, the characters in fairy tales face impossible tasks as well. They must pick up sacks full of seed, for instance. Or win the hand of the princess . . ."

I spit my toothpaste into the cold bowl of the sink. This might be information I could use. The psychologist continued rambling on, enumerating this difficult strait and that, obstruction grinning at the characters at every turn.

"But what do the characters *do*?" I asked the radio.

"Many learn the language of animals," the psychologist said, as if in answer. "The animals then come to their aid, accomplishing the tasks themselves, or maybe whispering direction. Their help always appears when circumstances for the character seem overwhelming and beyond hope."

"Aha!" I said, the light dawning. "Animal-ese!"

In the short distance between my apartment and the subway, it occurred to me that if fairy tales were such sterling tools for emotional growth, it would be worthwhile to publish a line of the classic tales. We could issue the stories in picture book form. Assign our best illustrators to the project. Princes would chop their way through brambles to come upon princesses as kind and good as they were beautiful. Simpletons would inherit kingdoms, live happily ever after. That morning, when Jake called the editorial meeting to order, I shot up my hand first thing.

"Yes, Codie?" Jake looked surprised.

"I have a great idea I'd like to propose." I blurted this out enthusiastically, but Jake interrupted me before I got another word further. He said that there was other business needed attending to first, and turned to a young woman who was sitting to his right. Her hair was tightly pinned, Her gaze, vacant. She wore a suit severe enough for an ex-nun. Funny, I hadn't even noticed her.

"I'd like to introduce you all to Jasmine," Jake said. Right away I was wise to the fact that something was awry. The name was a little on the unlikely side for a woman looking neither exotic nor flowerlike in the least. "Jasmine is joining our staff as an editor," Jake said. He went on to explain that this "fragrant *fleur*"—his actual words—"comes to us straight from Dickering and Deeling," a house I knew by reputation to be one that traded in highly commercial books. After Jake introduced her, he asked Jasmine if she would like to say anything herself. From a bag beside her she pulled out a line of books she had been

responsible for in her last position and fanned them across the
table. The saccharine faces of licensed characters smiled out at
me from the front covers. Jasmine said a few words about her
"philosophy of publishing," words like "revenue" and "marketing blitz." She smiled at Jake, who returned the smile and
interjected, "Jasmine's expert contribution to our list will indeed
be welcome."

Jasmine lowered her eyes in the least convincing display
of modesty I've ever witnessed, and, to cap her presentation,
said, "I guess I'd just say like to say that I'm very glad to be
aboard ship. Once I get my bearings and am on course, it's full
speed ahead. I can't really think of anything to add, so I guess
I'll just turn the wheel back over to the captain."

Jake looked visibly, disturbingly aglow. "So, Codie," he
said, "why don't we just move right on to you and you can
present this burning idea of yours."

Suddenly I didn't feel much like proposing my idea. "I
think I'll pass," I said. Me without the courage of my con-
victions.

"Pass?"

"I seem to have had the wind taken out of my sails." I
saluted Jake. "Anchors aweigh." Jake shot a worried glance at
Jasmine to see if she'd taken offense, but he needn't have worried. Went right over her head, my little joke did. Witless, I
thought. To boot, the girl's witless.

I did make a contribution at the end of the meeting, when
Jake recalled, suddenly, that there was another important per-
sonage of whom the staff should be made aware. "Do you want
to tell them who's coming, Codie?" he asked.

"Who's coming?" I asked, playing dumb. I knew exactly. I
just liked to give Jake a run for his money.

"I'm talking about the person who's flying down from the
north country to work with you on the *book of the year.*" Jake
gave the last words emphasis beyond their due. Therein lay the
key.

"Oh," I said. "Fay Wray."

"For those of you not lucky enough to be keyed into Ms.

James's sense of humor, that's Eva, the gorilla lady, who, I'm happy to report, is coming to work with Codie on the manuscript for our big fall book about the talking gorilla."

"Not talking. Sign language."

"And when is it exactly that Eva will be gracing us with this visit?"

"The whole of this week, you'll be happy to hear. Arriving this very afternoon."

There was probably no one more impressed than I that, in a sudden spurt of industry, I'd arranged Eva's visit down to the last corporate detail. I had a car and driver meet her at the airport and deliver her to our door. I'd made a lunch reservation at a swank restaurant to welcome her upon her arrival. From the supply room, I'd secured fresh notebooks for the two of us, new pens and pencils, two pink erasers. As if leaves were turning and it was the start of school. As if I'd been granted, inexplicably, the opportunity to start fresh from square one.

Eva in the flesh was different from how I'd experienced her on the videotape, her presence in person less imposing. Her skin was pale and had a translucency to it, and the effect was aggravated by the odd fact that she seemed curiously hairless. She did have hair, of course—short, brownish, drab—but what she had gave an impression of sparseness. And also evidenced a disquieting lack of attention to grooming, as I complained, that night, to Dee. "You'd think a person would bother to wash her hair if she's making a trip to the big city."

Eva arrived wearing sneakers and a jean skirt, askew because it was too loose for her waist, as if she had somehow shrunk under its weight. With these she wore a pullover and wool stockings, both frayed and too heavy for the season. I was unhappy to see that Eva had brought with her, in a plastic supermarket bag, her own manuscript. What we did that week, every day of it, was sequester ourselves in a conference room while I tried to make sense of the text she had written and asked her questions to flesh out the information. What we accumulated was a mountain of material, material that may have interested me for the span of a moment, but seemed overwhelming the next. It depressed me. Or maybe it was Eva's obvious and disturbing attachment to Simeon that flattened my spirits. She brought up Simeon's name often, as one might a missed, absent lover. Which could, I suppose, explain the clothing. I guess a person doesn't have to attend too much to what she looks like if the object of her affections is a gorilla.

"Beauty and the Beast," another editor joked when she'd caught me alone in the hallway. A reference that took a moment to register, as Eva was hardly a beauty. Shriveled, pinched. Maybe the other editor had meant her as the Beast.

It was not until the last day of Eva's visit that I found the voice to put to her the questions really on my mind. Something in me loosed without my planning it and I was surprised to hear myself fire away. "Is Simeon happy?" I asked. "Does he miss his jungle home? Does he remember enough to dream? Are you awakened by his cries?" Someone-not-me prosecuting Eva for crimes might as well be war-. I paused dramatically before adding, "Why have you forced his own language into secrecy? And what measures has he taken to preserve it?" Eva looked at me alarmed, suddenly frightened, or so I hoped, that perhaps she'd carelessly let information slip into the wrong hands, the hands of a spy. But as quickly as I'd put her on guard, I disarmed her with a sweet smile, and also by signing, "Simeon kiss Eva." Let her think the rest was but illusion.

Jake wandered in to join us that last hour, happening in with both of us smiling and appearances deceiving. "Just stopping in to say goodbye?" he said, inflecting it as a question, as if he were unsure whether or not he was welcome.

"By all means," I replied, inviting him in. I had nothing to hide. My mountain of notes looked like work done.

"So, Eva," said Jake, ever gregarious, the interested, attentive host. "Are you looking forward to getting home?"

"Not for my sake," she said, "as much as for Simeon's. When I spoke to him last night on the phone, he was extremely anxious for my return." Eva excused herself to visit the bathroom. I looked at Jake, waiting for him to voice his reaction to her. It was not forthcoming.

"Well?" I asked.

"She seems a tad off, doesn't she?" he asked.

"A tad?"

"Maybe it's her first time on the planet," Jake offered.

I looked at him blankly.

"I bet you it's her first time here."

I saw Eva off, ushered her to the car that would start her journey home, and found myself feeling softened, somewhat, by Jake's assessment of her, which was frank, certainly, but also seemed accepting, more so than mine. As I walked back to my cubicle, it hit me that my judgments of people were becoming increasingly harsh. Then and there I resolved to try to be more openhearted, more tolerant of the diversity of humanity, more trusting. I was so absorbed in the sentiment of my resolution that at first I didn't notice that there was someone in my cubicle.

"She seemed really nice," said a voice. It was Jasmine. She was sitting at my desk, flipping through a glossy promotional folder with press materials about a new license. "Eva seemed really nice," she repeated.

Jasmine, in territory that was mine, not hers, as if, for some reason, she'd just been waiting.

"Nice enough," I said coolly.

One of my tenets: with the enemy, never let on.

That night, at home, I watched wildlife on TV. Animals grazing, mating, preening, stalking prey, caring for their young. Wildlife once removed brought to me by my government funded channel. I was still thinking about what that psychologist had said, the one on the radio a few days back. One thing she said had been worrisome, and, naturally, that was the thing that I'd fixed on. The psychologist had indicated that there was a wrong kind of fairy tale and a right kind. The right kind preserved the rich symbols of the time-honored tales, while the wrong kind sanitized the stories, stripping them of blood and violence and retributive ending, and thereby of their power. I knew that my mother had read me fairy tales as a child, but the question was, which kind? And the more important question masked by that one was, did I have, encoded somewhere in me, the means to befriend forgotten parts of myself and therefore live happily ever after?

Or did I not?

Dee came home while I was staring at the TV, mired in that muck. First thing she did was pick up the remote and, without asking, switch to a sitcom. All one and the same.

"What's the matter with you, blue?" Dee asked, disappointed, I'm sure, that I hadn't put up a fight.

"There's a new person Jake hired at work," I said moodily. "And I don't like her."

"Codie, you don't like anybody lately. You've been downright irritable, you know that? Your disposition is nasty."

"Maybe it is, maybe it isn't. Doesn't change the fact that I don't like her."

"So what exactly don't you like?"

"She's portentious."

"You mean pretentious?"

"No."

I meant exactly what I said.

23

I suppose, at any point along the route of the relationship, I
might have considered talking to God. About this Dee-tour I'd
begun to fear I'd taken, I mean. But years ago I'd soured on
ever asking God for help. When I was younger, I'd once gone
to God. I'd asked Him to send a few angels my way. Fly me to
the moon is all I asked, not even. Actually, what I asked was
to be delivered to the stage. Which was, if one thinks of these
things in a grand, heavenly hiring-hall sort of sense, no more
than the post to which He'd assigned me in the first place. Instead I found myself at my grandmother's, drawing one unlucky
card after another.

My grandmother played a spade. She'd served pot roast for
dinner, then called me to a game of cards, neither of which I
had much taste for. When I'd tried to insist, "Thank you very
much, Grandma," but I didn't really like to play cards, she'd
told me, "Well, you'd better learn to like 'em. Else you won't
have a social life worth speaking of when you get older."

Opposite us, on my grandmother's mantel, was a ship's
clock, and I watched the hour tick toward six, the hour at
which, by rights, I was supposed to be downstage center. I
thought of the tutu in its box behind the furnace, where I'd

slipped it for safekeeping. And I waited for this angel I'd requested, the one I hoped would snatch me up and speed me home, deliver me somehow already costumed to the stage of the civic auditorium, where all of my friends would be clustered in the wings, wet-palmed, flutter-stomached, listening for the piano cue that would tell them to step onstage and start the dance we'd rehearsed together those many months. Miss Rose would have long since counted heads and found mine missing. Who would take my place in line? Who would do the special jetés Miss Rose had assigned specifically to me? Had anyone called to tell her what had happened? Or would she think I'd just forgotten?

Six o'clock came and went and, big surprise, no angel appeared. My grandmother played nine spades, ten. And as the night wore on and the hour for my recital passed, it dawned on me for the first time in my young life that God had abandoned me.

I couldn't understand it. God the Father.

The largesse of a drunk.

The day that followed my disappointment, I slipped outside by myself to sit in my grandmother's backyard. The air was chill because it was nearly Christmas, and the ground beneath me was as hard as if it had been plowed and paved. After I'd been sitting there a while, I noticed a white rabbit in the neighboring yard, nosing my way. I sat as still as I could so as not to scare it and in hopes that it might come a little closer. The rabbit spied me. But instead of running away, as I assumed it would, it hopped directly to me and sniffed at the open hand I slowly and tentatively extended. The rabbit was trying to tell me something. Rabbit and young girl. Communing.

Now, the thought that leapt immediately into my ever-suggestible little head was that I had just tamed a wild animal. In the same way that Saint Francis of Assisi had. If I were set to emulate one of the saints already on the books, Saint Francis was a choice plenty romantic. Wild creatures ate out of the man's hands, birds lit on his shoulders. Not only that, he had

had the stigmata. Which someday, if I were good, and lucky to boot, I might be blessed with as well. Maybe God had allowed me to be wrenched from dancing only because He had an even greater stardom in store. Sainthood.

This scenario would've been enough and more to buoy my sagging spirits, had not reality, in all its mundanity, imposed itself. Truth, the great interloper. This time in the guise of the neighbor lady next door. Who came out her kitchen door, sighted the rabbit which had, at this point, hopped onto my lap, and called out, "Cottonball! There you are, you naughty little bunny you! How'd you get outside?"

A house pet. The rabbit was a house pet. In a twist on the talking bunny motif, it wasn't wild at all, but already tame. If it's not one miracle being shot down, it's another.

The afternoon of the illicit incident, the one that prompted my removal to my grandmother's in the first place, I'd been alone in the house with my father, my mother having escaped the house on some holiday errand. Bits of gold foil dotted the high-piled carpet. Gold foil and red ribbon. It was Advent, that's why. A time to wait, to expect. The coming or arrival.

My father was in the living room reading the Sunday paper, and I'd stationed myself quite near, trying, unsuccessfully and for quite some time, to get his attention. I was always a child for a challenge. I'd tried the obvious ploy first, addressing questions directly to him. The questions I posed were engaging, polemical, or so they seemed to me. "Daddy, does God love all people, even Judas Iscariot?" When that failed, I tried a lighter approach. I opened the funny papers at my father's feet and laughed loudly for effect. None of this won his attention.

At that time, my family had a dog. Scheherazade was her name. That day, as I was quick to note, Scheherazade succeeded where I failed. When Scheherazade ambled up to my father and whined at his shoe, my father set down his paper to pet her. Then my father picked a length of ribbon off the floor and tied it to Scheherazade's tail. The dog twisted around to try to bite off the ribbon, and my father watched a while, chuckling, before he snapped his paper back to retreat again behind its folds.

Inspired by the scene I'd witnessed, I clamped a strand of ribbon in my teeth, crawled up to my father on all fours, rubbed my head against his calf, and whimpered. When my father peered out from behind the paper, I sat up on my haunches and panted.

"Codie," said my father, clearly irritated, "I'm trying to read."

"Ruff, ruff," I said.

"Go watch television, why don't you? Go do something."

The television was in another room, a room we called the family room. I slunk there, hangdog. When I turned on the TV, what sissed to the screen was the Sunday afternoon movie. The movie was set during World War II and featured American service women. Waves, they were called, in a polite throwback to idolatry. At the point I tuned in, the unit of women had been surrounded by enemy soldiers, and the soldiers were moving toward them through the brush, thrashing aside branches with their guns, every minute closer.

One of the women took off her uniform cap and lifted out her hair. "We'll let them know we're women," she said to the others. "They might not shoot us. It's our only chance."

One by one the other women followed suit. They took off their caps and shook their heads so their hair fell freely over their shoulders. The one who was their leader unbuttoned the top button of her blouse. Then a second button. And a third. Cleavage showed, a lacy bra.

"Boys," she called, in a voice suddenly different, seductive. "Don't shoot, boys. We're women. Here we are."

As the camera pulled back and away, the music swelled loud and threatening. Then the screen went black and the women were left in that Japanese jungle, undefended, prey to soldiers who looked different from the men they knew but who were, in the end, men. The movie was over, but its effect on me lingered. Something about it disturbed me. Disturbed and fascinated both.

After that, two men came on representing the sponsor of the show, a local discount store, and shouted out "Low! Low! Rock Bottom Prices!" The men held up items of merchandise, then flung them back over their shoulders in an advertising frenzy that suggested hysteria. As part of the commercial, a telephone rang. I picked up an imaginary receiver and held it to my ear. "Hello?" I said out loud. "Yes, this is the orphanage. . . . We have plenty of orphans here, a whole bunch."

Next to the TV was the toy chest in which my dolls were stored. I reached in and pulled them out one by one, tossed them over my shoulder, as I'd seen the men on TV do, as they hawked their cheap merchandise. The head of one doll was tangled in my jump rope. Another's leg was bound in the elastic strap of my plastic high-heeled shoes.

"Come on, orphans," I said, my voice sugar-sweet and singsong. "Time for your bath."

I gathered up as many dolls as I could hold in my arms and headed up the stairs to the bathroom. When I passed the living room, my father stayed fortressed behind his paper, did not, apparently notice the orphan dolls dropping dramatically from my arms along the way. In the bathroom, I opened my arms and dropped the dolls into the bathtub. I stripped them of their clothes and squirted dish soap over them. I filled the bathtub with water.

I don't know how long I was in the bathroom washing the dolls, but it could have been quite some time. To keep the orphans' attention, I started singing. The real words were Latin, but in my version they translated as something else. "Key-ring-A A-Lady's son," I sang deliriously, carried away with the heady responsibility of my mission and my charge. "Crisco A-Lady's son."

Suddenly, as in cartoon animation when a shadow passes over a character, I felt that I was not alone. I turned around to the door. There in the doorway stood my father.

And a mother not wanting to hear that nothing happened. Not a thing, Mom. I'm innocent, I tell ya. As innocent as a father and daughter together taking a harmless afternoon shower.

I suppose I can safely say that it was incidents like this that wore away my mother's jangled nerves. Incidents like this that ultimately drove that woman to distraction. One distraction being sewing. Sewing ballerinas was the hobby she took up.

Sewing them shut.

24

Anwa tells me I am daughter of the moon.

"How do you know?" I ask.

"Because you're so keen on make-believe, on dreams."

One bright night, Anwa lay with me on my mat. She'd been excused from service that night, the Mukarrib having requested another. Our midnight fortune.

"Look," whispered Anwa. "Look out the window." Her breath smelled of mint, of the sweet leaf she'd been sucking. "Of what do all those stars in constellation remind you?"

I pinched the flame of the plant pith we'd lit as wick, the better to see the sky.

"They remind me of hunters," I said, "of beasts." I rattled off all the obvious things. "That cluster, of scales."

"No." Anwa poked her finger teasingly at the spots that had lately erupted across my pubescent face. "Scattered across the sky, the stars are like so many blemishes dotting youth's complexion."

Anwa settled cross-legged on my mat, and I snuggled into her, my back to her front. She planted one hand on my belly, then worked the other one under me and up me. Insertion.

"Don't move," she whispered in the dark. "Don't move, don't make a sound."

"Ohhh!" A moan escaped me.

"You lose," Anwa declared.

According to the rules of our game, rules we had authored together over the course of many nights' play, I then had to do to Anwa whatever it was she requested. I pretended defeat, but I never truly considered this my loss. For I had appetite to do anything Anwa would request, and when the requests were new, I simply found myself developing new tastes. Following the rules of our game, after Anwa was satisfied, I had to take equal "punishment" from her. I always asked for the same thing.

"Your mouth and tongue, please."

"Sari, you always ask so prettily. 'Please.' As if you're asking someone at table to pass a bowl of relish."

"I see no reason not to be polite."

"Because this is 'punishment.' And why do you always request the same thing?"

"Because I like it."

"Request another."

"I can't have your mouth?"

"I'll give you my mouth after. First you need to request something new."

I turned over on the mat and lay flat on my belly. "You lie on top of me," I said, "and give me your fingers from behind, like mating animals."

"Sari, you've requested that before."

"Not for some weeks."

"You've requested it *many times* before."

"Because I happen to like certain things. And when I like them, I request them."

Anwa obliged me, but not without a sigh. All in play, of course. Another of our games. Children are nothing if not playful.

Afterward, I lay cradled in Anwa's arms and watched the patch of sky that in its turn watched us. My heart was flooded with a sudden sense of how happy I was. What I was thinking was: *I want nothing to change.*

"We should leave," Anwa said suddenly. Her reaction opposed to mine. Directly opposed. I can't say that this sort of thing happened rarely.

"Why ever would we leave?" I asked. "We're happy. And not only that, we are cared for, fed by the court's abundance. It was here, don't forget, that we had the fortune to find each other."

Anwa snorted at what she loved to call my naïveté. "But can we walk free?" she asked. "Can we leave the court at will?"

"And why would we?"

"Sari, listen carefully. I have a dream for us. In my dream, you and I live alone in an unsettled land. We make our home at the edge of a clear, cool lake. As bed I stretch a hammock between two trees, and there we sleep, lulled by the hammock's gentle sway and nuzzled by its curve into each other's arms. We have no roof, no walls. Nothing to shield us from the world, or it from us. At night, before we sleep, I point up at the vast, star-studded sky, and I say, 'Look, Sari, look at the vastness of which we are part. The stars shine down on us like love.'"

True enough the picture was pretty, but still I had my doubts. "What if it would rain?" I asked.

Anwa kissed the top of my head as if that were answer.

"We would get wet," I continued, supplying the answer she wouldn't. I snuggled closer to her. "I like being *right here* in your arms. That way if it rains we are protected."

"The air will warm us always," said Anwa, amending her fantasy to placate me. "And because there will be no others there from which we need hide, we will wear no clothes."

"No clothes!" This, to me, would be a great disappointment. "Could we not have clothes for when we wanted them and then just be able to take them off when we pleased?"

Anwa smiled slyly and put her mouth to my belly. "You'll have no time for clothes," she said. "I'll keep you clothed in my kisses."

"Still . . ."

"You don't like my kisses?"

"It's just that I would miss certain garments. My indigo sash. Among other items."

"You and your garments," Anwa scoffed. She poked at my

135

ribs to tickle me. "Come, tell me. Tell me you want to be clothed only in my kisses."

"No!" I laughed. "I want my sash!"

"My kisses!"

I curled up in a tight ball to escape her teasing hands, but against Anwa's persistence I had to surrender. "All right! All right!" I cried. "Your kisses! I want to be clothed only in your kisses!" When Anwa ceased tickling me, I put my lips to her ear and whispered one last time, "And my indigo sash!" At that, Anwa pulled me to her and once again kissed open my mouth, kissed me silly. When afterward I nestled in her arms to drift to sleep, Anwa pointed at the arch of sky framed by my window. "Look, Sari," she said. "Look at the vastness of which we are part. The stars shine down on our hammock with love."

I felt I could hear the lap of the lake of which she had spoken, and could sense the sway of the hammock. I imagined that it was its curve kept me in Anwa's embrace.

"If we leave," I asked, coming around to her way of seeing, "and go to this place where we lie about in hammocks, would I ever see my mother again?" I'd been thinking of my mother of late, of how I longed to see her.

"Your mother?" snapped Anwa. "Your mother is dead!"

Dead? What did Anwa know about my mother? About my past, she knew only what I'd told her.

"Hammock!" Anwa snorted irritably. "Have I told you you are daughter of the moon?"

"You're the one who said there was a hammock," I protested. "And what about the lake? And the stars?"

"A story," she said. "That's all that was."

"And the land then, the unsettled land? There must be such a place."

"We live in Felix Arabia," she said, shrugging off my hands. "This is where we'll stay." Anwa turned her back to me, her scarred, tale-bearing back. "Stop your dreaming, Sari. Go to sleep."

I did fall asleep. Eventually. But not as cozily or as securely as I had felt only moments before. I was certain there must be

136

someplace in the wide world would embrace us, though I had no idea how to find it. I burrowed closer to my lover's back, worried that there was something in her seemed unable to allow anything to rest.

Least of all herself.

"I'm thinking about Earl for the father," Dee said one day. Earl was a friend of hers.

"Father for what?" I asked.

"The baby."

"What baby?"

"My baby."

Dee dropped this information casually into a conversation we were having about another subject entirely, dropped it in the way a person might surreptitiously discard a candy wrapper on the street—hoping no one notices that she's crumpled the paper at her side and let it fall right there on the sidewalk. This was the first thing I'd heard about any baby, I'll tell you that. So I thought I'd best ask a question or two. Like how did she intend to proceed with this new project of hers, had she done any research into artificial insemination?

"Artificial insemination?" Dee threw me a look damning enough to condemn a heretic to the stake. "What are you talking? Dee conceives her babies the time-honored way."

"You mean you intend to go to bed with Earl?"

"Yeah." She shrugged. "Earl. Or whomever. Obviously I'm going to want to be very careful about whom I choose for the father of my baby. I'll tell you what I'm looking for, though. Smart. Whoever's the father has to be smart."

"But what about me?" I asked.

"Codie," Dee said as she clapped me on the back, "don't sweat even a drop. I've always thought you're going to make a really great parent."

As if this were my worry.

Dee went on to tell me that she'd already picked out names for this baby of hers. Bina was her choice for girl, Shamir if it were a boy.

"Shamir," I said sullenly. "That sounds like a girl's name. I don't like those names." I was curled up in the corner of the sofa, hugging a cushion to my breast. Why am I talking about names? I wondered. Names is not the issue here. The issue is Dee having a baby. Dee sleeping with a man.

"Codie!" Dee shouted, startling my thoughts. "The last thing I'm going to do is argue with you about my names. You got that? I've had these names picked out since I was sixteen. I've always known that I was going to have a baby, and I've always known that when I had one, these would be the names. You're not going to get in my way with this! So don't even try!"

Later, I thought of a crack I should've made, something about what kind of ship was this we were on, a relationship or a dictatorship? But I didn't say anything more at the time. I just sat there staring at Dee, wondering if I knew her, who she was. I didn't know.

So I didn't argue about the names. Or about anything having to do with the baby. Bloodless, I'd become. Instead, I argued about a dream I'd had. Go figure. What we argued about specifically was when I'd had the dream, whether I'd had it before I saw the newspaper article or after. I knew for sure I'd had the dream first, and had hard evidence to prove it. The dream had affected me so strongly that I'd written it in my journal, and had inscribed the date on top. *April 30th*, it said. As for the newspaper article, I'd saved it, too. It was datelined after, the beginning of May.

Dee, true to character, ignored the evidence. She insisted I'd seen the article first, that the article had triggered the dream. "You're all the time thinking about the article, Codie. *That's* why you had the dream."

"Look at the dates!" I yelled. "It's right there! In black and white!"

"Drop it about this dream already, Codie. You're obsessed."

Obsessed? Maybe. Occupied, more like it. I was dwelling on it. Dwelling, a word that means to make one's home, to live.

The dream I'd had myself, thank you, without any help from the press, had taken place in a ruin. "Tall columns," I'd written in my journal. "White marble spiking the sky." Oddly enough, though the edifice they'd once supported had long since crumbled into dust, the columns themselves were glistening, untouched by time. In the dream, I'd walked among the columns, tracing a path around them, picking up speed as I went, almost a dance. As I did this, it came to me that I was on the site of an archaeological dig. It was someplace arid, strong-sunned, sand-colored. A knot of archaeologists stood at the edge of a pit. They'd just unearthed something, and crowded around to show me. "Shards," one of them said directly to me, familiarly, as if I were in on this, privy to their concerns. "The shards have writing on them that none of us can decipher." One person in the group pushed her way through to me. When she cleared the others I saw that she was just a little girl. The girl was lanky. A long rope of dark hair brushed her waist. She took my hand. "They've never before seen this particular cuneiform," she said. "Codie, you're the one, the only one, who can tell them what any of this means." Though when I woke up, I couldn't quite imagine how that could be true.

So you can understand my being rather unnerved when, just a few weeks later, I saw the article in the science section of the *New York Times*. The lead story on the front page of the section was about an archaeological dig in Yemen. Ceramic fragments had been excavated there, and when the scientists pieced the fragments together, they found them etched with a form of writing never before seen. The writing bore no direct resemblance to any other ever catalogued.

I was at work when I read the article, and afterward I was distracted. I found it difficult, more difficult even than usual, to concentrate on stories that condescended to young intelligence. I had no idea how I could possibly play any role in this event taking place on the other side of the globe, an event that challenged even those with training and knowledge of the field. Nonetheless, I felt myself imbued with a strange sense of mission. I thought about the shards that had been unearthed and what they might say. "Lost language," I thought, a concept unutterably sad. To me it meant lost lives.

" 'To bring to light,' " I said, when reporting the coincidence to Dee. "In the dream, before she took her hand from mine the little archaeologist spoke those words, 'Your task is to bring to light.' "

"Codie," Dee snapped, "you're making me crazy. This dream you claim to have had is just one more manifestation of your ancient obsession. Which is tired. Overtired by now. Got it?"

"Clue!" I yelled out the back window. I could see that cat of mine in the alley two buildings away. She looked directly at me when I called to her, but she didn't move from the lid of the garbage can where she'd settled for a nap. I appealed to Wren, who was sitting at my kitchen table. "It's going to rain," I said. "They're predicting. Clue doesn't realize that it's going to *rain*."

"Of course she knows. The air's heavy enough that even I can tell. And cats are far more sensate than humans."

"But she doesn't know I'm about to *leave*." I called Clue's name again. "I won't be home to let her in when the downpour starts. And I can't just *tell* her."

Communication between species, my standard sermon. Wren had seen me in this state before. "Has she ever come home drenched after a storm?" Wren asked. The truth is, she hadn't. The few times Clue had gotten caught in the rain, she'd found some sort of shelter and come home bone dry. When I ceded that point, Wren hit me with her real agenda. She suggested that maybe I was worrying so much about Clue because it was easier to be distressed about my cat than it was to worry about myself and how I was going to fare now that Dee had gone. "Anyway," she said, "I thought you liked storms. The way you've always told the story, I thought you were the self-styled Queen of Storms."

The way I tell the story I guess anyone might've gotten that impression. Back in my formative years in tornado country, I used to stand in the backyard, watching—eyes wide, awed— as the sky turned a color that seemed unnatural, though of course it was as natural as rage. My mother used to stand at the kitchen door and call for me to come inside—before the winds got high and lightning flashed its warnings. But, even inside, I'd stand at the windows where I could watch. I liked violent storms. Something about them quickened my heart. I liked living in a place where nature could level houses, or at least lay them bare.

Not so, my mother. She listened to radio reports, and tried to instruct me in the difference between Tornado Watch and Warning. When the man on the radio said the word, my mother would shepherd me to the basement. There I could no longer see the rain, but I'd hear it pelt the window wells. Sometimes the electricity would flicker and fail, overpowered. Then we would light the votive candles my mother stored on the basement shelves. For emergencies just such as these.

One year, though it was late spring and the weather had long been warm, the skies let loose with hailstones. My mother, fright-eyed, taut-voiced, called me to the basement as she had many times before. We sat through the storm, and when it passed, I followed my mother back upstairs and outside to the front yard, which, in the aftermath of the storm, was littered with branches felled from trees. "Our siding," my mother moaned. She ran her hand across the slats of wood that sheathed our house. "Our beautiful siding." The siding she was mourning was now pock-marked. Pocked by hailstones the size of fists.

As our neighbors came one by one out of their own front doors, there were more reports of damage. Someone's swing set toppled, someone's birdbath blown away. But the story I liked best concerned the house that faced ours. This house had had white columns fronting its porch. Not for support, but to distinguish it from the other houses mass-produced in the development. A conceit which had not impressed the storm that had blown through. The storm's high winds had blasted the columns right out from under. According to later reports, the columns were found dropped around the neighborhood as randomly as spice. Word was that one turned up in the church parking lot, a distance of more than two miles away.

"What's this?" Wren asked. She was still at my kitchen table, tracing her finger over a child's scrawl etched like fossil record into its soft pine. I looked over her shoulder to read what was written.

"Original sin," it said. And beside that, "Sacrificial lamb."

"Words laid down to throw me off," is how, after a pause, I explained them to Wren. "False evidence. Veiling what I knew to be real."

I am on my way to Wren's, one of us abandoned, one afraid. When I woke up this morning, Clue was lying on my pillow, curled around my head. She'd been purring there while I slept, and the vibrations of her purrs, thick and fleecy, folded down and blanketed me. I woke up equilibrated and dialed Wren to see what she was up to. It turned out she'd taken a fright. So afraid, she was, her voice was shaking.

"God," she said. "Am I jumpy. When the phone rang, I leapt a mile." All it was that scared her, if you can imagine, was a little music. A little music early on a Sunday afternoon.

As Wren explained it, she'd been fine until she'd turned on the radio. "I was expecting, I don't know, world news, nothing special." Instead, she happened on a music program, and the theme of the program was scores from films. "I was kind of enjoying it," Wren reported. "As background music while I was puttering around the house, cleaning. When I finished, I'd gotten a little filmy myself. With dirt, I mean. So I decided to take a shower. I had my clothes off, one foot on the bath mat, one foot in the tub. When what did the host of the program decide to air next but the music from *Psycho*. The shower scene music. That violin riff where the woman gets stabbed and blood streams down the drain. Forget it. Fat chance I was going to get in the shower after that. Know what I mean?"

Yeah. I do. I know exactly.

On my way to Wren's, I catch the drift of live drums. I round a corner and come upon two men playing African congas. Maybe it foreshadows something, I find myself hoping. The rhythms of the drums, though, do not signal anything clear. I consider the possibility that perhaps music just is what it is, but this is a concept that seems too unraveled to ponder.

When I have listened a while, I put a dollar bill in the gourd the men have set in front of them, even though I am now unemployed. (More on this to follow.) After that I proceed to Wren's, where we will drink strong coffee and eat the persimmons I pick up on the way at the corner fruit store, and the two of us will talk about the future though we have no idea what it holds.

"Your daughter is remarkably musical," Miss Rose once said to my mother, "and quite a quick little study." At that time I had only an inexact sense of how the word "musical" might relate to dance, and even less idea what "quick study" meant. But I knew that my teacher must be complimenting me by the way she smiled at me as she spoke and by the way she tugged affectionately at the ponytail in which, for class, I'd bound my hair. My mother, who'd come to take me home, took my hand and led me out of the studio. When we got to the car, I asked her to explain what Miss Rose had meant. "Did she mean I'm a real ballerina?" I asked. I was hoping that was the gist.

My mother stood outside the car looking distractedly across the parking lot into the intersection beyond. "She means you don't have to study very hard to get A's," she said.

I wasn't sure what that meant, either. "Get A's?" I asked. "You mean we're going to be tested?" This prospect had never occurred to me.

My mother opened the car door and then, though she was still standing outside, slammed it shut just as quickly. "Life is a

145

test!" she shouted at me. "Everything is not pretty, like your little ballet class. Life is not some fun little dance!"

When we got home, my father was still in bed. I went to my room where I could close the door on my mother and my father, the anger of their argument surging down the hall.

This mother, who in graveled parking lots laid me low, was the selfsame one who went out and bought me ballerina fabric, the same good mother who sewed me ballerina everything. Our class was scheduled to have a recital, and, in the pointed way of the time, it had fallen to the mothers to sew the costumes. My mother had been the first finished. She'd brought the completed costume with her one day when she came to pick me up from class, and paraded it in front of the others as she might a newborn infant rival. When the other mothers crowded around, my mother lifted the lid of the box in which she'd nested the costume. Slowly, the better to present it. Inside were the pink net tutu and the thin-strapped leotard with sequined bodice. The mothers fingered the stitching. The other girls oohed in awe. I got pushed to the edge of the crowd, though I didn't particularly care. I was still tired from all the fuss the night before.

My mother had completed the costume in the wee hours of the morning, after having worked on it, painstakingly sewing on each spangling sequin, for the better part of a week. I'd awakened in the dark to see my mother at my bedside, whispering excitedly that I should come with her to her room, she had a surprise. In her bedroom, I blinked at the bright, artificial light still blazing. My mother pulled my nightgown up over my head, after which she helped me first into the tights and then into the leotard and elasticized tutu. "Get the camera, Tom," she directed my father. But my father didn't take my picture. Not that night.

A lesser mother might've capped the sewing she'd done for my sake once she'd completed the costume, but something unnamed got triggered in her, and when, soon after, she went on a shopping spree, she returned with a bolt of material, material she'd happened upon at the fabric store, how fortunate for me.

"Come here, Codie," she beckoned. I was standing in the doorway of the dining room, and instinct screamed at me not to go anywhere near, but my mother had a pattern piece in her hands and said she needed to hold it up to me, measure it against my waist. "I'm making you some things," she said, a tight smile masking her face. "See what a soft-hearted mother you have? After your shenanigans in the shower the other day, I should be disciplining you, not making you presents."

"What are you making?" I asked with suspicion.

"A ballerina nightgown. And then, I think, a ballerina bathrobe. After that, I might make a ballerina sundress, some ballerina pedal pushers, and a ballerina swimsuit. And if there's any fabric left over, I might whip up a little blouse as well and maybe a halter top, too."

"What about her underwear?" joked my father. I hadn't even heard him slip up behind me.

My mother ignored him. "Aren't you a lucky girl?" she primed me. Mother Amok.

I nodded, but didn't take one step into that room. The bolt of fabric she had bought was now unwound and falling over the edge of the table onto the floor. It was printed with tiny ballerinas, ballerinas pirouetting every which way across its length.

"I know you like ballerinas," my mother coaxed me. But these ballerinas seemed to be marching toward me, like a regiment, a ballet army. "Come here."

In the days that stretched out like dough under her holiday rolling pin, my mother started up one pattern after another, though she never actually finished any, abandoning each at various stages of incompletion. One afternoon when I came home from school, I was disturbed to see my mother dragging the outside garbage can into the dining room. She pulled it flush with the dining room table and, with one sweep of her arm, wiped the table clean of the lot of half-made pattern pieces, every one. Then she dragged the garbage can into the next room, opened the closet door, and began pitching other things, whatever it was she found at hand, things it seemed to me we would probably need. Scarves, jackets, the green felt decorative skirt she'd made for the Christmas tree. After that closet she went to the next. And on to another. She was on the way to my room, to my closet, when I got the idea I'd better run in before her and rescue the box which she'd stored at the back, the box that contained the tutu for my recital. I tucked the box under my arm and stole downstairs. My plan was to hide it in the basement. Clever girl, I slipped the tutu into the crawl space behind the furnace. A mother would have to be cagey and more to look there.

The night of my recital as I sat playing rummy with my grandmother, I could think of little else but that box. And I'd been naive enough to think that the music I'd heard warned only the women on the quiver-imaged screen of our TV, everything in black and white. But if I'd even the slightest suspicion that I myself was at risk, I distracted myself with another tune.

Stepping over orphan dolls to get to the shower. Wet, naked orphan dolls. When my mother came home, she had to step over them, too.

"I leave you in charge for only a couple of hours!" she shouted at my father.

"It's only a little water," my father yelled back. "A bathroom is *supposed* to get wet."

"I'm not talking about the bathroom!"

"What are you trying to say?" my father prodded provocatively. "Do you think something happened? What exactly are you saying?"

My mother jerked me out of the shower and carried me in a cross-chest carry to my room, where she pulled my nightgown on over my head, though I was still dripping wet, and where she drew the shades at my windows, though it was the middle of a winter afternoon. She pulled back the covers of my bed and ordered me inside.

"But I'm not sleepy," I protested.

"Yes you are," said my mother, her voice pinched. "I think one little girl has had a very tiring day. I think one little girl needs to go to bed right now." Sentenced to bed with the sun still shining. By the very woman who, short nights before, had wrested me from deepest sleep.

From my bed, beyond the door my mother closed behind her, I listened to my parents and the argument they skirted, no one daring to say anything directly. I heard my mother throw something against the wall. I heard my father stomp downstairs and slam the front door. A car engine floored. Its wheels screeched out the driveway and down the street. Then all was still, or so I thought, until the door of my bedroom blew open as if by wind and my mother's angry face appeared almost disembodied in the doorway, shouting, "Are you pleased with yourself? Are you pleased with the trouble you've caused?" After which she slammed the door on what would've been my response.

"Mom?" I called after her. "Mommy?" I was only asking the chance to explain.

The late afternoon sunlight poked in around the edges of the shades and fell on my bed in weak slats. Me, I didn't move from the bed where my mother had put me. My muscles, stiff. My body, armored. My whole being rigid as, oh, I don't know, let's just say rigid as fear.

One lime from a basketful. Who would ever notice? As time
went on, quite a lot of things in the khan would be reported
missing. Anwa would take to filching things. On one occasion,
she'd steal a whole day. She'd take me to a place I'd never been
before. The sea. So that I could forget the leer of a porcelain
monkey and the memory of someone's sour breath upon me as
if I were his.

The thieving Anwa would take up was extravagant, and
the gifts she'd give me, valuable. Some were gilded, others
gems. Over time they'd prove more expensive than we could
imagine. Anwa and I, we'd planned to marry. But it proved the
wrong wedding and a different bed entirely.

The summer I speak of, there was a wedding at the khan.
The one wed was a man named Ghil-Azn, chieftain of a neighboring tribe. News of the wedding flashed through the hareem
as swiftly as fire through tinder. I was told the news by Iman,
who rendered broad impersonations of the two men, overheard
in conversation, soaked in wine.

"You will wed here!" the Mukarrib had insisted, now further intoxicated by the sound of his own generosity. "For your
celebration, I extend you the entire premises of the khan."

With his reported gesture, the Mukarrib put not only the premises of the khan in service of the wedding, but its staff as well. Including its hootch-kootch girls, as Iman told me he had referred to us. Which is how I would come, once again, to be hootching and kootching before a full Hall of assembled guests and the Mukarrib's lustful eye. The things we do to earn our keep.

Mind you, I was not complaining. Far from it. So innocent I was, I thought dancing pleasure. As innocent as a virgin, for that was still my state. I put my mind to nothing of more consequence than my costume. I'd beaded it with silver spangles I'd purchased off a caravan that had recently passed through. The trader who'd sold them to me claimed he'd got the lot from some seaman. "Sailed from a darker land," the trader told me.

Anwa had happened into my room while I was trying on the dress. "I am quite keen on my costume," I said aloud, thinking I was alone.

"Eye yam quite keen on my cost-yume," Anwa echoed, her voice in exaggerated mimic of mine.

"Tease all you want." I spun around. "I know you love me largely because I wear costumes like this and wear them well."

"I'll tell why you love me," she said. "You like my fingers."

"You make it sound as if that's all."

"You like how long they are. You like the way they probe you."

"So what if I do?"

"No one else has fingers that read you as mine do. And what they mine is mine."

I picked up my scent pot and hurled it at Anwa, proud as she was. Anwa ducked, though she needn't have bothered. My aim was far from true and the pot barely grazed her.

"And what do you know of the sea?" she asked. She was laughing. "Have you been there without my knowing?"

The fragrant powder that the scent pot had contained was scattered now, dusting the crevices of the floor as it might the creases in a wise woman's face. "You know I haven't," I said, sulking.

Anwa grabbed me around to kiss me. In those days, disputes that fired between us served us innocently, were quickly transformed into just cause for us to reconcile, reason enough to give kisses in apology. Disagreement no more than a prelude to rub and lick.

Anwa ran her hands down the sides of the sheer silk of my costume. She pulled my hips to hers. "And do you love me, Sari?" she asked. How quickly Anwa could change a subject. And how it perplexed me that she asked for answers so evident. Love her? As if the melt of my body against hers did not inscribe it for all time.

"Love you?" I said. "It's you that beats inside me even now." Then I let my lips and tongue whisper their own reassurances. To the tips of Anwa's fingers, to her neck, to the hollow under her ribs. It seemed she wanted something more.

"To prove the depth of my love for you," I said. I had no idea what it was I was going to say, even as I spoke. "I will take off this costume." I caught her eye so she'd see the glint with which I added, "And you know how I favor it so."

Then I wriggled down her length to set my lips and tongue working in the furred, scented recess of her. A sort of cooing escaped her, a sound unlike any I'd heard from that handsome woman before, or in the weighted days that followed. I suspected suddenly that it was something pent up inside her I heard. And I, foolish enough to think that love could free it.

"Anwa," I said impulsively, "this wedding . . ." Reckless I was, tempting the gods at every turn. "This wedding for which the whole of the khan is preparing? I propose that it be ours."

"What?" asked Anwa.

"The dance, the feast, the ones that have been planned for the marriage of Ghil-Azn? I think they're meant, really, for us. Doesn't it make perfect sense? You and I have been joined together by the gods. Should we not be linked by law as well? What I propose is simple. When Ghil-Azn and his bride take their vows, we'll take ours as well. No one need know what we're up to. We'll mouth the vows and mean them for each other. And when, afterward, we eat the food and drink the wine? The union we'll be celebrating is ours. When we come back, to bed together, that will be our wedding night."

"But, Sari . . . who would I ask for your hand? Not your father. Not the Mukarrib."

"Ask me," I urged. "Ask me now."

"You?" she said, incredulous.

"Aren't I mine to give?"

Anwa scrutinized me, trying to discern whether or not I spoke in jest. Doubt clouded her face. She ventured the question. "Sari," she asked, "will you be my bride?"

It was a long pause I took before I answered. "Well," I hemmed, "that's a proposal I'd entertain, certainly, but one I'd need take some time to consider."

"Sari!" cried Anwa. "You're the one requested that I ask for your hand. If you're going to ask me to propose marriage to you, it's obvious you should agree to it when I do."

"Well, I wouldn't want to consent so hastily to a course of such consequence. There are factors to consider."

"Such as?"

"If I'm going to marry, I'd want to make sure I'd be marrying someone who'd be able protect me. I'm not so physically strong and—"

"You're an athlete."

"A dancer. Which is quite different."

"You're every bit as strong as an athlete."

"At any rate, I'm small. And vulnerable in the wider world. What if, for instance, I were one day to be out gathering fruit in the fields, and wolves were to attack me?"

"I'd tear them limb from limb."

"You would?"

"Indeed."

"Well, what if enemy soldiers were to attack the khan and the invading forces wished to invade me as well?"

"Just let them try."

"What if the burliest among them were to sling me over his shoulder and carry me away?"

"I'd smite that soldier."

"Are you equal to that? What weapon would you use?"

"If need be, I'd wrest his own weapon from him. I'd fix it so he had nothing to invade you *with*."

"You'd protect me no matter what?"

"You can rely on it."

"Well . . ." Here I paused to consider what other perilous situation I might fabricate. I glanced sidelong at Anwa to gauge her reaction. "What if Iman should decide she wants me for wife herself?"

Anwa grabbed me up and slung me over her shoulder, as I suppose I myself had suggested with my fictive soldier.

"No!" I shouted. "Let me down!"

"Iman will never have you! You are mine!"

"So then," I said, captive, "ask me again to wed you."

Anwa groaned. "I'm not going to ask," she said, "if what you're going to say is no."

"Go ahead," I urged. "Ask."

Anwa set me down. She seemed unsure whether or not she should continue. "Sari," she sighed, "will you be my bride?"

I flung myself into her arms and pressed my lips to her ear. "Yes," I said. This answer slid sibilant and happy off my tongue. "Oh yes. Yes, yes, yes, yes, yes. My answer is yes. Now we are betrothed." And so we were. "You know," I said, the idea suddenly occurring to me, "by letter of the law I am a virgin. It's a virgin you'll be getting on your wedding night."

"I'll need teach you how to love," said Anwa.

As if she already hadn't.

The hot hareem light glinted off the spangles in my skirt. During the wedding, I myself would have to keep quiet, but the costume could speak for me. As loudly as alarm.

What it would say?

Come and get me.

28

I won't linger on the details of the wedding. In most respects, it might have been interchangeable with any other. Ghil-Azn, a man with thinning hair, married Ralima, a girl of thirteen. Nothing unusual in that. The ceremonial transaction took place in the temple between the groom and the bride's father, the bride sequestered elsewhere. Typical enough. After the ceremony, when we gathered in the Hall for the feast, the bride's father made loud, sentimental speeches to any within earshot, speeches about the Mukarrib, his beneficence and accomplishments. But behind this veil, I mouthed my vows to Anwa, and she, hers to me. The wedding guests guzzled their wine.

The morning of the wedding, the khan had been shrill with preparation. Animals were slaughtered, bound by their feet, hung upside down, their throats slit. Blood streamed like time into sticky, fly-sweet pools.

At the feast, the bride and groom received the first plate of lamb, charred and crackling from the spit. The Mukarrib had seated himself between the two. Strategically so. This arrangement had not escaped the notice of the women of the hareem. We, too, were displayed as assets, seated together across the Hall. As the night wore on and the Mukarrib, increasingly intoxicated, began pawing Ralima, we kept a sharp eye on him. Watchful as weasels.

"Poor thing," someone said. "She'd be better off a hareem girl. Then she might at least look forward to a more pleasurable wedding night, of the sort Sari and Anwa have planned."

Anwa glared at me, irritated that I'd revealed our secret.

"Pleasurable wedding night?" another laughed, looking at Anwa and me. "Loud, you mean."

Here, I spoke up. "If the Mukarrib would dismiss Anwa at a better hour, she and I could get an earlier start, and then all of you would get the sleep you so desperately need. To maintain your fading beauty."

"I don't think even that argument would deter him," someone answered. "The reason he keeps Anwa in his chamber is his member. And where his member's concerned, we'll have no measure of leeway."

At this comment, the discussion disintegrated into some frivolous banter about members and measure, and someone suggested that Anwa bring a knotted string with her next time she was called to service the Mukarrib. To use as gauge.

We laughed, our attempt to have as merry a time as those around us. Our grouping that night might be likened to a small, undefended and pregnable island in a vast drunken, celebratory sea.

Because we'd let our attention wander, we didn't at first notice that across the room the Mukarrib had lifted himself up and was looking our way. He was beckoning to Anwa. Or so we thought.

"It appears he's remembered full well that he's not to have the young virgin sitting next to him. When he's ready to retire, look who it is he calls to him."

"No imagination, our Mukarrib. He is like one who requests the same menu every night for dinner."

"Anwa," I grabbed her arm and whispered my meaning, "I'll wait for you in my room."

"Don't forget the white sheet," she teased. "I'll wave it out our window to display the crimson stain."

Anwa and I now bonded together. Through and beyond time.

When Anwa reached the Mukarrib, she perched herself beside him and whispered in his ear. I looked away. My eye fell on the center of the room where two men had hoisted Ramira onto their shoulders. Ghil-Azn stumbled about beneath his bride, biting at her toes and grabbing her legs. The young girl clutched frightenedly onto the heads of the men who held her. Though she had been plied with wine, it was evident that she was still conscious enough and plenty to feel fear about the night that awaited her.

I turned to leave, thinking I would excuse myself from the festivities, go back to my chambers and bathe, festoon my room with the flowers I had earlier collected in honor of the occasion. I was stopped from leaving, though, by a slave boy who delivered the message that I was wanted by the Mukarrib. I looked back across the room. Anwa was trying to soothe our drunken ruler, as if making some appeal. She was rubbing herself up and down the front of him in what I soon realized was a desperate attempt to get him to turn his attention to her. But the Mukarrib's attention was not on her. He was pointing to me.

"He wants me?" I asked the slave boy. My tone implied that there must be some mistake, though it was clearly as he'd said.

"He calls for Sari," said the boy.

I fell silent, as did everyone around me. Iman stepped between me and the boy.

"Someone else volunteer to go," she said. "I'm too old, or, in an instant, I'd do so myself. Capture his eye. Hurry!"

The others did put themselves forward, making no small effort at seduction, but the effort was doomed. We all knew who it was the Mukarrib wanted. And we knew why. The Mukarrib was pointing at me.

Because there was no escaping it, I walked toward the man who owned me. I kept my gaze fixed on Anwa, hoping to catch her eye and there read some communication from her. But

Anwa would not look at me. She clung to the arm of the Mukarrib.

"What good a virgin?" I heard her plead. "You're better off with someone who has the experience to know the subtleties of your tastes."

The Mukarrib pushed her back. With great effort he lifted himself up, grabbing onto those around him for balance, and fell toward me. Though he barely had balance enough to stand, he somehow summoned enough and more. He grabbed me by the waist and hoisted me to his hip as if I were no more than an unwieldy satchel. Anwa ran up and grabbed at me, but two of the Mukarrib's henchmen tore her away.

And so the Mukarrib carried me off to his bedchamber. Which is where that night I lost the status of virgin that had made me such a delicacy in his hareem. Men of wealth and power ought always have a virgin in their stores. In case there's a wedding. When a virgin is as necessary an ingredient as flour is to bread.

It was probably not a time of much length I spent that night in the Mukarrib's bed. The man was drunk and had not the stamina for prolonged play. To me, though, it seemed a moon or more. He pawed at me, and left a trail of sticky spittle across my stomach and breasts as he slobbered on me in what passed for kisses. When, soon after, he pushed my head down to his member, I put my mouth around it as I had often overheard the other women in the hareem describe what it was they did to him. But the Mukarrib did not let me finish my work so cleanly. He tossed me on my stomach and hitched up my rump. In the far corner of the room was a porcelain statue of a monkey. The monkey watched our jerked ballet and seemed to be laughing. I kept my eye on that monkey the whole while the Mukarrib worked his way into me. I kept my eye on him as the Mukarrib pumped me with his seed.

When the man was through, he withdrew himself, but did not roll off me. I stayed pinned beneath him. The acrid smell of him suffocated me, and another foul smell wafted up from where he had been between my legs. Seconds after he was done, the Mukarrib was snoring. I shifted, trying to extricate myself from under him without waking him, but each time I tried, he clutched me more tightly. Finally, I managed to free myself and roll off the cushions. As I stood up, a gummy mucus spurtled down my leg. I picked up my costume from where the Mukarrib had tossed it to the floor and left that bedchamber differently than I had entered it. I left it quietly and on my own two feet.

Anwa was waiting for me when I got to my room. She lay on my mat beside the urn of flowers I'd intended to arrange for our celebration. I knew she was awake. Her eyes lit the dark.

"Sweet," she said hoarsely, an endearment that reached out for me across the room and by which I felt already taken in her arms. I spoke no word myself, but fell upon her and buried my face in the crook of her shoulder. She held me close and smoothed my hair. It was some minutes before I could talk.

"You never told me," I said. "Why didn't you tell me? How can you go there? Night after night?"

"Shhh." Anwa's lips pressed my forehead. "Shhh." The sobs that had grown in me welled up and convulsed me. When finally I exhausted them, I fell asleep in Anwa's arms. The tears that wet my cheeks stuck to hers as well and glued us together.

The next morning I awoke sore and spent. I lay on the mat and touched myself gingerly between my legs, perhaps to confirm, but more as comfort, and when I did so I noticed that a dark spot of blood stained my sheet. Anwa looked down. She saw the blood, too, and saw that I saw. With a hesitant smile that begged apology, she cupped the dome of my belly in her hand and said, "Sari, your hymen is broken. I guess that means it was, indeed, our wedding night." And I, complicit, answered, "Anwa, now you are mine, I am yours, and we are one." For with her hand firm upon me, I knew it to be true.

Always, when the world proved harsh, we worked to create a different one, our own.

29

Anger, anger everywhere. Molten anger. The city no more than a mirror. On the uptown IRT, two guys appear in my car. Young guys, tough-looking, thick gold chains around their necks. One is wearing a T-shirt with big, block letters across the front that proclaim, FUCK YOU, ASSHOLE. The other wears a large button, as big around, say, as the days before Christmas. It says, YOU'RE UGLY. Ugly is right, I think. Ugly as sin.

But the city where I live has two faces. On the avenue that intersects my street, for unclear municipal reason, the tar of the pavement is embedded with pieces of glass. Glass that, at night, sparkles under the illumination of the reedy, statuesque lamps that line the street. I like to think that the lamps were installed just to set the glass shining.

Perhaps that's a feeling warmed by the memory of the night Dee first kissed me. It was on that avenue, on my corner.

"What are you doing?" I'd asked hoarsely.

"Taxiing you to Love Land," she said.

Lit by lights like diamonds. Brilliant, blinking, blinding me to any impulse but love.

When I was a child, I once drowned. Or at least that's what I told my friends when my parents brought me home that day from the swimming pool. I guess I hadn't yet mastered the nuance of language, didn't have the sense of the word exactly, that to satisfy drowning, death is required. Obviously, it wasn't true that I had drowned. It was only true that I'd almost. I'd been rescued, pulled by my ponytail from the deep end of the pool by a broad-shouldered lifeguard. My mother had warned me against going in the deep end; I didn't yet know how to swim. And it wasn't that I disobeyed deliberately, simply that I somehow bounded beyond where I could stand and found myself in water over my head with no way to buoy myself or keep afloat. I knew I was in trouble. But I didn't shout for help, as would have been the obvious thing. Instead, I mimed a distress signal I'd learned from cartoons. When cartoon characters drown, they go down once, twice, thrice, each time holding up the corresponding number of fingers. The third time down, they stay down. Bubbles rise to the surface to indicate they're still breathing. And then the bubbles stop.

After the lifeguard rescued me, he told my mother that he'd seen my signal, but hadn't immediately jumped in after me because he assumed I must be playing. It was only when he glanced back, scanning the pool, and no longer saw my head bobbing that he realized I'd gone under. That's when he dove in and pulled me out by my ponytail. Which felt to me, I later told my friends excitedly, like a caveman dragging his wife by the hair.

The thing I have to say about being young is that there's an awful lot to learn, and quickly. An alert child picks up things where she can, imitates what she sees, but it's sometimes hard to cull out which voices to listen to and which not. Your average child's been instructed to look to adults for guidance. But it could very well be that all they've got is a chronological edge and a good bluff. So, in retrospect, it doesn't really seem so outlandish or misguided, my having turned to animation, having looked to characters popping off the screen, larger than life.

It was my idea to make a celebratory dinner for our anniversary, and Dee's to cast the celebration as another occasion altogether. Turkey, she wanted. Turkey with all the fixings.

"Turkey?" I said. A heat wave had been plaguing us. The temperature hadn't dipped below ninety in over a week. The menu I had in mind was more along the lines of cold poached salmon and yogurt soup. "Turkey is for Thanksgiving," I protested.

"I thought you liked Thanksgiving dinner."

"I like it fine at Thanksgiving, but . . ."

"So what's the problem?"

"It's not a problem. It's just that . . ."

"Turkey," Dee cut me off. "Turkey it is. And all the stuff we'd normally fix with it. Yams . . ."

"They're not really in season."

". . . those creamed onions like you made last year, cranberry sauce, pumpkin pie . . ."

"We'll have to use canned."

"Codie," she said. Her eyes glassed over. She stared dreamily off in the distance. "It really is an unbelievably great idea when you take a moment and think about it."

"What is?"

"That we have each other to be thankful for, and that that's what Thanksgiving's all about."

"Thanksgiving's all about our anniversary?" I asked. Sometimes my only defense was to play dumb.

"Babe," Dee said. She'd set me straight with a tone reserved for speaking to the dullest of God's creatures. "Don't you get it? It's the other way around. Our *anniversary* is all about *thanksgiving*."

"Oh," I said. I smacked my head.

Later that night, after Dee'd fallen asleep, her lips in my lap, I found, somehow, that I'd actually begun to glimpse the wisdom in her plan. I made out a shopping list. Cheesecloth, turkey baster, onions, stuffing. Items that imbued the other, everyday things on the list—toilet paper, lemon ammonia—with a certain festivity. The next morning, I opened my eyes to a bright wash of light stretching across our wall. Dee was sleeping next to me, smelling like sex. I leaned over to look at her. In her stillness, the colors of her face set together like a painting,

162

the mauve of her lips against the smooth, even brown of her skin, her thick lashes a crisp black accent. I kissed the nape of Dee's neck and brushed my lips against the tight black curls that sprouted there like seed.

At the supermarket, we wheeled our cart down the aisles and talked about what we would buy. Dee never asked, she just threw things in.

"Wait a minute," I said. "Artichoke hearts? We have three cans of artichoke hearts. Every time we go to the store you buy a can and then we never eat them."

"We don't have three cans."

"Yes we do. In the cabinet. Next to the three jars of capers."

Dee shrugged. She rested her forearms on the bar of the cart and jutted back her rear end, her way of pushing it, off-hand. She cocked her head to scan the aisles.

When we got to the poultry section, I was relieved to see that the store had stocked a few turkeys. The chill in the refrigerated store air raised gooseflesh on my bare arms. "Like November," I fantasized, anxious to make sense. "Like Thanksgiving." I rolled the turkeys over to compare the weights and prices on their labels. But at the other end of the poultry case, Dee was picking up a roasting chicken and tearing back the plastic wrapping. This was something Dee always did when she bought a chicken. She liked to smell it to make sure it was fresh.

"What are you doing?" I said. "We don't want chicken."

"Why not?"

"Because we're having turkey for our anniversary. We won't want turkey and chicken in the same week."

"Okay," she said, tossing the package back, "so we won't buy it."

"Well, but you already opened it."

"What do you care? Are you a major stockholder in the A&P?"

I picked up the chicken from where Dee had thrown it. It was slippery inside its plastic. It didn't smell like anything. The skin was too yellow, reminding me of the color urine gets when it's tinted by vitamins or other fashionable stimulants. A twentieth-century chicken. I dropped it back in the refrigerated case and steered our way into the next aisle, cat food. There, I was the authority. Dee could never remember what Clue eats and what she doesn't.

"No chicken," I said. "No fish. Oh, except tuna. Tuna, beef, or liver."

Dee threw in one can of turkey with giblets, the expensive brand.

"For our anniversary," she said. "So Clue can celebrate alongside."

Hearing Dee say this set whatever residual worries I had at ease. It made me feel that we were, indeed, a family. Dee must have been reading my mind. Or independently she must have been thinking family, too, because the next thing she said was, "Maybe I'll get pregnant soon."

I pulled the turkey baster out of our cart. I held it up and raised my eyebrows questioningly. This was my idea of how we should go about things. "Or we could adopt," I said. I pictured us adopting an Asian child or a Latin one. I imagined us a happy, United Nations family, perhaps the subject of a photographic essay on alternative families. I did not want Dee going to bed with some man.

"Kenshaka told me recently that he'd consider fathering the baby," Dee said casually.

"Kenshaka? Who's Kenshaka?"

"Kenshaka McCoy."

I did not know any Kenshaka McCoy. "Who is this guy? How do you know him?"

"A fare."

"A fare!"

"Calm down, Codie. I knew him before. It was a coincidence. I was cruising up by Columbia and he happened to flag me down. We got to talking, he asked me what I've been up to, and I told him I was thinking of having a baby."

"What, you asked him to be the father or he just up and

volunteered? I don't understand. How's he considering fathering the baby?" My voice sounded tinny, as insubstantial as a disposable pie plate.

"He's a good candidate. He's tall, he's good looking. And he's smart."

I walked blindly through the dairy aisle, forgetting butter for basting, forgetting cream for the pearl onions.

At the check-out line, Dee picked up a copy of *Family Circle* and leafed through. I scanned the headlines of *The National Enquirer*. "Turkey Laced with Razor Blades." "Baby Born with Monster Head." "Woman Gnaws Lover."

The automatic doors slid open for us to leave the chilled air of the store. As I stepped outside, the late summer heat blasted me in the face.

Heat searing, as blistering as burns.

The summer before I started school, I went to church one Sunday with my mother. In front of us, ahead a couple of pews, was a gaggle of nuns. My mother pointed out the nuns and in a church whisper told me it was probable that one of them would be my teacher when I entered first grade. I stared at the nuns with horror. I may have been young, but I was wise enough to know that it would not be safe in the least to entrust myself to a coven of women who covered their hair and wore heavy black robes in the heat.

Where I live now the summer is torrid. The sun reflects up off the sidewalk as white-bright as if it's reflecting off sand. I wear a straw hat I buy from a street vendor who sells hats and other straw things imported from hot countries across seas. The street is lined with vendors who are dark-skinned and foreign-featured, themselves having arrived from lands as timeless as their wares. The vendors call to me as I pass, the street a marketplace, New York a busy crossroads on today's trade routes.

I cock the brim of the hat so that it shades my face and eyes. At my feet, in the gutter, I notice a mound of mango pits, striated with dried strings of the fruit, strings tenacious enough to have clung on despite the insistent scraping of teeth. No mistaking I am in New York, but in the window display of the large, chain discount store I pass, Day-Glo rubber sandals are exhibited on mannequins dressed as desert nomads, drab and dusty. It does feel hot as the desert here, I think. Though the humidity makes for a closer heat.

I stand on the sidewalk, looking in the window of the discount store, and as I do a guy comes out of the store. He's carrying a large box on which is printed a picture of an electric fan. Though his package is heavy and unwieldy, he stops and smiles at me. I know a come-on smile when I see one. If I were to smile back, he might walk alongside me a while and suggest we stop for a coffee at the stand on the corner. But I have no intention of smiling back. I'm hot, sweaty, and irritable, so I scowl at him. "I already have a lover with a fan," I mutter. "I'm looking for someone with air conditioning."

Dee and I have been fighting. The incident that sparks our fight is Dee telling me I'm nearsighted, as if I don't know. She scoffs at me when I take out my contact lenses and have to hunt, squint-eyed, for my glasses. She says, venom in her voice, "What is it with my girlfriends? They've all been nearsighted. Every one."

"Telling," I spit back. I think, for some reason, of the nuns of my childhood, the way they had to swivel their heads to see anything, their peripheral vision blocked by their wimples. "So what if I'm nearsighted," I blunder on, all bristle and defense, all incongruity. "At least I have peripheral vision!" I throw in the example of the nuns to bolster my position. About this, Dee couldn't care less.

"You and this Catholic thing," she sneers.

In the city where I live there are prophets on the subway. Blind men, the poor who it's said are always with us. And cripples, a word I use only because the Bible does, though perhaps, over centuries, something's been lost in translation. I am on a subway car and a man walks through. He holds out a blue-and-white waxed cardboard cup, the sort in which coffee shops dispense take-out, and announces that he is homeless. He is thin and his skin, lesioned. "New York is a leper colony!" he cries out, his voice ringing through our car. "Or so the rest of the country would have us believe. Would have us believe that this island we inhabit is home for undesirables deserving of an ugly fate. But I have come to bring truth to light," he says. "I am here to tell you that the dying live. And that the wretched will find peace."

I close my eyes for a moment to listen to this man. He is velvet-voiced, golden-throated, his message resounds to reach those seated in the farthest reaches of our makeshift chapel. When I open my eyes, I am captivated by his face. A face dark and etched, reminding me of someone I once might've known. I dig into my pocket and hand the man a quarter, but he gives me much more in return. "The wisdom of the ages wells up within you," he says. "All you need do is to tap it."

I am so moved by his words that at first I don't notice we are stopped at Forty-second Street, the crossroads. The man passes through my car, moving on. In his stead, a woman glides through the open doors of the car and takes the seat next to mine. In her arms she carries an ample spray of flowers. They're freshly cut and someone has fixed wet paper towels and tinfoil around the bottoms of the stems, which is, by coincidence, the way my mother used to fix the bouquets she cut for me to carry in the May procession, the procession in which yearly I honored the goddess of growing things, the Virgin Mary as she was billed at the time. Though I am in Manhattan, though we are traveling in tunnels carved under a concrete city, the flowers the woman carries are field flowers. And it is that sign that helps me hope that what the prophet told me is the truth.

On the way home from the subway, I pass a florist. The proprietor steps outside to set a bucket beside the front door, and in the bucket, full to spilling over, are Queen Anne's Lace. A dollar a stem, he's asking. Pretty weeds from my childhood. Once wild, now costing.

In bed that night, I yell at Dee to get her sweaty leg off mine. Tempers high as temperatures. Days later and still our apartment smells like turkey. Food rotting in the refrigerator because it's too hot to eat yams. Dee gets out of bed and gets herself a beer. She puts on a T-shirt inside out and a pair of torn underwear to climb out on the fire escape. Not enough clothes but who cares. Clue climbs across my chest. The fur she sheds in the heat sticks to the sweat on my skin. After a while, I get lonely being angry, so I climb out on the fire escape to join Dee. I don't say anything, just reach for her beer and take a sip.

Dee and I watching late-fading light.

Listening to passing radios.

30

Yeah, and another thing. One morning, as I was on my way to work, I ran smack into a passel of 'em—white men in suits. An unexpected surprise in a subway station that can best be characterized as having a friendly, neighborhood sort of charm—urine dripping from the rungs of the exit turnstyle, a homeless couple curled up in the corner like kittens. In the midst were these guys, belted, buttoned-up, briefcases in hand. Looked oddly out of place they did, but ain't it always the way. That whenever I wake up angry at life, ready to spin out, and poised, however irrationally, on the brink of some blind fury, I'll spy just the thing I need to push me over the edge.

"It went for five hundred grand at auction," one was saying.

"First printing of a hundred and fifty thousand," another chimed in.

"All the chains'll push it."

What d'ya know. In publishing, they were. And me on my way to write product. Will coincidence never cease?

"Good morning," said Jasmine, as I tried, unsuccessfully, to slip unnoticed past her on the way to my cubicle. She smiled at me expectantly and I noticed she was wearing a navy cross-tie at her neck, the sort that I remembered worn by boys in Catholic grade school, circa 1960. Wrong on two counts, decade and gender, so I felt justified when I answered her but barely. I hoped my cursory greeting would discourage her, but as I was uncapping my take-out coffee and wincing at the growing list of things to do accumulating on my desk calender, she appeared in my doorway, newspaper in hand.

"Hurricane Hugo is wreaking havoc in the Caribbean," she said. I didn't answer. "I was just reading this feature here on the naming of storms."

"That so?" I said in my most disinterested tone.

"Remember when they only named storms after women? Can you believe the ignorance that revealed? As if women were all viragos?"

Apparently she wanted to female bond, and so early in the morning.

"We women have to stick together," she went on, "don't you think? Strike a blow for feminism."

"Feminism?" I whirled around. "More like imbecilism!"

Jasmine started, the desired effect. I barreled on.

"This whole business of naming half the storms after men has done nothing but confuse the issue. Go ahead! Throw off the wisdom of the ages! But storms most certainly have gender! All things in nature have gender! As anyone with any sensitivity to it knows full well! Everyone knows the moon is female!"

"Codie, I only meant to—"

"Everyone! Or are you going to stand there and deny it?"

"I—"

"And the sun is male! Undeniable! Volcanoes are female. As are oceans, rivers, and streams. Thunder is male. But storms themselves? Female! Every time! And if some misguided feminists want to throw away what's ours in the name of some homogenized equality, I'm here to tell you that they're wrong. As loudly as I can and for anyone to hear!"

Jasmine was backing, stiff-smiled, out of my cubicle.

"The ignorance," I muttered. "Handing away what's rightfully ours as if it has no value." And when I was sure Jasmine was out of earshot, "Named for a flower and what does she know? Wearing a bow tie like some schoolboy."

I guess I told her.

Wren, ever my gauge in emotional matters, advises me that, of late, I've been sounding a little excessively on the angry side.

"Really? I have? Angry?"

"I'd say."

It's not that I like being angry. It's only that I seem to have a fairly large reservoir of the stuff from sometime earlier when something maybe got damned. So, big sin, I happen to keep a little anger on supply. And it can hardly be my fault that when I'm not paying much mind it goes and attaches itself to the least little thing.

"What are you doing, Codie?" my father asked. I didn't think I was doing anything. At any rate, nothing I would expect to get in trouble for.

"I had to wash all the orphans. Their faces were dirty."

"And look at *you*," my father said.

I looked down at my own clothes. By this time they were sopping. My shirt was sticking seasonally to my belly like wax paper to cookie dough.

"I'm not dirty, Daddy," I said. "I'm just wet."

"Sopping wet," my father said. "What's your mother going to say?" I looked down at the floor to escape the accusation in his eyes, but there I was confronted by the bathroom rug, matted and sudsy. Rivulets and streams irrigated the surrounding tiles. My father checked his watch. "Your mother should be home any minute now," he said. "What are we going to do about this?"

I kept my eyes fixed on the floor. My father repeated the question.

"Come here," he said.

The fear I had when he called me to him was a child's fear, that my father was going to spank me, but after I'd walked slowly to him, he did the unexpected. He yanked at my shirt and jerked it up over my arms. Then he pulled off my corduroy pants and my underwear with them. To hide myself, I stepped one foot over the other, my arms and legs twisting around themselves like some sort of pretzel mangled in the making. My father began taking off his own clothes. He drained the bathtub, lifted out the dripping dolls, and laid them on the rug. Then he turned on the shower to wash the soap bubbles down the drain. The long while of this I tried not to look at what dangled between his legs, exposed for any young daughter to see.

"I'm cold," I said.

My father said nothing. He stepped under the spray of the shower and gestured for me to come in, too.

"I take baths," I said.

"Codie," my father said sternly, "you have made a complete mess of the bathroom, and your mother is due home any second. If I were you, I'd do as my father says. Christmas is only a week away, and Santa always finds out which children have been naughty."

I had to step over the orphan dolls to get to the shower. Wet, naked orphan dolls.

Though I'm not sure that anything really happened in the shower. After that, everything got a little misty.

So I decided to go to a psychic.

"Sidekick?" Dee asked when I reported home, though she knew full well. She just liked to remind me that she comes from the Abbott and Costello school of spiritualism. Dee knew exactly where I'd been. I'd told her before I left. Which is why I didn't even bother to answer, just threw her a look. "A psychic, huh?" she came around. "Yeah? So what'd she say?"

When I'd asked the woman about past lives, she'd closed her eyes, a different way of seeing. At length she said, "You're on a ship. You're very young. You've gone in search of someone and the seas are rocking wildly." She paused before adding, "This life I'm describing was one you cast quite tragically."

"Cast? Me?"

"There's been enough of that." She drew a breath and

waited, as if trying to divine more detail. Finally, she said, "The end is rather murky." Then she asked, "Did you know that once you drowned?"

"Drowned?" My voice cracked. She must've got it wrong. It was only true that I'd almost.

That I'd bounded into waters over my head.

31

Wren suggests, frank friend that she is, that at this late hour, with all the elements of this mystery laid out for suspicion and the evidence pouring in, we might very well discount and dispense with any details having to do with my Catholic upbringing.

But I still think Catholicism could be key. Taught by women in age-old garb, saints proliferating like gods, masses said in mumbo jumbo. Each morning the dusty caravan of busses deposited us at the door not of the school but of the church. We entered God's temple bound against a numbing cold by bulky coats, bookbags strapped across our chests to arm us against dark and insistent tides of ignorance, lunch boxes resolutely in hand to stave off centuries of hunger. No matter that it was cold outside, it was too close and confined for me bundled in my coat, squeezed into a pew, the church hot and stuffy. No air.

"I don't know," says Wren, ever skeptical. "Sounds like a lot of hooey to me. I think you might be throwing it in as ruse, wily subterfuge, as *distraction*."

What can I say?

"Go on," says Anwa, to encourage me.

I grope. "Tell me about the sea."

It was just this sort of question, bruised and stung, that suggested the idea of the trip to her; it was not usual for women of the hareem to be granted license to venture without escort beyond the bounds of the khan. But Anwa had access to the Mukarrib's nether organs, including his ear, and secured dispensation, outrageous as it was. To take me to the sea.

The morning we were to leave, I chased after Anwa, who strode to the river path. Already I felt lighter.

"Like boys!" I laughed as I skipped at her side.

"What do you mean?"

"I mean so *free!* Don't you imagine that this is how boys feel? Anwa, play this. As we walk, let's pretend that we're two boys out together on adventure."

"And what of your fur?" she asked, amused.

I hadn't thought of that. I would not want to give up my fur. "Boys with fur," I said, my extravagant solution.

I loosed my sandals and slung them over my shoulder. I burrowed my toes in the cool, moist earth.

"I thought you said we were going to the sea," I said. "This is the path of the river."

"River leads to sea," said Anwa, as if all directions were no more than a poem.

Beside us, the river was swollen from recent rains.

"Like the belly of Yasamen," I joked uneasily, recalling the death that sometimes still haunted me.

Our journey was long and took half the day's light. We passed pockets of women bent over the riverbank, fishing out raffia they'd soaked overnight, now supple enough to weave. We passed children fetching water and men spearing fish. Above us, clouds feathered the sky. A flock of birds flew past. I stopped to wonder—who is it that choreographs the skies?

"And when is it we'll get there?" I asked Anwa.

Another poem: "When the mouth of the river opens to the sea."

As we neared the shore, the air took on a different quality. I could feel it on my cheeks, on the breeze that ducked under my skirts.

"Brine," Anwa said, intuiting the question I would ask. "What you sense is the brine of the sea."

The trees that lined the river's banks thinned. When we turned a bend, the river waters widened and spilled into a harbor. The harbor was dotted with boats, and even the largest among them were bobbing. For what they lay in was the great, vast sea. As the expanse of it met my eyes, a small gasp escaped me. Anwa laughed.

"It extends forever," I tried to articulate. "Like land."

Beneath my feet, dirt gave way to sand. The sands were strewn with things unfamiliar. I picked up something green, slippery, and frondlike.

"Seaweed," Anwa told me.

"Seaweed," I repeated.

A hard-shelled, clawed creature skittered past my feet.

"Crab," said Anwa.

"Crab," I repeated.

In this way, I began to acquire a glossary of words for all the various forms of sea life. Anwa gave me more names.

"Whelk?" I asked, trying to keep the names straight.

"Urchin," Anwa corrected.

"Urchin," I repeated. "Conch. Seaweed. Crab."

Anwa turned and strode to the shoreline, skirting the tents erected for seasonal trade. At the edge of the water, the waves washed up over our feet, tickling them.

"Waves," said Anwa. "Surf."

As she spoke, the waves pulled back, spiriting away the ground beneath my feet.

"What is that?" I asked, alarmed.

"What is what?"

"The water pulling. My feet pulled, too."

"Undertow," said Anwa.

I felt it again. "But what does that *mean*?"

"It means what you said. The pull of the sea."

"But why?" I asked. " 'Undertow' is only a name. It doesn't explain it."

Anwa looked at me queerly. "It's a name," she said simply. "Like the others."

Anwa waded farther in and I followed. Tongues of water licked at my fear. Anwa and I knotted our robes higher, wading in until the water came to our waists. As the waves rolled in, we jumped to stay above them.

"Hey!" came a voice. It startled me. Enveloped so by the sea, I had forgotten that Anwa and I might not be alone. The voice was a man's. He was standing on the deck of a ship some ways away and was waving to us. The man was young and dark-skinned, like Anwa. He called out again, this time with words I did not recognize, though they reminded me of ones I heard from Anwa when I walked in on her alone and singing songs she remembered from elsewhere.

Anwa smiled broadly and waved back. The young man dove off the side of the deck and swam toward us. When he reached us, he stood up and shook the water from his hair.

"Like a dog," I thought with disdain.

It vexed me further when he embraced Anwa, took her head in his hands and kissed her. As the waves receded, I saw that he was wearing only a brief cloth knotted around his waist and then again between his legs. The fabric flapped in the water and I saw the tip of his member poke through.

I did not like this man. Neither his scant costume nor the familiar way in which he handled Anwa. Worse yet, Anwa allowed it. She seemed happy to see this man. It was with growing suspicion that I watched their interaction.

Anwa and the man exchanged more words in the tongue they shared that excluded me. Anwa said something, nodding to me, and the man laughed heartily. Then he dove back into the water, as suddenly as he had initially intruded, and swam in the direction from which he had come.

"Who was that?" I asked Anwa, my voice flat with displeasure.

"Xam," she said.

"And who is Xam?"

"He's gone to get a skiff," said Anwa. "To bring us to the

ship. I told him it was too far a distance for you to swim, that you are used only to the span of rivers."

"He found that reason for laughter?"

"No. He laughed at other information."

"Which was . . . ?"

"I told him that you are my wife."

"Anwa!" I cried out. "You told this man, this man with the too-familiar ways and the phallus bobbing in the surf that I am your wife?"

"The word I used means wife only inexactly. I used a word in my language that is closer to bedmate."

"Anwa!" I was mortified.

"What would you have me tell him, that you are my sister? I am afraid he would know better."

I turned away from her, my cheeks flushed and hot with shame. Anwa laughed and skimmed her hand across the surface of the sea to splash me.

"A sailor on a ship," I said, "and you tell him that you have taken me in bed. Did you tell him, too, where it is you kiss me?"

"No," she teased. "I told him where it is *you* kiss *me*. And with what passion."

Xam was at the ship, lowering a small, raftlike craft over its side. When the raft dropped in the water, he jumped in after it, hoisted himself inside, and paddled toward us.

"Why are we going to the ship?" I asked sullenly.

"Wouldn't boys?" asked Anwa.

When Xam reached us with the raft, I saw that it was made of goat hides, stitched together and inflated for buoyancy. Anwa clambered easily over its side, but when I tried to pull myself up, the raft rocked and I slipped back into the water. Xam grabbed my arm to assist me.

"Does he do this for all girls or only for your lovers?" I asked Anwa.

"Ask him yourself," she said. "He speaks both languages, as I do."

Xam smiled at me and bowed his head in mockery of introduction. "Any bedmate of Anwa's," he said, "is friend to me as well."

I turned from them both and covered my face with my hands. As the raft plowed toward the ship, I peered through my fingers. The sun glistened on the surface of the water. Liquid sun on satin sea.

"It's safe, Sari," Anwa teased. "You can come out now."

I uncupped my hands from my eyes and lifted my face to the sun. A lone gull glided above the raft, her wings outstretched, accompanying us. When we reached the ship, Xam called up to some men who lowered a rope ladder over the side. Anwa caught it as it swung toward us, and climbed up. I grabbed a hold of the rope and started up, too.

On board the ship were men, a score or more, and at the unexpected presence of two women, they swarmed around like fish at feeding. The ship was rocking, and with it, my stomach. One of the sailors pushed his way up to me. He grabbed my breast and pinched it hard.

"Ta'ib!" Xam said. A warning or a name?

The sailor pinched again.

As quick as a breath, Xam drew a long-bladed dagger he had sheathed in the thick bush of his hair. One of the other sailors pulled one similar from his belt and tossed it to the man Ta'ib. I jumped back.

"Don't worry," Anwa said to me. "It's sport."

"Sport? They have knives!"

"With sailors, sport is edged."

The group of sailors crowded into a ring around Xam and Ta'ib, who circled each other, crouching low. When Ta'ib lunged, Xam knocked him with one deft shove through the others and up against the bow of the boat. He poised his knife at Ta'ib's throat.

I feared Xam would kill the man. Instead, he threw down his knife and laughed. Ta'ib laughed, too. The two clasped each other in a good-natured embrace, as if no conflict had passed between them. Xam flashed Anwa a toothy smile.

"You can see I've not lost physical prowess," he said.

"Nor pleasure in displaying it," quipped Anwa.

After that, the sailors dispersed to their work. As Anwa talked with Xam, I sat on the resin-rough deck, watching the sailors move about. Some tugged on sails, others climbed up rigging. To a man, they had ease and assurance. Their cheeks were chapped, their muscles exultant. It struck me then: they navigated a different world than I.

I sat back, leaning to rest on a stack of crates that towered behind me. The faces of the crates were inscribed with characters foreign to my eye, the inscrutability of the writing a testament to the rich diversity of trade that reached our shores. Beside me stood a tall alabaster jug. It was plugged with a stopper and sealed with clay. I ran my finger over the earth-gray seal on which was printed a miniature relief, a continuous, serial picture, made, I knew, by rolling an etched bead over the still-wet clay. A slight nod to art by commerce, detail peculiar to our trade.

Steadily, almost imperceptibly, the air around me grew heavy, like a tree weighty with fruit. Above the ship, the threat of a sudden storm unexpectedly clouded the sky.

"We'll need to go," Anwa decided, coming to get me.

So soon. "But we just got here," I said.

Anwa reminded me that monsoon season was soon to be upon us and this might be its first fury. "Sea travel and overland caravan alike halt with the onset of monsoon," she lectured, as if I didn't know. "Are you more hardy than they?"

"Would that I were," I said with a pout.

Our freedom, fleeting as memory.

Xam signaled Anwa to wait for him, then disappeared down the hull of the ship. He returned with something cupped in his hand and extended it to Anwa. Inside was an oddly shaped piece of abalone etched with a crude likeness of a leopard and tied to a leather thong. "For amulet," he said.

"Amulet!" I snorted. The very thought. Xam's cult was, apparently, as specious as Anwa's. "Whoever heard of a leopard affording protection?"

Xam ignored my mockery. He slipped the amulet over Anwa's head and straightened the charm at her collar.

Thus protected, though dubiously so I thought, Anwa made her way back down the rope ladder. The three of us climbed back into the small vessel that was flapping in the water, tethered to the ship, and Xam rowed us ashore. When we reached the break of the waves where the sea shallowed, Xam sliced one oar into the sand as mooring. He and Anwa exchanged farewells, and I was surprised to see Anwa's eyes brim with tears. The sight disturbed me. I had never before seen Anwa cry. I watched the two closely as they again embraced. Anwa held Xam tightly, as if she didn't want to let him go. When finally they disengaged, Anwa and I climbed out of the boat. The warm seawash lapped our legs. Xam pivoted his craft and sighted it back toward the ship.

"Anwa, who is that male?" I asked. "How is it that you know him?" She did not answer, but kept her eyes on his receding form. This vexed me more. "And why is it he can never keep his phallus covered?" I asked. "He seems to like it hanging out for all to see."

Anwa turned to me, her face impassive. "His phallus is nothing I haven't seen before," she said.

"I knew it!" I shouted, anger leaping like flame. "I knew that he was your lover! And still you care for him, I dare you to deny it! I saw the way you embraced him! I saw your eyes well up with tears!"

"My lover?" said Anwa. "Sari, what demon advises you? You know full well that in my tribe, same as any, it's taboo for brother and sister to bed down together."

"Brother? Xam is your brother?"

Anwa turned and waded out of the surf. I again felt the undertow at my feet and an equivalent feeling like a pull at my heart with each step Anwa took in distance. At the water's edge she stopped and leaned down to pick something up off the sea's floor.

"Sari," she called. "Something more for you to name."

In her hand Anwa held a rock, smoothed from the pounding of the surf. On top of it lay a reddish creature in the shape of a five-pointed star, its legs curled tightly around the rock's rounded edge.

"Starfish," she said. She handed it to me.

I ran my finger over the creature's bumpy back. Its tentacles grabbed the rock more tightly. If we took it with us, it would die.

"We'll leave it here," I said.

Thunder rumbled in the sky. Anwa and I ran up the path to the river, attempting to outrun the storm, though we couldn't. It caught us quickly and soaked us through.

When finally we arrived at the khan, Anwa stumbled into my room and fell belly down on my mat, her arms and legs sprawling, unable to contain her exhaustion. I shed my wet robe and flopped myself onto Anwa, my belly to her back. I spread my arms and legs on top of hers.

"Sari," complained Anwa, "be still."

"I am a starfish," I giggled.

The sharp call of a heron startled the air. Anwa rolled over and hugged me to her, and it is that way we fell asleep, tentacled tightly.

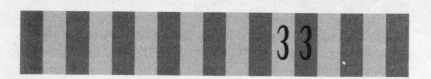

33

Light bulb.

One day, I got an idea. Though there was some difference of opinion about the significance of the idea. Dee read the whole thing as a signpost—of my unhinging. But I saw it in a different light. I felt this idea of mine brilliant, ground-breaking. I fancied myself front-runner in a vanguard. The idea in dispute came to me one night as I was soaking in the bathtub, that site of such fluid conductivity.

I had in the tub with me a dictionary, in order to do the research required for this project I was hatching. I'd been careful to make sure that the dictionary I consulted was mine, not Dee's. Lord help me if Dee caught me in the bathtub with her dictionary. I can hear her now. "It's a reference book, Codie! Not some dimestore paperback!" This time, though, Dee wouldn't see what I was up to. Or so I hoped. Dee wouldn't see because she wasn't home.

When I cracked the dictionary, it fell open to the middle, which seemed as good a place to start as any. I began scanning the pages, and jotted down all the words I came across that jibed with my idea. Gewgaw. Jimjams. Willynilly. Liblab. Loveydovey. Mangelwurzel. Mangelwurzel didn't follow exactly the pattern of the others, but it had its own quirky sound, so I kept it. When I'd collected a long list, I played around with the words, putting them together in different combinations. After a while I had what I thought might be the text of a strong first page. I copied the words carefully onto a clean sheet of paper.

"Codie!" My jig was up. Dee'd come home. She was calling my name from the hallway. "Hey, Code, where are you?" The bathroom door swung open and there she stood. My beloved. Slur-speeched and soused. Looking greatly amused, as always, at what she liked to remind me was my predictability. "As if I couldn't have guessed," she said, shaking her head.

"Close the door," I said irritably. "You're letting in all the cold air."

Dee took her time doing what I asked. When she came in, she flipped down the lid of the toilet and sat on it. Then she toed off her shoes and set her feet on the lip of the tub.

"Got to rest these dogs," she said. "Maybe I should soak 'em." She dipped one foot into the bathwater and skimmed it across the surface to splash me.

"Hey!" I cried. "Get those dirty dogs out of my clean water!"

"Wha'd you say?" Dee snorted. Now she was set to make fun of the way I talked.

"You heard me."

" 'Get those dirty dogs out of my clean water'?" Dee repeated this in the whitest voice she could muster. "You're too much. Can't even say 'dogs,' can you? Out your mouth sounds like you're talking about doilies."

"Maybe I like to say it my way."

"You know, Code," she said, diverting the focus, as she was so adept, "you and me, we're going to be some funny old ladies together. When we're eighty and counting, we're going to be walking down some street still squawking away at each other like two nasty-tempered crows."

Promises, promises.

"Hey," she said abruptly. She'd spotted the piece of paper I had in my hand. "What you got there, the ballerina story?" Another raw nerve.

"Which you never commented on, by the way."

"Well . . . that's because I've been thinking about it."

"Oh yeah? And what've you been thinking?"

Dee took a long time answering. Stumped her there, I had. "I've been thinking . . . ," she said. Stalling. For inspiration. "I've been thinking that you're looking awful cute in that bathtub there. I may have to jump your bones."

This was one of Dee's tactics, sex as distraction. Believe me, by that time I was wise to every trick. So what I said was, "Fat chance I want you in my bathwater. All you'll do is churn it up."

Challenge enough for Dee. In seconds flat she had her clothes off and was in the water, leaning over, trying to kiss away the rumblings that presaged my mounting anger. Though her kissing didn't last long. Because there wasn't enough room for Dee to stretch her legs. And the water was too hot. Or too cold.

"Not wet enough?" I suggested.

"What is it with this faucet keeps stabbing me in the back?" she complained. No, there was nothing got Dee agitated faster than a bath drawn for soothing. I made a mental note to buy a bottle of bubble bath for her birthday. As a joke.

"So, come on," she said, "tell me what you're working on."

It must've been the kissing that softened me. I've always been a sucker for kisses, and Dee's were sweet, like some memory of home. I gave a glance at the paper in my hand and on impulse, however ill-considered, decided to share it with Dee. "It isn't the ballerina story," I said. "It's a piece called 'Abracadabra.' " I hadn't actually known that that would be the title until I said so. "Want to hear it?" I asked.

"Sure."

Wet and naked as I was, I sat up tall. I cleared my throat to indicate the importance of what I was about to read, and caught Dee's eye to ensure her attention. Then I read what I'd written, the words strung together like pearls on catgut. "Willynilly, loblolly, lickspittle, liblab. Gimcrack, jimjams, clapperclaw." After which I stopped. Because that was it. The sum total of what I'd written. At any rate, so far.

"It's text for a picture book," I explained. "Each page will have some words strung together like this, just a few. And they won't make any sense together, but the sounds will give a little tickle to the ear. The meaning isn't important, see. It's the sounds I'm after."

Dee furrowed her forehead. "But what'll the story be?" she asked.

"No," I said. "No story. It's just the words."

"But they don't make any sense."

"I just said they don't."

Dee considered. "This is for children?"

I stopped Dee short to suggest to her that the way she was deliberately being thick about my intent was not the most helpful way to go about discussing someone's work. Dee answered back that she wasn't being thick at all, insisted that the only sin she was guilty of was trying to make sense. "And where's the sin in that?" Now, me, I've always been a reasonable person. Able to recognize that, in this case certainly, the text I'd written might be something of an acquired taste. The string of words was short; they barely hinted at the scope of my vision. So I decided it might clarify the piece if I gave Dee a second exposure. I read it again. "Willynilly, loblolly, lickspittle, liblab. Gimcrack, jimjams, clapperclaw."

"But they're not even words," said Dee.

"Of course they are."

"Jimjams?" Dee asked incredulously, seizing on the one word she might well have recognized. "Jimjams?" I handed Dee the *Webster's.* She paged through the J's. " 'Jimjams.' " She'd found it. " 'An overwrought condition. Delerium tremens.' " Dee laughed out loud.

"Okay, okay," I said. I tried to grab back the dictionary, but Dee held tight. " 'Clapperclaw,' " she read gleefully, flipping forward. " 'To scold, revile; to claw with one's nails.' *Ha!*" There was nothing more annoying than Dee thinking she'd gained ground. "There's no story here!"

"As I already explained to you," I said, my voice betraying just how vincible I felt my position had become, "it's not the meaning of the words that's important. I picked them for their sounds."

"This is not a children's book," Dee said flatly.

"Oh, pronouncement from on high."

"I don't really think it's any kind of book, but there's no way in hell it's a children's book."

"And who asked you?"

"Don't get all huffy, Codie. I'm only trying to help."

"Well, you should listen to the way you say things ninety-nine percent of the time. It doesn't sound much like help."

"I'm just telling you that it's not a story you're writing, it's more like, I don't know, an incantation."

"Yeah, well, maybe that's what I want it to be. Words have power, sounds do."

"What, you want these kids conjuring up something?"

"They're not going to conjure anything up."

"You're the one said words have power. You're going to have these kids incanting God-knows-what."

"Incanting?" I shrieked. "Incanting?" I had her there. I opened the dictionary and looked it up. "Incantation, yes. To incant, no. There is no such verb. It's not a word."

"Who cares if it's a word?" Dee simpered, mocking me. "It's the sound I'm after. In-cant-ing." At that moment, I hated Dee, and the look I threw her must've said so and clearly. But Dee, she just looked at me cool as a beer chaser and said, "You know what, Codie? You're losing it. I think maybe you're already a goner, taken leave."

"Get out of the bathtub," I said suddenly, surprising even myself.

"Whatchu talkin'?" Barricade in black talk.

"You heard me. I said, get out of the bathtub."

Dee leaned back in the tub and smiled. Never mind that the faucet was skewering her back, she settled in as if it were the most comfortable place in the world. So I got out. I grabbed up the dictionary and my papers and paraded out of the room, my towel trailing behind me in indignant retinue.

"Hey!" Dee shouted after me. "What'd you do? You brought my dictionary in the bathtub?" This detail just dawning.

"*My* dictionary!" I wheeled around and shouted back. "*My* dictionary!"

"It sure *better* have been yours! It sure better not have been *mine!*"

I tore open the cover to flash my name where I'd written it on the flyleaf. Dee let fly some character slur the gist of which was, what's the matter with you, Codie, can't you ever take care of your things? And then I did lose it. When I heard her say that, I threw the dictionary at her. It splashed down in the bathwater and sunk like a stone.

Not a lot to deny here. Hair trigger, I'd become. At the slightest whiff of arrogance and its attendant, alcohol. In that apartment, there were skirmishes, border wars, outbreaks in every room. Though never about the issues actually stoking me. Never betraying the white-hot fire at the core. My anger, it came through the cracks.

"Really, Codie," says Wren. "You sound incredibly angry at men."

"Men?" I say. "I've been talking about Dee."

"That's beside the point." Wren looks me straight in the eye to add, "Though Dee is about as male as they come." I let this comment pass. Easy mistake for Wren to make. She's never been to bed with Dee. It's nigh impossible for Dee to pass herself off as male when I've stripped off her clothes, when I mush my face between her full breasts and catch scent of exactly what it is she has between her legs. "This man thing is a problem," Wren insists.

"Do you realize," I say, "that there's no word in this dictionary that means 'man hating'? No male equivalent to 'misogyny.' Doesn't that just say it all?" I am trying to derail Wren's train of thought, but she stays right on track.

"Something is going to have to break," she persists. "We share the planet with these guys. Can you even think of one that you like? Go ahead. Name one."

It's not so very long I pause. Not so long a time at all I take to think. "Jake," I say resolutely. "I like Jake a lot."

34

It's my guess that the thing that first raised Jake's hackles was the ice pack. The poor guy probably had to put a lot of energy into looking the other way. It must have been awfully hard pretending he didn't see when one of his employees—by this of course I mean me—was parading around the office wearing an ice pack tied around her ankle with a leg warmer.

"Tendonitis," was the answer I gave anybody who noticed and asked me what was wrong. "Of the Achilles'," I sometimes added. No cause for worry, this minor inflammation of mine. Just a little something that started acting up once I first started putting one foot in front of the other, so to speak.

The first reckoning came one morning when, ice pack in place and hobbling pointedly around the office in ballet slippers instead of shoes, I ran smack into Jake. I was on my way into the ladies' room just as he was coming out the men's. "Codie," he said. Not hello, not good morning, just my name. The way a person does when he's taken a bit by surprise. Jake was staring at my foot, and I noticed that my leg warmer was coming undone and dragging behind me on the floor. I knew that my appearance was questionably office-appropriate. For that reason I felt I owed Jake a bit more than the stock explanation I'd been handing out to others like some street-corner giveaway.

"The doctor said I have to ice it as much as I can." Limp, Codie. Worse than that. Lame.

"What's the matter with it?" asked Jake. He was staring at my foot. Not taking his eyes off.

"An old war wound." Like my daddy taught me: When at a loss, joke. "It acts up every now and again. Unpredictably. With the weather."

Jake nodded uncomprehendingly. I flashed a smile and limped into the bathroom. It occurred to me that maybe I was carrying this new role I was trying on too far. That maybe, if I really felt I needed to ice my recently inflamed tendon, I should restrict myself to doing so when I was at my desk, shielded by those sometimes useful ramparts, the office partitions. I decided that I'd definitely remove the ice pack for the editorial meeting. For the editorial meeting at the very least.

I arrived at the meeting a few minutes late. The rest of the staff was already assembled, seated around the table. The room was attentive, listening to Jake, who was talking bottom line, which meant that the meeting was well under way. There were no seats left near the door so I had to angle past Jake and squeeze down the narrow aisle to get to the one empty chair at the end of the table.

"Well." Jake stopped what he was saying to call attention to my entrance. I could feel the collective eyes of the room follow me as I made my way. "Tiny Tim," he said, after a considered pause. "So glad you could join us."

All the other editors at the table tittered. Just waiting for the chance, I'm sure. Every one of them had, at one point in the past few days or so, questioned me about my limp. No matter. I knew how to take the stage. I smiled a saccharine smile. "God bless us every one," I said. I took my seat.

The meeting proceeded harmlessly enough in its usual meandering fashion. Jake's "bottom line" gave way to a design discussion about point size, which led to Jasmine's arguing over cover concepts, which segued into another editor making a case for acquiring a young adult manuscript he waved in hand. The manuscript, as he summarized it, told the story of a techno-whiz kid who breaks into the computer files of the local florist shop. The kid looses a scandal when he threatens to go public with records documenting exactly who in town is sending flowers to whom. "Contemporary plot," the editor argued. "Lightly comic. And our list is short a 'boy' book."

When all matters had seemingly been dealt with and, normally, Jake would have dismissed the meeting, he announced, rather ominously, that he had one final item of business to discuss with us. The V.P.s upstairs, he said, had recently become concerned about the number of long distance and other calls being made from office phones. Apparently, the bill each month was quite high and whoever was in charge of this sort of thing noticed a lot of questionable calls among the listings. Calls to staff members' hometowns, calls from the mailroom to Jamaica, that sort of thing. Jamaica the island, not Jamaica, Queens.

Jake pulled a long computer printout from a file folder he'd set on the table in front of him. "What I have here," he said, "is a list, by employee, of every call that that employee has made during the past month. The list," he went on, "includes local calls as well as long distance." I was paying enough attention to notice that as Jake was saying this he was looking directly at me. I scrolled through a mental list of the phone calls I had made recently. I wasn't guilty of any hometown calls. I hadn't made those since my mother died some years back. Local calls were different. There'd been that extended call to Dee, the one in which I'd stayed on for the duration of a talk show. But that was months ago. I remembered a few times Dee called me during the day from pay phones around town and I'd called her back. But everyone in the office made personal calls. What were the V.P.s going to do, hang me at dawn?

At this point, Jake began tearing off sheets of the printout. He called out the name of the employee listed at the top of the sheet and passed the printouts down the table. Jasmine was looking over hers.

"These are all licensing calls," she said defensively. "They expect me to call the licensors, don't they? How do they expect us to do business?"

Another editor, the one who'd been pushing the techno-scam novel, exploded in outrage. "You mean they've been sur-veiling our calls without telling us? Aren't they required to warn us before instituting a policy like this? This has got to be illegal! You can't just use information like this to nail people!"

The room quieted as everyone examined his or her print-out. I was the last to receive one. Mine was four pages long. I looked around. I noticed that everyone else had only one page or, at the most, two.

"The calls are listed by phone number," Jake explained. "Which means that if you called a given number more than once, the listings for that number will be grouped together. Next to each is the date and time of the call."

I unfolded my printout. I was alarmed to see that three whole pages were taken up with one number, 976-1616, which was the number to call to get a recording of the exact time. A little something I'd taken to doing quite frequently, the evidence right there. Calling time every few minutes or so. At a certain point in the afternoon. Day upon day.

Well, if a girl's going to make a habit of sneaking out of work day after day, she'd better be careful to get the timing right.

I thought Jake might haul me across the carpet then and there, but he didn't. He dismissed the editorial meeting. I slipped guiltily past him while he was reassuring Jasmine about her calls. "Call the licensors ten times a day," he was saying. "That's not the sort of call they're concerned about."

When I got to my cubicle, the ice pack was melting all over my desk, where I'd left it when I'd taken it off. The leg warmer was sopping. I dumped the ice pack in the wastebasket. And wrung out the leg warmer there, too.

35

Let me backtrack a moment. To the day I first made my getaway from work to the ballet class, the one that had been beckoning to me right through my window. The move was something of a small, personal triumph. Craft and cunning from a girl earlier too timid to skip study hall. It happened on the day the head of the marketing department visited our editorial meeting, just the straw I'd been waiting for. No accident I happened to be wearing my leotard under my dress. I'd scouted out the route from my desk to the back elevator more times than one. Believe me, I had the route down.

During the editorial meeting, Jake called on me to report on the gorilla book—the status, the schedule, how it was coming along. "All systems are go," I said brightly, which didn't quite give Jake the specifics he was looking for, nor was it exactly true.

"Manuscript to production?" Jake asked.

I consulted the schedule I had worked out with Eva, looking for the due date. "Two weeks," I said. I hadn't really even started.

I'd like to make it clear here that I'd meant to start. Each morning I arrived at work with my take-out coffee and every intention. I'd managed to muster a fair amount of energy for the project the week Eva had jetted down from the tundra to work with me. But the real task remained. To write the thing.

In what was left of the morning's meeting, Jake turned the floor over to the person sitting to his right. "A man who needs no introduction," Jake joked, "because you all work with the guy." The man he introduced was Barker, the company's marketing whiz, a man who'd made appearances at our meetings before. The last time he'd come around, he'd tried to sell us on series, those books that reproduce themselves like cells gone malignant, the publishing biz's answer to sitcoms or soaps. He'd wanted to impress us with the marketing intelligence that, "Series are highly profitable, and the editorial time you spend developing them will be exceedingly cost effective. Much more so than time spent on single titles."

"Single titles?" I'd interjected. "You mean books?" Barker had winced, but I noticed Jake crack a smile. In spite of himself.

This time, Barker'd come to make another pitch for series and an even more directed suggestion. The marketing department, he informed us, had just concluded "a ground-breaking study," or so he billed it, in which they'd tracked the sales figures of juvenile titles. "What we found," he said, "is that books with certain words in the title sell remarkably well. These words are a hook, and one well-placed word can snare a whole market. We've found one word that, on the strength of its presence alone, swings the door wide open to a whole market. The girl market. Can anyone guess what that word might be?"

"Boys," someone suggested.

"Babies."

"Ballet," I guessed.

"No," said Barker. "None of you have taken the extra leap here." He waited. None of us seemed able to make it. "The word is 'wish,' " he said.

"Wish . . . ," murmured Jasmine. She was taking notes.

"These four little letters are a magic key," Barker went on. "Work 'wish' into our titles, and we'll have cute little fillies grades one through twelve stampeding the aisles to buy our books. Look at the titles that prove the rule. *One Girl's Wish, Wish You Were Here, The Case of the Mystic Wish, Last Wish at Ocean's Edge.* Success stories, every title. The phenomenon sweeps the genres. Romance, mystery, adventure . . ."

Barker pulled out a stack of computer-generated graphs to substantiate his claim. He threw around sales figures, confounding the atmosphere with numbers. Then he said, "But we can't very well get away with putting out a list in which we've obviously manipulated every title to include the word 'wish,' now can we?" I closed my eyes. I could hear the rest coming. "So what we obviously need to do to really capitalize on the supremo sales power of the word is to create a new series, one that could generate a book a month, maybe more."

"But what would the series be about?"

"Doesn't matter. Could be about the dark side of the moon. As long as it has 'wish' in the title."

Barker leaned back, finished, and smiled. He looked smug and satisfied with himself in the way a cat does when she lays a stiff-bodied bird at your feet. I wondered if perhaps it was simply Barker's nature to view the world in terms of profit. Maybe, before me, sadly enough, was a man being true to the reaches of his self.

"Whatever happened to the old-fashioned way?" I heard myself ask aloud. "Acquiring books based on character, impelled by stories begging to be told?" This time Jake didn't smile or even hint at the possibility. Possibly right then I thought: Escape, take my chances.

To get to class, I had to pass through the mailroom and take the freight elevator. I cut through that day, and enough others afterward that the guys who worked in the mailroom no doubt suspected something, though they never said. A sly smile was the most they ever let on. "Yo, Codie," they greeted me as I wore my path, their winks trumpeting my triumph.

I can't say that my first day in class was exactly the exalted experience I'd dreamed of. When class started, I didn't even know the basics. I kept my eye trained on the teacher. "We'll begin in second position," he said. It had been a long time since I'd heard that instruction. I couldn't remember, exactly, what second position was.

The teacher's name was Will. He threw around a lot of French words, ones that rang vaguely familiar, but for which I could recall no concrete referents. When we finished the barre and the class moved, unsupported, into the center of the room, I hung toward the back, hoping to be able to follow the more complicated steps without fully participating. I was afraid that Will might notice me, that he might suddenly point at me and single me out for ridicule. "Whatever made you think you belonged in this class?" I imagined him saying. But suddenly he was standing directly in front of me, frankly scrutinizing my attempt at the exercise he'd given. "You don't have a clue what you're doing, do you?" he asked. He was smiling as he said this, though, and something about his manner intimated that we were somehow in this together. He put his hand at my elbow to show me how to curve my arms and then at my thigh to show how to turn out the leg. When he moved on to correct the next student, I glanced in the mirror and got a glimpse of the ballerina that could be, the long line of my extended leg, the sure point of my foot. Something swelled in me and it felt like a memory. The room was resonant with music from an ancient upright.

"Ballet?" Dee scoffed. This was shortly after. She'd found out what I'd been up to. And not by accident, as I make it sound. She found out because I was fool enough to confess it, as if it were a sin.

"I've been taking ballet class," I told her. "In the middle of the day. When I'm supposed to be at work. I sneak out in the afternoon and I don't come back for a good two hours."

"Girl," said Dee, "you're gonna be some broken down ballerina. You have to start that stuff when you're *eight*, not twenty-eight. And now you're going to go risking your job for this foolishness?" I guess Dee only liked me skipping out and risking my job if it was on her account.

Dee didn't talk tyranny all the time, it was just a little something she had up her sleeve, a trick she pulled out when she didn't want me straying too far. Dee made magic, all right. Her rope trick was merely a warm-up for her disappearing act.

"So, where'd you get this fool idea?" she persisted. "However did you dream up this one?"

"A little birdie told me."

"I guess you took me literally," Wren would later laugh.

"When?"

"When I told you to look in the mirror."

"Codie!" Will called out to me. "Why are you flailing your arms? *Port de bras* is not semaphore!"

Will strutted past us, we hopefuls in this motley class of beginning students, and lined us up in arabesque. "Arabesque is an exquisite step," he lectured. "There's nothing quite like it." His lips twitched into a smile before he added, "Of course, there's nothing quite like it in this room right now, either. Some sorry approximations, maybe." A little good-natured sarcasm before he turned profile and demonstrated the physical mechanics of the position himself. I watched Will closely. Will was—still is—a beautiful dancer. "A ballerina with a difference," he likes to say. Will's favorite color is black.

On the break after barre, I passed Will rummaging through the carton marked lost and found. Between two fingers he held up a sock riddled with holes. From under the pile he extracted a thin towel mottled with bleach stains. "I guess I'm not going to get rich peddling anything here," he decided. After that he pulled out the cropped ballet sweater. "Wouldn't you know?" he said. "Just my luck. The only thing worth anything in the box is pink. Pink is not my color. Give me something bolder, more alive."

"Like black?" I said, looking askance. For then, as always, Will was wearing nothing but—black tights, black leotard, black T-shirt, black ballet slippers.

"Black complements my hair," he defended himself. It was the second time that month that Will had bleached his hair, and it'd turned dry and brittle as drought. I went to touch it, but he parried my hand. "Whatever you do," he said, "don't get a match anywhere near this hair. Lord help us. We'd all go up in flames."

Despite the fact that the sweater was pink, and despite the fact that it was made for a woman and way too small, Will slipped it on. The sleeves barely covered his elbows. "Like a glove," he said, looking down to admire himself. Then, with a sudden burst of energy, he swept back into the studio, hopped up on the piano, and leaned over to whisper something to the accompanist. The accompanist smiled and, before he began to play, stretched out his arms as if he were limbering up for the concert stage.

"All right," Will challenged us, "name that tune. Which of you prima ballerinas knows what this music is?" This was something Will liked to do, set things in context, impart to us whole histories, a practice that ultimately allowed us to pretend that it was we ourselves dancing *Les Sylphides, Serenade,* or *Giselle.* The music the accompanist was playing did sound familiar to me, but I was hard-pressed to name it. There was one girl in class, though, who knew, and she called out the answer. "*La Bayadère,*" she said.

I knew enough to know that *La Bayadère* is a ballet about an Indian temple dancer who dies when her lover abandons her for another. The ballet is most notable for the opening of its fourth act, an act which takes place in the Kingdom of the Shades. In this sequence the corps dancers file onstage one at a time, and as each enters she does a very simple pattern of arabesque and *cambré port de bras,* a pattern that repeats over and over again until all the dancers have fed onstage and joined the snaking line. The effect of the cumulative pattern is rhythmic, mezmerizing, a suspension of time.

From the top of the piano Will picked up a book about ballets and waved it at us. "You'll find it in here," he said tantalizingly. "All right. Line up. Toot sweet." Will then marked for us the very steps choreographed years before and performed by generations of corps dancers, directing us to do them across the floor, to feed on as real ballerinas would, one etheric phantom at a time.

When class was over, while everyone else was filing out

the door, I lingered in the room, though I couldn't have explained why. Across the room I spied the book Will had brandished, still in its place on the piano. I went to pick it up and turned to the page Will had marked.

"Hey!" Will appeared in the doorway. "What do you think you're doing?" As if I had my hand in a verboten till.

I looked up, but the light was in my eyes, and blinded me as might an apparition. "I don't know," I answered. Though, actually, I thought I very well might.

"Catch!" yelled Will. He peeled off the sweater he'd fished from the lost and found and tossed it to me. I caught it against my chest.

"Don't you want it?" I asked.

"Not my color," he said. "Pink. Looks more like yours."

After class that day, when I got back to the office, there were five phone messages left on my desk. "Dee called," said the first. "Dee called," the second. "Dee called." Et cetera. The receptionist who'd taken the messages had written them on little pink slips and had noted the time at the top of each one. Anyone with an eye out could see that I'd been gone for the better part of the afternoon. The office phone always figuring to expose me one way or another.

As I stood there, slips guiltily in hand, Jasmine peered around my partition.

"Quick question," she said. I stuffed the pink slips in my pocket. But before Jasmine could even ask me what it was she wanted, the phone rang.

"Excuse me," I said. It was Dee.

"Where've you been?" Dee asked gruffly.

"A meeting."

"I thought those meetings you all have are first thing in the morning."

"Today was different," I said, not exactly a lie.

Dee's voice was muffled by the sounds of traffic behind her. I knew she must be calling from a pay phone, some corner somewhere, could've been any borough, since her job took her far and wide. I never did figure out what it was exactly that made her then and there start to suspect. It might've just been too alarming, someone breaking free, someone you've made a pact with doing something outside the rules.

Jasmine lingered in the doorway of my cubicle, listening in on our conversation. I was worried that she might've come looking for me earlier, before I'd returned, and seen the mounting pile of my messages. I even worried that there might be a conspiracy afoot, that Jasmine might be a spy, plotting to gather evidence against me and hand me over to the corporate authorities.

I always do manage to intuit when trouble is rounding a corner. But somehow I'm always looking the wrong way.

That night when I got home from work, Dee was sitting in wait. In one hand she held the story that I'd given her months ago, the one I'd written about the young ballerina laid waste by historical event. In the other hand she held a red pen.

"Codie!" she cried. Her eyes were aflame with something like zeal. "I've been going over your story. I think it's good."

"Yeah?" I asked suspiciously.

"Yeah. But there're also some major structural problems. So I decided to rewrite it." She waved the manuscript in front of me, the pages flashing red now, like a cape before a bull. "I think you'll like what I've done."

36

One star-spangled night my father came to fetch me from my grandmother's. My mother had returned home from her breakdown, so I was allowed to come home, too. My father packed me into the car and drove the long, level road home to Middletown. When we pulled onto the highway, he fell silent and snapped on the radio.

The station my father turned to was a classical station. The announcer introduced an Aaron Copland score, a piece distinctly Americana. I stared out the side window at the seemingly endless fields of corn standing up to the stars. In the distance, on the horizon, I could see fireworks displays. They followed us home, as if they were fixed in the heavens, stars themselves, when actually, of course, they were finite, illusory, set off by the consecutive towns we passed along the flat stretch home, farm communities all. "What's red and white and blue all over?" my father asked, the start of a joke. It was the Fourth of July.

"Wait a minute. Wait a minute," says Wren, to whom I have been telling this story. "How long did you say it took your mother to get over that breakdown?"

"Oh, I don't know. Six weeks. Eight."

"But you implied she had it sometime around Christmas."

"Christmas? Did I say that?"

"You indicated it was shortly after the Advent incident."

"This part's where I get confused."

"So how could you have been coming back on the Fourth of July?"

"Maybe it's more the *emotional* truth."

"Are you saying this is a lie?"

"Can't be. I'm not allowed to lie. My mother warned me never to tell stories."

"When was that?"

"When I tried to tell her what happened in the shower."

One evening, as I wended my way home after work—something I did slowly, in order to forestall actually reaching home (meaning Dee)—I wandered into a small boutique, beckoned off the street by a mannequin in the window. She was dressed, on the whim of some downtown stylist, in harem pants and toe shoes. As I walked in, a woman behind a counter took my bags. As claim check, she handed me a playing card. Nine of spades. I took one look and handed it right back. "I'm sorry," I said. "At the risk of sounding crazy, this card is bad luck. Would you mind giving me another?" She obliged without blinking, but still I felt compelled to excuse myself. In a stage whisper, as if I were talking about a third, quirky party over whom I had some charge, I said, child of my time, "Too much tarot." After which I pressed to the back of the store and combed through the crush of clothes on the carousel rack.

I tried on a succession of dresses, emerging from the dressing room in each to execute a few quick and contained ballet steps in front of the long mirror—to determine if the skirt moved when I did *frappés*, if the cut allowed me to easily bring my leg up into *passé*. (Did it make me look like what I wanted to be?)

"A dancer?" the saleswoman asked me.

"Not professionally," I said. A little trick of mine: Imply more than you say.

I decided on a dress that was full-skirted and tulle, with a bodice tight as a leotard. As if I'd had a choice. Next to the cash register was a basket of leg warmers, impulse items, like candy bars or gum at the supermarket, so I threw in a pair, just because. But when I got home and picked up the mail, I began to suspect that nine of swords might be the fate awaiting me after all. Propped against my door was a package from my father. A box long and thin. I opened it up to find a knife inside, one I recognized. In the box my father had included a note. It said, "Your mother would've wanted you to have this." Years had passed since my mother had died.

I did the thing anyone with any life experience would do: I threw the knife away. But when Dee came home and saw it sticking blade-down in the garbage can, she pulled it out. Maybe it looked like Excalibur. Or at least as if it would come in handy.

"Hey," she said. "This is a great carving knife. It'll be perfect next time we do turkey." She rinsed the knife off and laid it in the dish drainer.

"Oh no you don't," I stopped her. "The knife goes."

When I was a child, my mother had said two things about that knife. The first, sharp and pointed, she'd said to my father the night he gave it to her. "You call this an anniversary present?" I'd heard her scream. "Eight hours late to take me to dinner and you call this an anniversary present?" But a few days later, when I found the knife in the kitchen silverware drawer and asked my mother about it, what she said to my face was a different story entirely. She'd smiled, her voice sticky as a glue trap, and said, "It's new, sweetie. Isn't it nice? Your father gave it to me for our anniversary."

Any object with two faces like that is not honest. It's lying a chunk of the time, and probably a lot more than half. I didn't want the knife in my house. I didn't care if Dee did put up a fuss. As far as I was concerned, Dee had lately begun putting up a fuss about a few too many things. Like the morning she'd failed to wake up to her alarm and barked at me, "What's the matter with you? Why didn't you wake me?" Trying to make me think it was my responsibility to take on hers. Who'd she think she was, the Queen of Sheba?

Then there was the morning she'd gone into the kitchen and discovered there was no coffee ready in the pot. For this she woke me up out of a sound sleep. "Codie," she said, "*I'm* the one who has to be to work early. If you finish the pot of coffee, make a new one so there's always some for me."

"But I finished it yesterday morning."

"Doesn't matter. Make it whenever. I only have time to heat up the coffee. I don't have time to make it."

"Well, if you're the one wants it, why can't you make it the night before?"

"I told you! I don't have time!"

So whoever gave her the idea I was the wife?

Things were getting a little unreasonable around that household, and it was starting to wear thin. If I were in the mood for theatrics, Will's brand was a lot more entertaining.

"Codie!" Will called out to me as he scrutinized my fledgling attempts at a pirouette. "I only have one thing to say to you. Keep your day job!" Which was, of course, not the only thing he had to say to me at all. He went on to show me how to shift my weight, pull up on my leg, how to spot. "I love you dearly," he said to me, "but day after day I hound you not to look at your feet. If you don't keep your focus up and out, I'm going to blind you. You're going find yourself out on Eighth Street selling pencils."

I'm not sure why, but nights, when I'd go home, I'd often tell Dee about class. Maybe I did it to spark her interest in me, let her know that Will was paying a lot of attention to me. But I don't think Dee liked to hear about somebody paying me attention, someone who wasn't her. Mostly, when I talked about ballet, she changed the subject. And when I'd set myself up in front of the mirror in our living room to practice whatever steps I'd learned that day, Dee'd set about trying to distract me. She'd call me in to look at what she was watching on TV, or she'd pull out the story she was working on—a little bagatelle about gangland murder—and insist that I read it then and there.

One night when Dee and I had ordered in take-out Chinese, she started up yelling at me about the way I'd taken to dressing for work—black tights for stockings, cropped dance sweaters instead of a blazer. She launched into a lecture on the difference between costume and clothes. I ate quickly, accelerated the trail of my chopsticks as if that might fan the sting out of listening to my lover tell me I didn't know how to dress myself. In the carton, next to my plate, were two fortune cookies. I studied the cookies knowing full well that one of them held my fate. I began to pick up one of them, had my fingers on it in fact, but at the last minute changed my mind and chose the other. I cracked it open and read the fortune. It said, "There is growth in pain."

"What kind of fortune is this?" I railed. "Cookies are not supposed to dispense doom!"

"Let me see that." Dee grabbed the slip of paper from me and read the fortune. "Well," she said, "this doesn't specify that you're going to be in pain. It's just a proverb. All it says is that there's growth in pain."

"Yes, but it *implies* I'll be in pain."

Dee shrugged and opened up the other cookie. She read aloud the fortune that was hers by default. It said, "Your dearest wish will come true."

"That was supposed to be mine," I said sullenly. Dee threw me a skeptical look. "It really was supposed to be mine. I almost took that cookie. That was the cookie I was first drawn to, but I went against my instincts."

One thing about Dee, she was tolerant when I whined. "How old are you now?" she asked.

"Four," I admitted.

"Try two," said Dee. What I was occasionally reduced to.

No doubt I was just scared, getting a pain-promising fortune so close on the heels of a knife in the mail and a card in the suit of swords. "I'll protect you," Dee promised, when I tried to explain.

There. Nothing bad could really happen.

It was right around that time that I came across a slip of paper with a note scribbled in my hastiest hand. "The Littlest Harem Girl," it said, "A Cautionary Tale." It was the note I'd initially jotted down for myself when I'd first got the notion to work the idea into a children's story. I knew I'd gone on to take more pages of notes, ones I'd recorded as I blissfully soaked up solvents in the bathtub, and I rooted around to find those notes, too. But for the life of me, I couldn't locate them. Not in any of the places I'd have been likely to put them.

I was late to meet Dee at the coffee shop on the corner, so I set off, feeling vulnerable, frightened somehow. A vague premonition was beginning to haunt me, events suddenly threatening to spiral. The day was blustery. As I walked down the sidewalk, a bubble gum wrapper gusted past my nose and fell at my feet. I picked it up. Most of the wrapper was printed with a comic, but squeezed beneath a rule at the bottom was a fortune. "What you think can't happen can," it read.

Dee noticed right away that I arrived under a dark cloud. When she asked me what was wrong, I showed her the fortune. "What does that even mean?" she asked.

"I don't know." I shook my head. "But it doesn't sound good."

That night at home I found myself beset by a fierce and relentless anxiety that came on with the force of a fever. I paced our apartment, edgy, antsy, rattling the bars. Thinking it would allay my fears, I took a walk to the newsstand on the corner to consult my horoscope. The monthly magazines lining the walls were all agreed. Difficult aspects, dissension and trial, ruler in retrograde. I turned homeward apprehensively to report my destiny to Dee. As I waited to cross the street, a car sped by. Its license plate read DAETH. The anagram barely disguised.

"Come here, baby," said Dee, in an unexpected offer of solace. I was standing at the window. I'd drawn the curtains tightly, and was peering through a slit. Dee took me in her arms. She smoothed my hair and kissed me. The next night she came home with presents for me, a bottle of Wild Turkey and something wrapped in a box.

"Presents?" I said. "What for?"

"No reason."

I savored the heft of the present in my hands.

"Are you going to open it or what?" pressed Dee.

I tore back the paper, gold as flame.

"You're going to love it," Dee blurted out. "It's very you. I couldn't resist."

Inside the box was a clay pottery vase, chipped, with cuneiformlike pictures of dancing girls bordering its rim.

"It's beautiful. Where's it from?"

"Second Avenue."

"I mean originally."

"Second Avenue. It's not really old, it's faux ancient. That's what the woman at the store called it."

"Oh yeah?"

"Right away I thought of you."

I set the vase on the table and opened the bottle of Wild Turkey, which Dee had probably thought was a present for her, but which I was in the mood to make mine. I drank a tumblerful before dinner, another after, and downed a third while I was doing the dishes. All that alcohol prejudicing my system had me slopping dishwater all over the kitchen floor and deceived me into thinking it would be a good idea to practice my ballet at the same time as I was washing the dishes. I took a running leap and tried a *grand jeté* in a space not grand enough at all, slipped on the wet floor, and fell on my hip. Pain shot through me, pain so sharp that at first I couldn't raise myself up.

Dee ran in from the other room. I picked myself up quickly and did a turn in attitude for her, my hip still smarting. Dee applauded.

The irony of the story is that, as I grew more frightened, Dee seemed to soften. She even began throwing compliments my way. One night, when I went up to *passé relevé*, she grabbed me around the waist and hugged me to her like a looking doll. She told me what a pleasure it was to watch me dance around the apartment. She called me her beauty, her little slip of a thing. She called me her ballerina.

"You're mooning at me," she noticed, pleased.

It was true. Basking in Dee's warmth and light, all my fears seemed groundless. Somehow, at last, I found the voice to bring up directly a rather delicate concern I had, one that had been worrying me, actually, for quite a long time. Close-held in Dee's arms as I was, it felt as if I might be telling just another bedtime story.

"Baby," I said, "there's something I need to talk to you about."

"Yeah?"

"Let me just start off by saying that there are a lot of things I really love about you. I appreciate all your many good qualities, really I do."

"Cut to the chase."

"I love you, Dee. It's just that sometimes in this relationship, sometimes . . . well, sometimes I feel . . . stepped on."

"Stepped on?"

"I guess I mean . . . I feel . . . a little . . . well, a little like I'm being sort of bulldozed. You're a very powerful personality. And I love that," I added quickly. "But sometimes I feel . . . I guess what I feel is that your energy sort of . . . well, that it overpowers mine."

"What are you talking about? You have loads of energy."

"No, I don't mean energy like energetic. I mean *energy*. Who you are. How you move through life. You have a particularly fiery energy, you know? And sometimes I just feel that it scorches the um . . . the quieter energy that is me."

"You're not quiet," said Dee.

"No, what I mean is that I . . ."

"And I don't know why you're saying you have no energy. Think of all the things you do during the day."

"I'm not talking about ener—"

"You have plenty of energy. Where did you get this idea of yourself?"

"What I'm trying to say is—"

"Codie, I never realized what a low opinion you have of yourself. You're much more energetic than you think."

Dee and I, we didn't always speak the same language. Wide gulfs would rend us asunder. But before we went to sleep that night she grabbed me around the waist and pulled me to her, which felt like love.

The next night Dee didn't come home.

37

She was supposed to be having dinner with her friend Earl, and promised to be back at a reasonable hour. As the hour drew late, to pass the time, I brewed up a cup of hot chocolate. I was still looking forward to Dee's return. I was thinking that, when she walked in, I'd waylay her, run my lips over the smoothness of her cheeks. Just for starters.

All the world cozy as cocoa.

But Dee didn't get home at the reasonable hour she'd led me to expect. She didn't get home until sometime after three a.m. She called my name loudly from the outside hallway, and when she came through the door she let it bang shut so there'd be no one in the building wouldn't know her late hour. "Kiss me," she said. She crawled into bed with her shoes still on. I wasn't so keen on kissing Dee right then, but she didn't notice. She grabbed me to her and waggled her thick tongue inside my mouth. It wasn't only beer she tasted of, I couldn't tell what all.

"Where've you been?" I asked when she let me go.

"Planning our future, baby," she said. This was the lie I wanted to believe.

"Our future?"

"We're moving to Seattle."

"What are you talking about?"

"Codie, Seattle is the town for us. The place is crawling with dykes. I have it on reliable say-so."

"Where were you tonight? What are you talking about?"

"Ruby and Jinx say we're going to love it there."

"Ruby and Jinx? Who are they?"

Ruby and Jinx, it turned out, were two lesbians from Seattle on vacation in the Big Apple who'd had the questionable fortune to be Dee's last fare of the night. "Since I was knocking off anyway," Dee told me, "I decided to show them the town."

"I thought you were supposed to see Earl," I said.

"Earl? I'm not speaking to Earl."

"What do you mean you're not speaking to Earl?"

"I've ex-ed him out of my life."

"Since when?"

"Since he betrayed me."

"Betrayed you? What'd he do?"

"I don't want to talk about it."

Lost things. Sometimes Dee lost things. Like friendships of long-standing. Flowed right out of her life, they did, and other things flowed in. Like lesbians from Seattle. Dee went on to tell me that she took Ruby and Jinx bar hopping in the Village. She rattled off a string of clubs with startling names like Clit Clique and Burning Bush. She raved about Ruby and Jinx, about how much fun they were, how game. "They said that when we move out there we can stay with them until we find a place."

"What are you talking about, when we move out there?"

"You don't want to?" Dee pulled away from me and thrust her lower lip into a petulant curl.

"We never even discussed this. You can't just come home and snap your fingers and say we're moving to the other side of the country. This is our home. Moving is something we'd have to talk about for a while. A long while."

"You discuss things to death!" This exploded out of Dee without warning. "You never just *do* anything, Codie. You always have to analyze and pick apart. I will *not* live like that!"

Dee pulled all the covers out from where they were tucked

in at the bottom of the bed, and wrapped them around her, mummy-like, a cocoon.

"Your shoes," I said, my voice cold and hard.

"What?"

"Take off your shoes."

Not long after the fight with Dee I came upon two bubble gum wrappers with messages altered just slightly from the first, confounding the message of the original. "What you think can happen can," said one. The other, "What you think can happen can't." I studied these as I had the other, but couldn't make head nor tail. Neither did I find direction in my horoscope, though I'd now developed the habit of stopping at the corner newsstand every morning to consult the dailies. I even paid another visit to the psychic. The psychic told me that Dee and I had lived together other lives, all right. She told me a lot of things. But no one—not the psychic, not the dailies—no one at all predicted anything about any headband.

I think it might have been all the talk about sperm donors that threw me off. Dee reporting to me daily that this one had volunteered to be the father, that that one said he'd gladly stick his dick in her any day. Clever ruse, effective smokescreen. Dee's crafty way of getting me to look in that ever-tempting wrong direction. Dee had me on the lookout, see, for a black male. And I followed the scent, suspicious of any I saw walking down the street. Soon as I'd spot some guy brown-skinned and half-attractive I'd worry that Dee had already made his acquaintance. Maybe in some bar, maybe in the cab. I'd worry that they'd got to talking and that Dee had "interviewed" him as a "candidate," as she liked to put it.

Yes, ma'am, I had it bad. Bad enough that one day I nearly introduced myself to the guy sitting next to me on the bus. This guy was young, black, and good-looking. He pulled a book out of his pocket and I strained to see what it was. *The Rustle of Language*, the title read. By Roland Barthes. Smart. Dee had said she was looking for smart. I was so sure that this fellow must be the one, the sperm cast, the deed done, that I had to stop myself from putting my hand on his shoulder then and there. "I'm Codie," I wanted to say. "Dee's girlfriend. I'm sure she told you about me." I'd flash a pandering smile, chatter on. "I just want you to know that I'm the one who'll be the other parent, so don't worry about a thing. This baby will be in excellent hands."

The threat to me felt that absolute, and so audacious, that I thought that at any moment it might walk right up and take a seat next to me on the bus crosstown.

So the headband came as something of a surprise.

"What's this?" I asked. A red headband. It was springy and covered in grosgrain ribbon.

"What's what?" asked Dee.

"This." The headband was sitting on the nightstand. It was the kind of thing I remembered from high school, worn by girls with sunny smiles and long blond hair.

"I don't know," said Dee. She shrugged.

"Well, where'd it come from?"

"It's not mine."

"Obviously it's not yours, but it's not mine either, so where'd it come from?"

"Beats me." Dee could lie to the Lord.

"Well, I think it's very peculiar then that it's on our nightstand, don't you?"

"I don't know. Maybe I found it in the back of the cab."

"So you *did* bring it in?"

"I don't remember."

"How can you not remember if you brought something into our house?"

"I'm not like you, Codie! I don't remember how many Rice Krispies were in my bowl at breakfast! When you gonna stop bugging me about every little thing?"

Oh, Dee remembered what she brought into the house, all right. And it wasn't just a headband. One day, not long after, I came home early from work on account of Jake having fired me. And that day I found out as well. I was right, too. Blond. That kind of headband always belongs to a blond.

39

"The adagio's looking leaden," said Will. "I'd like to try to get the quality up. At least to wooden."

Taking Will's class in the middle of my workday afternoons. Each day this was engraving itself as ever more risky routine.

"You wouldn't talk in monotone," Will was saying, "so why do you dance in it? Quicken the connecting steps, suspe-e-e-end the extensions. What I'm talking here is phrasing."

Language. Always language. Reminding me (a little disconcertingly) about the small matter of the job I allegedly held, the one that paid my rent. Day after day, as I'd worn the stealthy path from work to class, I'd begun to feel a little like a sneak. Like some creature of darkness, a mole, a weasel, an animal that's been shamed into snitching pleasure, not one who can come right out and claim it by birthright.

"No!" Will was shouting. "When you jump, don't thud down and stay there. Come down *through* your foot and use the floor to spring back up. Imagine that you're barefoot. Pretend the floor is hot sand."

It occurred to me, quite unconnectedly, that maybe Dee might be right. About me jeopardizing my job.

"Codie!" Will singled me out. "With *glissades*, the dynamic is different. Stay on one level, *skim* the floor. As if you're carrying a basin of water that might easily spill. You're carrying it forward to a king, let's say." Will's eyes glistened impishly as he cautioned, "If you spill it? High stakes. It's your head."

Call it intuition, call it prescience, but a resolution suddenly flashed to my consciousness—that I ought to lay off dance for a while. Until I could figure out a way to make an honest living for myself and dance as well.

After class, Will braced himself to stretch out his calves against one of the pillars that rather gratuitously studded the back of the studio. I picked up my bag and walked over to him.

"This place reminds me of something," I said. "Or maybe it's you that reminds me of someone."

"Oh yeah?"

"I get sparks of déjà vu here. They flash and then, zap!, they're gone."

"Really? What triggers them?"

"I don't know." I let the thought trail off, a message in a bottle tossed to the waves for answer who knew where or when. Then I told Will what I'd really come over to say, that I was thinking maybe I'd be taking a break from class for a while.

"What are you doing, jumping ship?"

"You know, I do have a job I'm supposed to be at."

"So you say."

"That day job you advised me not to quit."

"What I don't understand, girl, is why they haven't fired you already."

"You and me both."

"What is this so-called job you have? I hope you're not in charge of national security."

"Books," I said. "Children's books."

"Oh, yeah?" he asked, interest perked. He mugged, angling to profile. "How I long for some rampion," he said. "From the witch's plot next door."

"Rapunzel," I guessed.

"Take the girl into the forest and kill her," he said, on to the next. "Deliver me her lung and liver."

I named the game: Mad Mothers through the Ages. "Snow White," I fired back. Two for two.

"Fetch me a pumpkin," Will continued, a muddle of fairy tale cues.

"That one's not a mother," I objected.

"Of sorts, it is," Will said, grinning. "I'm a fairy."

"What?" I wasn't sure I caught his drift, or even heard him right.

"I'm your fairy *god*mother. Come to lead you back to dance."

Will entwined his fingers in mine and I took that opportunity to pull him to the long window at the end of the studio. "There," I said resolutely. "There's where I work." I pointed across to my desk, the lamp above it blazing optimistically, as if to light work that might actually take place. I was unnerved to notice also that my cubicle was not empty. There was someone standing in front of my desk—Jake. And he was staring out the window directly at me, just as I was staring at him.

"Oh shit," I said.

"What?" asked Will. He saw me blanch.

"I'm cooked."

Jake didn't give me a warning or put me on probation or anything like that. He asked, "This is not the first time, is it?" and I didn't answer because I couldn't tell him any different. I knew he knew. And he knew I knew that he knew. "You've had one foot out the door for a while now," he said. "Why haven't you just quit?"

"I thought about it," I admitted. "But I chickened out every time."

"I'll tell you what," said Jake. "You're fired. You haven't left me a lot of leeway here and this way at least you'll get unemployment."

Jake gave me two weeks' notice, but that afternoon I left early. I headed home because I'd started crying. I guess I was crying because of the irony of it all and also because nothing in life was going the way I'd planned.

Neither did I expect to find Dee at home in the middle of the day. She was supposed to be driving her cab, cruising, maybe she just got thrown off by the slang sense of the word. But there they were in bed, Dee and some blond, the blond looking not exactly as I'd pictured from the headband. This girl had a tattoo on her upper arm and a studded leather jacket slung over the arm of the chair. I got one glimpse of the sordid scene and backed out the door of the apartment. Dee called after me, but without much conviction. I heard the blond giggle. I heard Dee say to her, "Just a minute, baby. I'll be right back."

I headed for the subway because it seemed like the best way to get far away fast. I knew I had a jump on Dee. I was already wearing my pants, and she'd have to pull hers on. When I started down the steps of the station, I heard footsteps behind me. Much as I wanted to get away, there was probably some part of me half hoping. Suddenly, from up above, a bottle came hurtling into the stairwell and shattered on the steps in front of me. I covered my face to shield myself from the glass that shot up like shrapnel from a shell. I looked up to see a man leaning over the bannister, leering at me. Drunks a dime a dozen and on parade.

I rode the rails a while, but eventually I got tired and headed back home. Dee wasn't there when I got there. She came back sometime between midnight and morning. I sat up in bed listening to her fumbling with her keys in the locks. She dropped them a couple of times. She kicked the door and cursed. When finally she listed into the bedroom, she looked surprised that I was there. Then, before I even had a chance to say a word, she started yelling at me. "*You*, Codie! *You* have driven me to sleep with other women!" Underscoring it with the accusation that I never loved her. This, she shouted to the walls, to the ceilings, and to anyone beyond them whom she'd happened to wake up. She told me she couldn't stand it anymore, watching me waste my life, told me she wanted me to know that she wasn't about to let me drag her down as well.

"I'm going to have my baby, Codie," she said resolutely. "I know you don't respect that, and so there's just no room for you in my plans. I've got my future to think of, my child, my responsibilities as a mother."

Some exit line. After she delivered it, Dee lurched out of the bedroom and toppled onto the living room couch, a bit of choreography I witnessed through the door. She hugged the cushion by the arm and, within seconds, was asleep. This I knew because I heard her snoring. The sort of snores I'd recognize anywhere. The snores of someone who's sloshed.

The next morning, when she stumbled slit-eyed off the couch, Dee announced to me that she was moving out.

"Where are you going?" I asked.

"What do you care?" Dee shouted. She called me names I won't repeat. "If you cared anything at all about me in the first place, this would never have happened!"

I told Dee I thought it was a little ridiculous for her to be shouting me down when she was the one who'd been fucking somebody else in our bed, but Dee's response was to shout even louder. It was clear to me what was happening. Dee was ripping out of my life with gale force. She was leaving and I couldn't stop her. I could sooner have lassoed a tornado, changed the course of the moon, held back the tides. Dee's nature. I never did get a handle. In one week's time she had all of her things out of our apartment. She left only a slip of paper with her telephone number, no address. "I've forwarded my mail," she said, "but give this to anyone who calls."

The night she moved out the last of her belongings, I didn't quite know what to do with myself, so I switched on the TV. And what did I chance on but *The Newlywed Game*. There was Bob Eubanks, smiling, as if nothing in the world had altered. He was asking the wives this question: "Wives, since you've met your husband, in what way would you say he's proved perfidious?" The first wife didn't know the meaning of the word, and asked what it meant. Bob flashed a smug smirk to the audience and said that, according to the rules of the game, he wasn't allowed to explain anything, all he could do was repeat the question. "Perfidious . . . ," the wife murmured, stalling for time. "Well, Bob," she offered hopefully, "yesterday he cleaned out the bird cage."

I left the house to wander the streets, hoping for more reality there, or at least a blanketing comfort. Somewhere in the course of my wandering, I can't say on which street or in which section, an old woman stepped out of a darkened doorway and touched her hand to my arm.

"Is it day or night?" she asked.

"Night," I answered. Just that natural. As if someone had simply asked the time.

40

Anwa slipped the choker around my neck. Rubies, brilliant as blood. I kissed the bulge of her belly, and tried to impress upon her what I'd already told her numerous times, that it was not necessary she pass on to me every single gift proferred her by the Mukarrib. She snapped close the clasp.

"I take, now," she said, steel-eyed, "for two."

The roundness that had begun to show on Anwa was telling, articulating something small and dependent that had stolen inside her. Anwa whispered the news to me, then shouted it to the world. She alerted our king in the bargain. The way she chose to tell him was in kind.

One morning, as Anwa quit the Mukarrib's chamber and the night's work she'd done there, the soldiers followed her to my room. They'd grown suspicious that the bulges they'd noticed each morning beneath her robe were a bit more pregnant than befitted even her ripe belly. Under her robe, they discovered an ivory urn Anwa had indeed concealed. And that's not all. In my room they uncovered a cache of pilfered treasures. Filigreed lamps. Rings, braziers. All hoarded over the angry course of months. The soldiers had stumbled on a prize. As even the blind could see.

"Kill me!" Anwa challenged the soldiers. They didn't kill her, though. They manacled her. And would have done so to me as well, clear accomplice that I was, but Anwa shouted, "Let her free!" Anwa told the soldiers she'd lied to me, convinced them that I thought all our stores were come by honestly, presented her by the Mukarrib. "Sari knows nothing," she insisted. Which was and wasn't true.

The soldiers wrested Anwa, live and wailing, from my room. Anwa's shouts and protests drew all the women from their rooms and we fell in train behind the soldiers, the lot of us keening loudly. Our cries brought the Mukarrib to his window. He looked down upon the courtyard and shouted to the soldiers the order they already knew. "Don't kill her," he said. "She's full with my child."

"It's not your child!" Anwa called up to his window. "Not your child at all!"

"Then whose?" asked the Mukarrib.

"A sailor's."

"You're on high land, my dear."

"I consorted with plenty the day I traveled to the sea," Anwa called back. "Any one of ten could be the father. Or twenty. As Sari is my witness."

"Is that true?" the Mukarrib called down to me from his window. I looked at Anwa. I could not bring myself to see her killed.

"No," I said quietly.

"What?"

"We were there only a short while." I spoke more boldly. "She bedded with no one. Later with me."

I turned my head. Out the corner of my eye I saw the soldiers right a bamboo cage in the center of the courtyard and throw Anwa inside.

The soldiers did not beat Anwa's back, as would have been their custom, she so bent with child. They put their sticks to work, instead, on her feet. And when they finished, they herded the rest of us back to our quarters. I watched out my window. I could see the cage clearly. They'd set it in the center of the courtyard, where it was visible from most vantages in the khan. Which was, after all, the point. When at last, the stars pricked their way through the blue-black sky and night masked the day, I set to work. I draped a washing cloth around the back of my neck, filled a basin with water and hugged it to me as if it were the baby Anwa and I might raise together. Then I slipped soundlessly through the long hall and down the cold stone stairway that led to the courtyard.

Anwa's head was turned, her eyes averted. She would not look at me. When I reached through the bars and touched her arm, her muscles stiffened. I could not think what to say. It should've been something about my love for her, how deep it was, how true. Better yet I should have promised to free her. "Hold fast, Anwa," I might have said. "I'm executing a plan." Instead, the words that sprung from my lips were a feeble attempt at humor. "Anwa," I said, "look at the stars. They look like so many blemishes dotting a young girl's face, do they not?" Anwa showed no sign she heard me. I wondered if somehow the beating had rendered her deaf. But when I dipped the cloth to wet it in the basin and asked her, "Give me your feet," she shifted and brought her feet, which she had hid behind her, out to the edge of the bars.

At the sight of them my voice caught in my throat. Anwa's feet were caked in blood. In places the blood was dried and brown, hardened into a crust. Other wounds were still open, deep and glistening. I washed Anwa's feet gently, at first not even touching them, just wringing water to soften the hardened top layer. When I did touch the cloth to her feet, Anwa did not cry out, though it must have pained her greatly. She closed her eyes, and in the bright moonlight I saw tears pool on the thick black lashes that Anwa had closed tightly against the world.

"Anwa," I whispered when I finished. "Bring your lips to the bars. Let me kiss you." She did not respond. I touched my fingers to my own lips to plant a kiss on them, then I reached my hand through the bars and delivered the kiss to Anwa's lips. She surprised me by taking my fingers in her mouth and sucking. She sucked hard like a hungry baby at a dry teat. Then, turning her head to look straight at me, she bit down into my finger, her teeth breaking the skin. When she let go, she held my gaze defiantly, as if she expected me to respond, as if what she'd taken, simply, was her turn in conversation and now it was mine. But this time it was I who averted my eyes, frightened by the steeled glint I saw in hers. I took the basin to the river and emptied Anwa's blood into its waters. I hoped the blood would somehow tell the river what had happened. I hoped the river would, in some way, advise me what to do.

I fell to my knees. There came no answer.

Just the rustle of the wind through the rushes on the banks.

In the days Anwa was caged outside, the khan was visited by a squall. The storm was unexpected; the season for monsoon had already passed. Nonetheless, the rains stayed upon us for days, seemingly ceaseless. I wondered if Anwa might have conjured up the storm—to express the fury she couldn't.

During the rains I visited Anwa each night to bring her food I sneaked from dinner. Scraps of flatbread, crescents of melon, whatever I could palm with sleight of hand. Each night I swabbed her feet with unguent of myrrh. Days? Days were helpless. I kept watch out my window in vigil, a vigil that grew each day more sympathetic. One day, I found myself reaching down to touch something between my breasts, something that wasn't between mine at all, but between hers. The amulet. The one made of abalone, given her by her brother. . . .

Xam. Xam was the answer. Why hadn't I thought it before?

That night, when I visited Anwa, I asked her for the amulet, and just in time. Someone must've noticed the melon rinds and seeds of grapes that littered the stone outside her cage. Someone must've suspected that Anwa was being cared for, for, the very next night, a guard was posted at her cage. And guards were posted there night and day thereafter.

The night I got the amulet, I slept with it around my neck. Which is how I carried it early the next morning as I stole out the unguarded gate and down the back path of the khan. A pale light broke through the fronds of the date palms that lined the path to the river. I turned in the direction Anwa had led me the day we'd walked to the sea. After I'd walked some distance, I was surprised to notice that the storm was not following me. Away from the khan, the sky was clear. Furious as they were, the rains were localized, contained over our city, supporting my suspicions. I hadn't time to dawdle, though, or ponder my observation. I had help to ask for, something to deliver.

The wharf, when I reached it, was bustling. The ships I'd remembered were not in the harbor, replaced by others. Any girl, however naive, knows that the nature of ships is to come and go, but I was nonetheless disoriented, expecting to see the ship on which I'd first seen Xam. When it was not there, I wasn't sure how to proceed. Far beyond me, the sea and the sky met in a thin line blurred by heat and haze. I sat in a tangle of thick-roped fishing net abandoned at the edge of the sea. The surf wet the hem of my robe and sopped my sandals.

As I turned back to the higher slope of beach, I spied a column of men marching. The men were carrying crates, moving cargo, apparently, from one end of the shore to the other. One of the men stopped when he saw me. He set down his crate and called out to me. It was Ta'ib, the sailor I'd met on the boat with Xam. When I recognized him, I ran up and held out the amulet for him to see. "Xam," I said. "Where is Xam?" He pointed far out to the water, which I'd already suspected was true.

We did not talk for long. The man who was overseeing the transfer of cargo shouted at Ta'ib, I assumed it to be an order to move on. Quickly I held my hands up in two vertical fists, in mime of a captive grasping bars. "Anwa," I said, to explain. I slipped the amulet over my head and gave it to Ta'ib, who fastened it around his own neck before he picked up the crate he had set down and moved on. As he fell back into line, Ta'ib called something back to me. I did not know what it was, but

I took momentary heart from it, as far-fetched as that seemed.

When Ta'ib passed from sight, it suddenly seemed nothing more than silly for me to have come all this way to deliver a worthless shell on a leather thong. I began to wonder what rendered me so foolish as to think I could help Anwa in any way, much less save her. There was now nothing for me to do but go back to the khan, back to the dark, dead nights in which I was now restrained even from visiting the one I loved. I kicked the shells at my feet. I headed back the way I'd come.

In the khan I sat and watched the days pass, days long and lifeless. I had no appetite and stopped eating, no longer even attended meals as I had when palming food to bring to Anwa. While I fasted, Anwa grew rounder, but it was with child. In that time, the khan was quiet, dampened, everyone huddled against the storm that still, unexplainedly, raged. The only one not quiet was Anwa. Above the din of the rain and thunder, Anwa began making sounds not quite human. They sounded like howls, wafted in through my window, became for me as much a part of the atmosphere and every bit as soaking as the rain.

The morning the storm suddenly ceased, I woke up to an eerie quiet in which there was sound neither of rain nor of Anwa's anguish. I jumped to my window and saw the door of the cage swung open and Anwa gone. The guard who'd drawn the lot of that night's sentry was splayed on the stones of the courtyard in a pool of his own blood. I ran out the hareem and down to the courtyard. In the guard's heart was a pearl-handled knife, one I'd seen before, pulled from the sheath of someone's sea-salted hair. It was Xam's knife! He'd come! Anwa'd been saved! I started, insensibly, to run. My instinct was to catch up with them, stow away on a boat with Anwa and Xam and sail to a different land altogether. I might even have made it, but for the morning guard who'd come out to replace the night. He took off after me and caught me up. He put his own knife to my throat.

"Murderer!" he said. "You've killed the guard!"

"It wasn't me!"

"Then who? Where's Anwa? You've set her free!"

"Would that I had," I spit out defiantly. "Would that it was I who loosed her from her cage!"

A guard found dead and me caught running from the scene. The man had no choice but to take me captive. He did not throw me in a courtyard cage, though. Instead, I was delivered to a dark cell in the bowels of the khan, a part of the complex I'd not even known existed. I can't tell how many days I passed in that tomb, for there was no window to admit the sun, and it was every hour dark. I marked time solely by visits from the jailer, who each day brought me food, food that smelled, at best, like slops for animals or the fouled fur of animals themselves. Alone in the dark, with no one and not much of comfort to touch, I ran my hand over the rough surface of the crude bricks that walled the cell. Stubs of straw bristled out of the brick as if they were whiskered. Sometimes other whiskers brushed my hand. Live ones. Rats. I wondered how many and if they were diseased, though after a while in the cell I lost the faculties for wondering much of anything at all. The only thoughts that kept me alive were of Anwa, and of what I would do when finally I was freed. I knew I wouldn't be held forever. Even to penalty there must be an end. I knew they'd either set me free or kill me.

One day, the same man who'd brought me bowls of slop now unchained my door. At first I didn't move from the corner in which I crouched, not knowing if what I'd be walking to would be my death, or my life, which would seem like death.

The jailer took me by the arm. He led me back to my room in the hareem, supporting me, as I was shaky on my feet. The sunlight hurt my eyes. I squinted at the light and blinked at my room, which was not quite as I'd left it. The covers of my bed were neatly arranged, though I knew when last I'd left I'd thrown the covers back over my mat in haste. I was also surprised to see that on my mat there lay a cat. She was sleeping. Near her was a crude dish filled with fish scraps. Someone had been feeding her. Later I was told that she'd appeared in my room shortly after I'd been taken away and that she'd stubbornly resisted all attempts to put her out. It was as if she'd set herself there to hold my place, one live thing standing in for an absent other, a marker in a text.

When my jailer deposited me in my room, Iman appeared, though I hadn't noticed her following us. As she approached me, I became aware of what I must look like, and how I must smell as well. Iman's expression betrayed her shock but barely. She grabbed up my basin and shouted a sharp order to the many who'd sprung up in cluster at my doorway, gawking. "Go. Fetch some fresh water from the river. And more than one basin. Fetch and keep fetching." The one woman who remained at the door, Iman enlisted as well. "Make some root tea!" she ordered. After that I was conscious only of the comfort of Iman's kind, tending hands—washing down my bone-thin body, changing my robe, combing my coarse, matted hair. When Iman lifted the cup of tea to my lips, I sipped, and the hot strength of it brought my wits back. I looked around the room.

"Where is she?" I whispered hoarsely.

"She's gone, little one. You know well as I. She escaped."

It was difficult for me to believe Anwa gone in a room so clamorous with her memory. Anwa cooing, moaning, wriggling down my length to suction her lips on my sex, mine already on hers. The two of us circling into each other. Like infinity.

And so will I escape, I resolved. I will follow.

I had not the strength yet to effect a strenuous journey. I consoled myself with the thought that, if I need wait a few days or even weeks to leave, it would be no more difficult to find her than already it was. In the days I had been jailed, Anwa would have had ample time to travel quite far. And so I rested, accepting the affectionate nuzzling of the cat who was my new companion, and allowing Iman to nurse me back to strength. Daily I confided my plans to Iman, and, as often, she tried to dissuade me. "You have a home in the khan. A roof and food." She reminded me what I already knew, that even if I could escape and take to the sea, I'd have no assurance of ever finding Anwa. But to every argument she had, I had one counter.

"The sailors seem to me like cats," I said, according an air of instinct to my plans. "They track each other's courses and have ways to communicate which are not ours. Someone will know where Anwa has gone. They will help me find her."

"Sari," Iman said carefully, "even if you should find her, Anwa might not be there. In some sense she was gone even in the last days she was here, and over that I'm afraid you have no control."

"Anwa is at sea," I exclaimed. "And I am the moon, or at

least her favored child. The moon rules the tides. Anwa told me so herself."

"I think that you are not a moon," said Iman, "but simply a young girl. A young girl who's experienced loss and sorrow beyond her years."

"I need to find her," I said. "I love her." It was the only argument I knew.

On the day I determined to leave, I brought the cat who'd kept watch over my convalescence to Iman's room.

"She looks black," I said, "but in sunlight she's henna. She will eat riverfish, but prefers the striped-tailed lizards that dart about the hareem. You can let her roam. Without fail, she'll return. And though she is female and somewhat small, she can protect herself. I've often found fur in her claws."

I stayed in Iman's room until the sun faded and cast its pink light on the yellowed walls. The cat curled herself at the edge of Iman's mat. I left her there and went to pack my bundle.

When the night was fully dark, I slipped out of the khan, escaping the walls of the citadel through the slack-jawed gate ever open to the river path. The fronds of the trees stirred and whispered. It was some hours before I reached the sea.

I had not seen the sea at night, only by day. The moon shimmered on the water. Beneath it, the pounding of the surf seemed louder, more rhythmic. Mute boats rocked in the harbor, while dark, solitary figures patrolled their decks. I knew I would have to wait until morning, until the dock bustled again with life. Then I planned to talk with the men, get information, secure myself a post on a boat, the boat that would sail me away, toward Anwa, wherever it was she had gone. I walked to the edge of the surf and let its cool swell wash my muddy feet. As they had that first visit, the waves pulled at the sand beneath me.

Undertow: named and defined, still not explained.

The water lapping at my feet helped me hope there might indeed be direction in the pull and pound of the waves. I set my sights ahead.

A vast and bewildering ocean unrolled itself before me.

43

Before I left the psychic's house, I felt I needed to ask her one last question. I just wanted something to leave with, a little something solid to hold. I tried to articulate some pointed, direct question, but found myself at a loss for words. The psychic sighed. She closed her eyes. "A cage," she said. "There's a girl in a cage. The food she eats is sneaked her through the bars." She opened her eyes and looked at me. "The girl is you."

Caged? Me? Something was wrong. Obviously the woman had confused me. With the one who was the white-hot center of my story.

"What else?" I asked, too quickly, anxious. "Is there anything else you think I need to know?" Guidance. All of us down here just grasping for guidance.

The psychic nodded. "Your pain," she said. "It's something about your pain. . . ."

"Yes?" I pressed.

She paused. She said, "It's that you romanticize it. You tend to romanticize pain."

That woman doesn't even know the half.

When we moved in, we had a yard, but no lawn. My father unrolled the pieces of sod and laid them end to end across the yard, fit them together like puzzle pieces.

My father was a drunk. And my mother? She had a couple of nervous breakdowns in response. At which time I would get shipped off to my grandmother's for however long it took for my mother to get back on her feet. Or at least for her eyelashes to grow back in.

All because my mother happened to walk in on everyone naked—me, the orphan dolls, and my father as well. Excess. It was always excess led to these lapses, and my mother took to sewing up a storm.

"What do you think happened here?" my father yelled at her. "What in your dirty mind do you think happened?"

No doubt, at this point, I've got everyone thinking my father molested me. That would explain everything, wouldn't it? My going to bed with women, my mother's breakdown. I bet everyone thinks my father fingered me, or rubbed up against me. I bet everyone thinks he stuck it in. Something unspeakable begging to be told. Otherwise, where's this story lead to—some vast desert nowhere?

When my father commanded me, that day I've oft returned to, to join him in the shower, I did. And when I was inside, he pulled the plastic curtain shut. I stood as far to the back of the tub as possible, afraid that my father might move toward me. But once I'd stepped inside, he paid me no attention. I watched him soap his body. I watched him lather his hair. My father stood under the spray, rinsing clean, when I heard my mother's voice call over the sound of the water.

"Tom! Tom, are you in there?" I heard the bathroom door open. "What's this?" My mother must've spied the dolls, and our clothes lying with them, on the floor.

At that moment, my father's lips twitched into a sort of anticipatory smirk. Still, he didn't answer my mother. He waited for her to pull back the shower curtain.

"Codie," my mother said, "what are you—? Tom, what are you doing in here?"

"What does it look like we're doing?" my father said. "We're taking a shower." He stuck his head back under the water to rinse out the rest of the shampoo.

My mother looked to me for explanation, but I didn't have one. "I'm finished," I said, as if that might somehow dissociate me from the scene. My mother grabbed me roughly under the arms and yanked me out of the tub. My father stepped out after me, onto the bath mat, kicking my dolls out of the way with his toe. And I followed the rest of the row from my bedroom, where my mother put me to rest because one little girl was tired, wasn't she, very tired indeed.

So what was my father's intention in this? To scare my mother is the only answer I've been able to come up with after all these years. A motive that's nothing if not in character. Just a joke. Along the same lines as telling a shy bride he was a Russian spy. The man who was my father never actually touched me in ways prohibited by law. He just frightened me. Frightened me but good.

There were other breakdowns and other trips to my grandmother's, but I've never had much patience for litany. Suffice it to say that each instance was founded on false promises. And hopes that would not die. And every little thing a threat to a fragile, glasslike world.

"So maybe it's not a lie after all," says Wren.

"What's not a lie?"

"Your story about coming home from your grandmother's on the Fourth of July."

"It was a childhood memory. Maybe I got mixed up."

"Or maybe it was another time your mother had a breakdown."

"Maybe."

"Didn't you say it happened more than once?"

I let out a small sigh. "You're a good friend, Wren. You forgive me a lot."

"Not unlike a helpful animal?" she suggests. Wren smiles

mischievously, as if maybe she's eluded a cat. I look at her quizzically. Apparently there's something I'm not getting.

"What are you trying to say?" I ask. "Am I missing something essential here?"

I notice Wren's voice ring with an odd trill I've not before noticed, a sort of warble, as she answers:

"Everyone in the dream is the dreamer."

44

Epilogue. In which our heroine steps out from the mystical cast and takes a frank look at herself in the chrome of a napkin dispenser in the coffee shop on her corner. "Needs a little lipstick," she observed. She pulled a tube out of her pocketbook and leaned in toward her reflection, the better to see herself, why else? *Très rouge* was her color. French. Like certain kisses only vaguely remembered.

A man was sitting in the booth next to her, watching. He smiled a half smile. And when our heroine noticed this man noticing her she hiked her skirt a little higher and crossed her legs to show some thigh. "Who knows," she thought, "maybe I'll start going out with men again." She was, after all, as she reminded herself, up for grabs. She checked to make sure the man was still watching and when she had satisfied herself that he was, she ran her finger around the edges of her lips to even out the *très rouge*, then turned to look him dead in the eye. "Do you think I look too much like a nun?" she asked. Coy. Our heroine is nothing if not coy. Though certain other charges leveled against her over the years have been blatantly false.

"I want someone who's there for me thick and thin!" Dee shouted, the night she walked out the door.

"And I'm not?" I yelled back. "You're saying I'm not there for you?"

"Codie, the last thing I need," she said, "the *last* thing, is some party girl!"

Party girl? Struck me dumb with that one. Maybe she was thinking about one of her other girlfriends.

The night Dee made this accusation, she had her duffel bag slung over her shoulder. As if she were going to war. When I knew full well she was only going to the blond's house. The blond. Now there was a surefire prospect for thick and thin.

After Dee left, I bought a couple of plants to keep Clue and me company. Plants were about the limit of what I was up for. My speed. Reliable. I watered the plants and leafed through old love letters. One day it hit me, the evidence right before my eyes. My relationship with Dee spanned a couple of postal rates. Nothing more, nothing less.

Seasons passed, as they will. Hot weather gave way to cold gave way to warm. Birds appeared, returned from a long absence, chirping in the branches of the one tree outside. Right around that time, the bar downstairs expanded beyond its walls, adding a sidewalk café. Intemperance. Right below my window. People laughing and carousing, keeping me up all hours. One night I took my plants out to the fire escape to repot them— partly to allow their roots room, partly for spite. Within minutes the manager of the bar was knocking at my door.

"You're dropping dirt on my patrons!" he yelled.

"How dare you accuse me!" I shouted back. "I'm inside my own apartment! Sitting on my couch! Reading my newspaper!" Though in my hands I held a trowel and my nails were caked with potting soil, as anyone could see.

Just at that moment, the phone rang, and it was someone inviting me last minute to a party, of all things. Must have been Dee got that party-girl reputation of mine around. I didn't much want to go, but, what with the guy from the bar in my face, shouting at me, I thought maybe I ought to. It scared me to be at home all the time. Crying. Or about to. So I got dressed and left the house.

At the party I could've done what I ended up doing with any number of the men who were there. There were plenty to choose from. What I saw when I entered was a lot of people milling, holding clear plastic glasses with wine, red or white, and no one looking lesbian in the least. "Remember, Codie," I coached myself, "up for grabs." I stood at the edge of the crowd, unable to enter at first, like a young girl gauging the speed and rhythm of a jump rope already turning. It hit me as I stood there that I was no longer in an age of innocence, no longer B.D. Time had shifted. To A.D. Which meant that if the night turned out to be one for collecting stories, they would not be ones I'd ever get the chance to share with Dee. Late at night, sheltered in her arms, lips alive. Without that prospect, there seemed so little point.

Across the room, people were dancing in tight groups of twos and threes. I made my way there, claimed an open space off the center of their circle, and danced, unsociably, alone. After a song or two I noticed a guy at the edge of the crowd watching me. He had a long, sloping nose and hunched posture. He was wearing a baseball cap, though, that I found, for some reason, endearing, familiar almost, its brim angled cockily to one side. When the music stopped he walked up to me and introduced himself. His name was Beau, he said, with a wink at the promise that implied.

Beau asked my name and I told him. "What's it short for," he quipped. "Buffalo Bill?"

"Codswallop," I said. A word I'd once found in the dictionary. In the days when I thought words like that had power.

"You're quite a dancer there, Codswallop," he said. "I mean, you move real well. Anybody ever tell you that?"

"I dance professionally. I'm a principal with the New York City Ballet," I said. Lies flimsy as veils.

Beau asked me to sit down with him and I agreed. I was barely settled before he launched into his life story, told me all about himself, about his job as a sales rep, about growing up in New Jersey, about having two older sisters and a mother who died when he was three. "I was raised by my aunt," he said, "my mother's sister, the Italian side of the family." I was beginning to regret my decision to sit down with him, and wondered if, with all the information he was lobbing at me, perhaps he'd mistaken me for someone else. Like maybe his biographer.

"Oh," he added, after the bit about his mother dying, "and I love baseball," information he apparently felt to be of equal value. I smiled vaguely and nodded at the cap. "Oh right, this," he said. He broke into a sheepish grin. "I bet you wonder why I'm wearing this." His voice got suddenly hushed and confidential. He glanced furtively around. "Actually," he whispered, "I'm wearing this because, um, because . . . well,"—more boldly—"I might as well just out and tell you. I had a hair transplant today."

With that, he flipped off his cap and bent the crown of his head toward me so I could see. On his bald pate were short plugs of hair in even patches. Where the hair had been inserted into the scalp were small puncture wounds, and the skin immediately surrounding the transplants was red and raw. That was when it hit me full. That I didn't want to be at this party anymore, not even another second.

"I've got to go," I said abruptly.

Beau righted his head and shot me a wounded expression. "But we just started talking," he said. "I was just starting to get to know you."

"I've got to go."

"It's because of the transplant, isn't it?" he accused. "It's because I told you I had a transplant." I stood up from my chair, but Beau clapped the baseball cap back on his head and grabbed my shoulder to restrain me. "Why don't we leave here together?" he urged. "Why don't we go for a drink or something?"

Because he was begging me to, I looked at Beau. I looked him full in the face. And I saw everything I knew about him. All he'd told me and more.

"Listen," he said. "Listen. We don't have to go out tonight, but I'd like to get your number. So we could go out another time." He pulled out a pen from his breast pocket. He fished in his pants pocket for a slip of paper.

I was too world-weary to have to explain to this person that I didn't want to go out with him and why. I just hadn't the earnestness left. So I gave him my name. "Codie James," I heard myself saying. "891-5712." The name I gave him was mine, all right, but not the number. The number was Dee's. Nothing pre-meditated, mind you, it just sort of slipped my lips. I pictured him calling, pictured Dee confronted with a strange male voice asking for me by name, or, better yet, leaving me a message. "I'm the one you met at the party," he'd say. There was some satisfaction in that.

A paltry satisfaction, but there.

But why a harem? The question still remains. Of all the myriad times and places I might've chosen to fix on, the question that's still begged is: Why then, why there?

The answer's small as seed.

Before my mother was pushed by pain to pluck out all her eyelashes and eyebrows, in the days when I still went weekly to receive pink instruction from Miss Rose, my father used to take my picture. I was, in fact, his favorite subject, a circum-stance that got its start the day I first came home from class and began to practice what I'd learned in front of the long mirror that hung on the living room wall. I stood back so that I could see the full length of my body and executed the precise steps that had French names, repeating in my head the corrections Miss Rose had given me. "Hold your arms as if you're embrac-ing something that takes up space," she'd said. "A wide world getting wider."

All this attention to form and line attracted the eye of my father, who appeared with his camera and told me, "Hold it!" My father preferred poses to steps in motion. He liked to cap-ture me still, immobile as a mountain. So I pointed my toes, stretched my legs long. My father's favorite pose was arabesque.

"Do that one—what's it called?" he'd ask. He'd make belly dancing motions with his hips, he knew as well as I.

"Arabesque."

"Ayrab-esque," he'd say, a joke that amused him each time he resurrected it. He'd jiggle his cigarette pack, a visual aid. My father's brand of cigarette was Camels.

And so I stretched one arm forward and the opposite leg back while my father shot whole rolls. My body, one long, angled line, "Like a slash against the sky," he said, though the background was really a couch and a wall and a ceiling far too low for panorama. Once my mother came to the doorway and looked on. "Don't hurt yourself, Codie!" she cried, as if a child standing on one leg were cause for alarm. "Tom! She's going to hurt herself!" Ballet can hurt a person, I know. Not the person who's dancing, but maybe her mother.

And in the end, none of these details matter—not the whodunnit, the what they did, or why. Because the details of a story, whatever that story's complexion, always add up to the same thing: All through time and every time, all a person aches for is to be allowed.

"You mean love, of course."

"That too."

One day my father called me up at work and whoever answered the phone told him that I no longer worked there. My father dialed my number at home, expecting my machine, I'm sure. It was eleven o'clock in the morning. I answered the phone.

"What are you doing home?" he asked.

"Right now? I'm drinking coffee."

"I just called the publishing house. They told me you no longer work there."

"That's right."

My father started asking a lot of questions, wanting to know what happened. So I told him the truth. That they fired me. My father wanted to know whatever would've prompted them to do a thing like that. I explained to him that, in fact, they'd been justified, that I'd pushed them to it by, among other offenses, slipping away from work for two hours at a stretch. "Sometimes longer," I said. "Sometimes three." My father demanded to know what kind of job I was looking for. I told him I wasn't looking for a job.

"So what do you intend to do?"

"Well, Dad, mostly," I said, "I guess what I intend to do is dance."

I knew full well this would not sound like much of an answer to the man who was my father. Predictably, he put up an argument, tried to talk some sense into me. He asked me what could possibly come of me spending my days dancing. "Where's that going to lead, Codie? Answer me that." I answered the only thing I knew, which was that I really didn't know. "Then where are you going in life?" he demanded.

A person can get tired of everybody bugging her about where she's going.

To be, Dad. I'm going to be.

Every once in a while, when I'd be walking down the street, going about my own life, whatever that might prove, I'd look up and there would be Dee. Dee and the blond. Once they were holding hands. Another time, Dee had her arm around the woman's waist. Always entwined and all the time smiling. The two of them, Dee and the girlfriend, on occasion, on the street, they'd sail right past. Just part of the landscape.

One day, some time later, I ran into Dee and she was alone. "Uncharacteristically alone," I said when we stopped to talk. Residual anger. I guess, when it needed expression, I could still zing it in. Dee shifted her gaze and eyed the earrings I was wearing, one a sun the other a moon. She took them between her fingers. "Two pierces," she said. "So you went and got two pierces in one ear." Dee-versionary tactic, new and improved.

"Dee," I said, "I got two pierces long before I met you."

"No," she said, incredulous. "You didn't."

"I had two pierces the whole time we were together."

Attention to detail. Dee consistently missed all of the questions that required any attention to detail. "Like the fact that I loved you," I could have said, but didn't. Or even, "Who I was at all."

Dee has always been, always will be, a global kind of girl.

Dee, she was like no other. Brown-skinned, nappy-headed, tall, sleek, and proud. Sometimes I threw things at her. A dictionary. A headband. Which only made Dee more proud still. One night, as Bob Eubanks was my witness, Dee likened my breasts to figs. "Figs!" she cried. "My wife's breasts are figs!"

But often I caught her gaze on them just before she'd fall on me with kisses.

Sweet nights, fleet nights, nights white with stars.

About this lark that is life, there is one thing and one thing only that I know for certain. And that is that a person can't move on from anyplace other than exactly where she is. Me, I was on the corner of Broadway and Houston. Come from the ballet studio, with counts to kill while waiting for the light. I started practicing something I'd just learned in class, when, wouldn't you know it, Will snuck up behind me.

"Hey, don't mind me," he said. Will was grinning. "Sometimes a girl just has to do an arabesque turn on the corner."

"I was just—"

"No, no, don't explain. If anyone should understand, it's me. But if you're going to do it, girlfriend, do it right. Lift from your chest. Like you've got a string attached there pulling you up. Come on." Will took my hand to steady me. I went up to my toes. "Okay, a little joke," he said.

A joke. How better to close?

"What reflects as well as a wall of mirrors and might even be more honest?" Will didn't wait long before blurting out the punch line.

"Give up?" he said.

I nodded.

"Partnering!"

The answer, pure and simple.

Not far from us, a homeless man was sitting on the corner,

watching. When we were through, he applauded. Will turned the man's way and took a low bow, so I smiled too and made a deep curtsy. *Révérence*, is what that's called, something I'd learned in class early on. A peculiarly apt word, to my devout way of thinking.

I've always loved to worship.

Long ago, in my youth, I fashioned myself curator of ancient record. Next to the driveway of the house in which I grew up was a wall built from stones indigenous to the area. And in a neighborhood so newly built it would pretend it had no history, these stones bespoke the lie. For on their faces were clearly printed the reliefs of sea life, the impressions of small shells. Some recognizable, like scallops. Others less familiarly shaped, small and branchlike, pieces of coral, perhaps. On lazy days I used to press against the wall and run my finger over the reliefs of the shells. I knew what shells were only because I'd seen pictures of them. I lived in a city locked by land.

It was my mother who first pointed out the shells to me. She told me that the reliefs were fossils of an earlier time. Her voice waxed romantic, mythopoeic, as if what she were about to do was take stage and spin a yarn. But instead, the words she spoke were scientific fact, that once, long ago, the whole of the state in which I lived had been under the sea, and that the shells of that sea had become embedded in rock and so had been preserved for us as relic of that time. After she told me, I took it upon myself to search for and collect all the fossils I could find. I examined rocks wherever we went, and found fossils in them, or so I thought. My mother confirmed that some of what I found were indeed fossils. Others, she said, were simply my imagination. My imagination. Which is a sort of sea life of my own, I suppose. Adrift in the depths, aching for preservation. . . .

And Sari, at last, stands at the prow. Land slips from sight. Sea surrounds. Her ship trails the wake of the moonlight.
She hopes it will carry her home.